BLACKSTONE FORTRESS

More Warhammer 40,000 from Black Library

ROGUE TRADER: THE OMNIBUS
Andy Hoare

CORSAIR: THE FACE OF THE VOID
James Swallow

• DARK IMPERIUM •
Guy Haley
BOOK 1: Dark Imperium
BOOK 2: Plague War

WATCHERS OF THE THRONE: THE EMPEROR'S LEGION
Chris Wraight

• THE HORUSIAN WARS •
John French
BOOK 1: Resurrection
BOOK 2: Incarnation

VAULTS OF TERRA: THE CARRION THRONE
Chris Wraight

• RISE OF THE YNNARI •
Gav Thorpe
BOOK 1: Ghost Warrior
BOOK 2: Wild Rider

• BLACK LEGION •
Aaron Dembski-Bowden
BOOK 1: The Talon of Horus
BOOK 2: Black Legion

WARHAMMER QUEST®

BLACKSTONE
FORTRESS

DARIUS HINKS

BLACK LIBRARY

For the author of the SF novel I read when I was nine. I can't remember the name. The one with the spaceship in.

A BLACK LIBRARY PUBLICATION

First published in 2018.
This edition published in Great Britain in 2019 by
Black Library,
Games Workshop Ltd.,
Willow Road,
Nottingham, NG7 2WS, UK.

10 9 8 7 6 5 4 3 2 1

Produced by Games Workshop in Nottingham.
Cover illustration by Mauro Belfiore.

A CIP record for this book is available from the British Library.

ISBN 13: 978 1 78496 928 8

Printed and bound by CPI Group (UK) Ltd, Croydon, CR0 4YY

It is the 41st millennium. For more than a hundred centuries the Emperor has sat immobile on the Golden Throne of Earth. He is the Master of Mankind by the will of the gods, and master of a million worlds by the might of His inexhaustible armies. He is a rotting carcass writhing invisibly with power from the Dark Age of Technology. He is the Carrion Lord of the Imperium for whom a thousand souls are sacrificed every day, so that He may never truly die.

Yet even in His deathless state, the Emperor continues His eternal vigilance. Mighty battlefleets cross the daemon-infested miasma of the warp, the only route between distant stars, their way lit by the Astronomican, the psychic manifestation of the Emperor's will. Vast armies give battle in His name on uncounted worlds. Greatest amongst His soldiers are the Adeptus Astartes, the Space Marines, bioengineered super-warriors. Their comrades in arms are legion: the Astra Militarum and countless planetary defence forces, the ever-vigilant Inquisition and the tech-priests of the Adeptus Mechanicus to name only a few. But for all their multitudes, they are barely enough to hold off the ever-present threat from aliens, heretics, mutants – and worse.

To be a man in such times is to be one amongst untold billions. It is to live in the cruellest and most bloody regime imaginable. These are the tales of those times. Forget the power of technology and science, for so much has been forgotten, never to be re-learned. Forget the promise of progress and understanding, for in the grim dark future there is only war. There is no peace amongst the stars, only an eternity of carnage and slaughter, and the laughter of thirsting gods.

BEFORE

How they would have wept to hear him. All those years of brutal tutelage, so many prayers meted out with an unsparing stick, and not one of their aphorisms had stayed with him – all that cant wiped away by the savagery of the war. Only one simple phrase, whispered to the rhythm of his breath, had kept him alive. *Through the needle's eye.* He could see it in his mind – a sliver of sanity, surrounded by a galaxy of madness. *I live or die.*

In place of a sky, it seemed Sepus Prime wore a dirty, sodden cloth, stained the same feculent shade of dun as the mud below. It sagged low over the fly-clad marshes, bleeding a desolate rain, crushing the mounds of dead and billowing around a shame-faced sun. Glutt waded through the filth, a slight man weighed down by a heavy coat. His face was a mask of dark, viscous mud, and his mouth was hidden by a rebreather. Only his eyes were visible – flashes of white beneath a peaked cap, scouring the trench for the shot that would finally kill him.

'Through the needle's eye,' he whispered, risking a glimpse

into no-man's-land, using his staff to haul himself over a broken trench wall.

Fumes lay heavy on the swamp, crawling lazily over shattered gun emplacements and crook-backed trees. Even through his rebreather Glutt could smell the chemical stink of enemy weapons. How many of the regiment were still alive out there? Betrayed. Clawing at their throats, calling for loved ones, begging for the help they were promised. The reinforcements that never came. They *never came*. They had all been fools, but he would be a fool no more. Anger fractured Glutt's thoughts, dangerous and raw. He recited his mantra with vehemence, clinging to his mind, weighing it down with words.

He pulled out a map and wiped it clean, tracing a finger over the gridlines, counting the miles. He was close. Another few hours and he would see the barracks. He had no desire to rejoin the regiment now, after all that he had seen, but where else could he go? He had no vox and he dared not risk any other method of communication, and this side of the valley seemed to have been forgotten. The earth shivered beneath a mortar shell rain, but it was a distant sound, like the echo of a storm.

An image flashed through his mind, so vivid he gasped – pale, ruptured flesh tearing over a clinker-black shell. He drove the vision down but it coiled beneath his thoughts, waiting for his guard to slip. He had seen it countless times over the last few months. It was horrific, but part of him was also fascinated. It was so clear. What did it mean?

He was about to drop back down into the trench when he saw movement in the smoke – half a mile away, near a bombed-out gun emplacement. He grabbed his laspistol and peered through the scope.

'Sorov?' he whispered, catching a glimpse of red sash.

There was another blur of movement, then nothing. Only the lolling, yellow fumes and the sporadic grumble of mortars. He had not seen a soul for two days. Perhaps he imagined the shapes? Then he heard a faint crackling – not the rattle of gunfire, but the white noise of a vox-unit. It came from the gun emplacement.

He dropped into the bunker, his breath coming in snatched bursts. Insurrectionists were everywhere. Snipers haunted every gully, masquerading as corpses, lying patiently beneath cold limbs, waiting for some fool to break cover. Again he heard the crackle of vox traffic, muted by the fumes but unmistakable.

He peered up over the scorched embrasure, looking through the gunsight again, trying to guess where a sniper might hide. There was a rusted tank chassis, halfway to the gun emplacement, jutting from the mud like an unearthed fossil: a Leman Russ, one of its sponsons still visible, pointing defiantly at the leaden clouds. Just the kind of place a sniper might wait. He looked in the other direction. There was a trench, parallel with his, about a hundred feet away. It had caved in, sporting a crest of broken joists and blast-warped girders. Again, exactly the kind of place snipers might hide. There were cadavers in the razorwire, swaying in the breeze like abandoned marionettes. It looked as though they had been thrown clear of the trench by an air strike, but he had seen traitors adopt that pose, then lurch into movement at the first sign of a target.

'Lieutenant Sorov?' he whispered. Could he still be alive? And if he was, why would he be here? The push on the civitate had started. Sorov always led from the front. Why would he be back here, so far from the front line? The thought that the lieutenant might still be alive shook Glutt's resolve. Sorov had stood by the men. He alone in all the regiment seemed worthy of trust.

Glutt hunkered in the trench, crippled by indecision. The image of torn flesh washed through his thoughts again, but he crushed it with his mantra, determined to think clearly. What if it was Sorov out there? Could there still be another route for him, even now?

Glutt bolted up the trench wall and ran through the smoke, head down, flicking his pistol from the tank to the corpses. His footfalls rang out through the smog. *Slap. Slap. Slap.* Flies whirled around him, drawn by his blood-black coat. Sweat pooled in his eyes. He tried to sprint, but his legs were wasted from lack of food and the mud gripped his heavy boots, leaching what little strength he had left.

Minutes passed until finally the gun emplacement reared up before him, brutal and angular, a slab of pitted rockcrete shattered by artillery. One side was intact, but the other was gone, leaving the surreal sight of a furnished room, split down the middle and hanging in the air. The furniture was undisturbed: a neatly made bunk, metal plan chests, a small dining table; all perched in the clouds, washed clean by the endless rain.

Glutt had almost reached the walls when he heard someone snap the safety off a lasgun.

He staggered to a halt, his heart thudding as he tried to pinpoint the sound.

'The savant?' The words were spoken quietly, but they echoed across the swamp, eerie and dislocated.

'Lieutenant Sorov?' gasped Glutt, still crouched, staring at the shifting clouds.

'Throne,' said Sorov, striding into view, flanked by Guardsmen, their lasguns trained on Glutt.

'In,' he snapped, waving for Glutt to approach.

Glutt staggered forwards, into the arms of the Guardsmen, who grabbed his filthy coat and hurled him inside the ruined tower.

As Glutt lay panting on the floor, Sorov and the others stood over him, scowling.

Sepus Prime could not touch Lieutenant Sorov. He shrugged it off like an idle threat. He was one of those officers with the inhuman ability to look clean, fresh and unperturbed as the galaxy went to hell around them. His hair was immaculate, oiled and gleaming beneath his cap, and the buttons on his coat flashed proudly as he moved. An old scar curved from the corner of his mouth to his ear, but even that looked deliberate – just another military honour. He studied Glutt through half-lidded eyes.

'Where is the rest of your detail?'

'We never made it to the front lines, lieutenant. The insurrectionists were on us before we reached Tadmor Ridge. I was able to–' He hesitated, noting the wary expressions of the Guardsmen. 'I was able to *disable* some of them, but there were too many.'

'You're a psyker?'

'Yes, sir.'

'You abandoned your men?'

'No.'

'They're dead,' said Sorov, his expression blank, 'and you are not.'

'I did everything I could, lieutenant.'

Sorov studied him in silence. No one helped him to his feet.

The silence was broken by the crackle of the vox-unit. There was another trooper crouched a few feet away – a comms officer, hunched over his vox-caster.

'Ten minutes until contact,' said the Guardsman, with the

handset held to his ear. There was a tremor of excitement in his voice. 'Everything went to plan.'

Sorov closed his eyes for a moment. When he opened them again he looked back at Glutt. 'Tell me, Glutt,' he said. 'If you were a traitor, why would you have stumbled over here and revealed yourself, rather than using your talents to kill me from a safe distance?'

Glutt struggled to keep his expression neutral. *Traitor.* Sorov had pinpointed the doubts that had haunted him for weeks. All he saw on Sepus were pitiable fools and callous, inhuman orders. His faith was gone. What did that leave?

'There is no reason,' said Sorov. His expression softened. 'You've done well to last this long, soldier. Not many have.' He nodded to his men. 'Pick him up. And keep an eye on him. He's a sanctioned psyker. Don't let him ruin this.'

As the Guardsmen dragged Glutt from the mud, Sorov headed over to the comms officer.

'Korbol,' he said, glancing up at the shattered floor of the room above their heads. 'Anything?'

'Nothing, lieutenant.'

Sorov nodded, and then glanced back at Glutt. 'Over here.'

Glutt tried to brush some of the muck from his coat as he rushed after Sorov, but it had dried into a thick crust. He moved with the clumsy, awkward steps of an automaton.

'Get me Kapek,' said Sorov to the vox-officer.

There was another burst of static, then a voice came through the speakers, ghostly and hazed by distance, like an old recording.

'This is Sergeant Kapek. We have–' The voice was cut off by a series of pops and whistles. *'We are no closer, lieutenant. Heavier losses than anticipated. The aerial strikes failed to knock out the lascannons. They're cutting us down.'*

Sorov grabbed the handset. 'Ten minutes, sergeant.' His voice was an urgent whisper. 'Ten minutes more.'

There was a pause on the other end, but it was not static this time; they could all hear the sergeant breathing. *'Ten minutes?'* he said finally, sounding shocked.

Sorov raised his voice, despite the risk of revealing himself. 'Throw everything you have left at them for ten more minutes. It's working. He's headed your way.'

This time there was no pause. *'Ten minutes, lieutenant. We'll do it.'*

Sorov looked pained and seemed on the verge of saying more, but he held it back.

'Lieutenant,' came the voice again. *'Are you still there?'*

'Sergeant.'

The voice sounded defiant this time, all trace of doubt gone. *'It was an honour, lieutenant.'*

Sorov's expression tightened. When he spoke again, his voice was as rigid as his face. 'High command will know, sergeant. Commander Ortegal will know what happened here today.'

Another series of pops and crackles hissed through the speaker.

'Kapek out,' came the reply, then the line went dead.

Sorov stared at the handset for a moment. Then he took a deep breath and handed it back to the comms officer, turning to face the other men. 'I give them five minutes, but it will suffice. By the time the insurrectionists wipe them out we'll have hit our target.' Sorov looked at the comms officer. 'Federak. These are the *exact* coordinates?'

Federak was wiry and short, with the slabby, knocked-about face of a prize fighter. 'This is the right emplacement, lieutenant,' he said. 'If Gorny got his maths right, the shuttle will pass right overhead.'

'Good.' Sorov looked around the group. One of the Guardsmen was carrying a rocket launcher over his shoulder. 'If you get even one clear shot, you'll be lucky.'

The trooper nodded. 'Sir.'

Sorov stared at him. 'We've thrown everything into this. There are a few hundred men left at the barracks, but you saw the state of them. There will be no more chances. This is it.'

The man saluted. 'One shot will be enough, sir.'

Sorov nodded, then waved at the damaged upper floor of the tower. 'Into position.'

He glared at the rest of the troopers. 'Am I so pretty you can't take your eyes off me? Watch the damned trenches. Keep yourselves alive for a few minutes and you might even get off this rancid planet.' He caught sight of Glutt. 'You keep out of the way.' He leant closer, tapping the eagle-shaped head of Glutt's staff. 'I'm no fan of witches, sanctioned or not. Throne preserve you if I catch you trying any parlour tricks.'

Glutt saluted.

Sorov nodded to the pistol at Glutt's belt. 'You know how to use that thing. Join the others and watch the bunkers.'

Glutt saluted and rushed to stand beside the comms officer.

'What are you doing out here?' he whispered, once Sorov had climbed up into the room overhead to join the trooper with the rocket launcher.

Federak gave him a suspicious look. Glutt felt like proving his suspicions right, showing him what a psyker could *really* do, but he thought of the needle, biding his time. He had no clear plan. He no longer believed in the regiment, but what did he believe in?

'The governor's going to pass over this way,' muttered Federak, waving his gun at the clouds. 'He thinks he's won. He's racing to Tadmor Ridge to deal with Sergeant Kapek and the rest of those poor sods. Sorov got a man into his inner circle. The pilot. We know the exact route he's taking. He's going to pass over this spot in a few minutes.'

Glutt could not believe the lies people told themselves to try to stay sane. 'You're going take down the governor? What difference will that make? They'll still massacre the rest of the regiment. The insurrectionists will still control the whole coastline. We've still lost.'

Federak forgot his wariness of Glutt for a moment and laughed. 'Not destined for high command are you? Think. Before Governor Narbo took control of the insurrectionists, what were they doing?'

Glutt bit down his rage and shrugged.

'Killing each other,' Federak elaborated. 'Always killing each other. Why do you think they used to be so easy to control? They all think *they* should be in charge. None of them will follow the others. It's only because Governor Narbo executes his opponents that they've become an army. There *was* no insurrection until Narbo lost his mind and pulled them all under one banner.' He nodded at the trooper with the rocket launcher. 'We're about to remove the glue that holds them all together.'

'But we'll have nothing left either.'

Federak shrugged. 'Once Narbo dies, the insurrectionists will turn on each other. They'll become a mess of squabbling warbands and high command will send us home with a chest-full of medals.'

'Sorov knew this would happen,' muttered Glutt. He looked up at the lieutenant. Maybe there *was* still a man worth following? Maybe he was making a mistake? No. One true man in a legion of liars was not enough.

'Of course,' said Federak. 'I don't know what Governor Narbo was smoking when he decided to join with the insurrectionists, but he should have known Sorov would never let him get away with it. The man has balls of steel.'

Glutt was about to reply when Federak frowned and looked up.

'Hear that?' he muttered.

There was a low, shuddering rumble drifting through the clouds – the unmistakable drone of promethium engines. Overhead, the lieutenant and the trooper with the rocket launcher shifted their position.

Everyone in the tower held their breath.

The sound grew louder as a dark smudge appeared in the mustard-yellow clouds. The lieutenant whispered something and the trooper raised his rocket launcher. The shuttle thundered right overhead – so low Glutt could see its markings.

A deafening blast rocked the tower and the sky turned white.

Glutt ducked, shielding his eyes.

Smoke enveloped the gun emplacement.

'Down!' cried Sorov. 'She's down!'

Glutt raced through the fumes and staggered out into the mud. The others were ahead of him, danger forgotten as they ran towards the downed shuttle lying just a few hundred feet away, engulfed in flames. It was on its back, but the wings were still visible. It was an Aquila lander – the governor's personal shuttle.

'Quick!' barked Lieutenant Sorov, dashing through the mud and waving for his troops to approach in two different directions. 'Make sure.'

Glutt ran after them, struggling through the mire, unable to keep pace. The excitement of the others was infectious.

It threatened to overwhelm him. 'Through the needle's eye,' he whispered.

Lieutenant Sorov was the first to reach the lander, halting a few feet from the blaze, his laspistol held out before him. 'Governor!' he cried, dodging from side to side as the ruptured fuselage spat flames at him. 'Are you in there?'

Part of the engine cowling collapsed, adding a fresh gout of flames to the blaze.

'Lieutenant!' gasped Federak. 'It's not safe!'

Sorov ignored him, squinting through the flames, edging closer, waving his pistol at every movement.

'There!' he cried.

A hunched shape dragged itself through the inferno.

The Guardsmen opened fire, launching a blinding barrage of las-shots at the struggling figure. The shape shuddered and fell. Then, as the shots died away, it lurched to its feet and charged, flames trailing from its misshapen head.

Most of the Guardsmen fired again, but Glutt's pistol faltered in his grip. The needle's eye suddenly grew in his mind, expanding and reforming, letting madness flow around it. Sparks flashed – arcing from his brain, splintering his vision, turning the world into a kaleidoscope. He stumbled, teetering, engulfed by colour.

As the flaming figure dived at the Guardsmen, Glutt staggered back through the mud, his staff rattling in his grip, infused with the energy that was lashing from his face. The others were too busy to notice Glutt's crisis. The burning figure stumbled through their shots and grabbed a Guardsman by the throat.

Reality slipped from Glutt's grasp. His peripheral vision vanished, leaving just the tunnel of garish light, centred on the thing that had emerged from the shuttle. It must have once been the governor. Most of his uniform was burned away, but there were enough scraps left to reveal that he was a high-ranking officer. Whatever he once was, Governor Narbo was now a nightmare. Glutt realised to his horror that *this* was the vision he had been struggling to hold back for days. Beneath his charred uniform the governor's flesh had ruptured and split but, rather than blood and viscera, there was a black carapace, bristling with spines, pulsing as it strained against its human cage.

As skin sloughed from the black shell, the thing snapped the Guardsman's neck and hurled him to the ground. Glutt howled and light spewed from his throat, ripping through the smoke. The force of the blast kicked him off his feet and he landed in the mud. The governor's head was lolling weakly from the creature's back, sagging like an empty hood, but another face had appeared in its chest where the skin had fallen away – a pool of black skin, rolling and bubbling around a canine snout.

The Guardsmen were still firing at the creature, but to no effect. The shots thudded into its stooped frame but it paid them no heed, lurching on, filling the air with blood.

'Warp spawn,' muttered Glutt, staggering back towards them, his voice flat. 'You can't kill it.'

The thing discarded its kill and lunged forwards, enveloping another man. The soldier howled briefly, before his cries were smothered.

Three Guardsmen had died in as many minutes. Two were left, plus Sorov and Glutt.

The final scraps of Governor Narbo fell away to reveal a coiled, serpentine hulk. It was impossible to make out clearly in the smoke, but Glutt caught glimpses: an insectoid face, twitching as it swallowed gore; a cyclopean eye – featureless and yellow, like an egg yolk, bubbling in tar. It toppled forwards, dragging another Guardsman down into the mud, tearing him apart.

Sorov and Federak fired furiously and the lieutenant cried out in disgusted rage.

Over the last few months, Sepus had gradually fractured Glutt's mind. The last time he had tried to use his gifts they had almost overwhelmed him. He had sworn not to try again until his mind was more stable, but now he saw no option.

Glutt closed his eyes, pictured the needle and stepped through its eye.

The immaterium rocked through him, exploding his atoms, whipping his flesh into an empyric storm. Now, finally, he heard the words of his masters from the scholastica psykana. Oaths of protection tumbled from his lips; psychic bulwarks, beaten into him as a child, reared from his subconscious like a suddenly remembered song. It was too late. Warp fire pulsed from his heart and flooded his blood vessels, igniting his flesh as he wrenched himself back into reality.

The scene was unchanged – the serpent-thing was still wading towards Sorov and Federak, guts draped from its jaws.

Glutt raised his staff and howled, opening his mind to the full violence of the warp. It ripped through him, rattling his bones, blistering his skin, sparking from his staff. The warp creature reared, but it was too late – Glutt's bolt had already hit home.

Spider legs burst from the creature's sides – dozens of them, scrambling frantically, trying to lift its sagging bulk – but as Glutt abandoned himself to the immaterium, his staff hurled ever-greater torrents of warp-fire into the struggling horror. Sorov and Federak backed away, guns lowered in shock.

The world fell into shadow leaving only the column of light, blazing from Glutt's staff.

Glutt's mind linked with the sentience that had mutated Narbo. To his surprise, he felt neither hate nor violence, but something else. For a brief moment, he saw the galaxy from an utterly alien perspective. He tasted ideas that would never have occurred to him: freedom, acceptance, liberation.

Then it was gone.

Unreality collapsed and reality returned. Glutt stood, swaying before the shocked faces of Sorov and Federak, then dropped to his knees in a pool of oil, surrounded by scraps of the governor.

Glutt was changed. He could feel it. There was a new layer of skin beneath his old one, simmering, ready to explode. What a fool he'd been. Holding back for so long.

'Emperor be praised,' whispered Sorov. 'You killed it.' He held out a trembling hand and helped Glutt to his feet.

They all looked at the remnants of the governor.

Glutt shook his head, his voice husky. 'It was never alive.'

Sorov stared at the pool, pale with shock. 'The governor's heresy ran deep.'

'Something found a way into the world through his flesh,' said Glutt.

Sorov frowned at Glutt, confused. 'What? What was it?' Then he shook his head and recovered his composure. 'We can talk later.'

Glutt sensed that Sorov did not really want his question answered.

The lieutenant seemed unable to think for a moment, staring at the charred remains and muttering under his breath, then he turned to the vox-officer, Federak. 'Share our news with the insurrectionists. They need a new leader. Set the dogs on each other.'

Federak looked even more dazed than Sorov, but he nodded and triggered the vox-caster, stuttering as he announced the governor's death across every channel.

By the time they made it back to the trench, the vox network was a cacophony of voices, all desperate to know if the news was truth or propaganda. The clamour grew as the governor's aides revealed that he should have reached Tadmor Ridge by now.

Sorov did not pause to celebrate his success. He waded through the stagnant pools that lined the trench, muttering calculations under his breath. For ten minutes he said nothing to Glutt or Federak, lost in his own thoughts. Finally, as the pallid sun neared the horizon, he paused and turned to Federak.

'Get me the barracks,' he said. 'Sergeant Baranov.'

The vox-caster whined and screeched as Federak struggled to find the right frequency, then a voice crackled over the speakers.

'Lieutenant. Sergeant Baranov here, sir.' The voice sounded flat and beaten.

'The governor's dead.'

'Yes, lieutenant. We heard.'

'He's dead, man,' said Sorov, confused at the sergeant's apparent lack of enthusiasm. 'Do you know what that means?'

There was a pause at the other end. *'We intercepted a message from Commander Ortegal,'* said the sergeant eventually. *'We know about the orbital strike.'*

'Orbital strike?'

There was another pause.

The colour drained from Sorov's face. 'Tell me, sergeant. Quickly.'

'Sepus Prime has been reclassified, sir. Designated unsafe for human habitation. Contaminated. There's a plague. Mutations. Linked to the heresy of the insurrectionists. I couldn't understand all of the terms. They do not intend to...' The man paused to clear his throat. *'They mean to leave us here, sir.'*

'Even when they start the bombardment?'

'We fall under the same designation, sir. Contaminated. The fleet is preparing virus bombs.'

Sorov leant against the trench wall, staring at the handset. The crackle of gunfire rang out across the network.

Sorov looked up at the clouds, as though he might see the cruisers overhead, readying their loads.

Federak took the handset. 'Is that las-fire? Are you under attack?'

'Suicides.'

Until that moment, Glutt had been in a kind of dazed trance, revelling in the new power jangling across his skin, wondering at the change he was experiencing. But at the sight of Sorov, winded by shock, staring at the sky, Glutt's transformation took a new turn. Anger kindled in his palms. He tried to stay in the present, grabbing the lieutenant by the arm. 'We have to get to the barracks, sir. This can't be true. Sergeant Baranov must be confused. Commander Ortegal wouldn't abandon the whole regiment when we have just handed him a victory. He wouldn't bomb his own men.'

Sorov stared back at him. 'Governor Narbo was a heretic. You saw him, Glutt. He was clearly infected by this "plague". And high command must have already known about it. They must have already been planning this reclassification.' Something flickered in his eyes. 'But they never told us.'

Glutt battled the black despair that was rising at the back of his thoughts. 'One traitor. They can't condemn us all for that. They can't condemn the whole planet.'

The trench shook so violently that it seemed as though someone had lifted it and slammed it back down again. Beams and girders tore from the walls, and earth slammed into the three Guardsmen, causing them to stagger and cough. The dusk deepened, smothering the trench in gloom. Aftershocks juddered through the mud.

'They've started,' whispered Federak, his voice brittle.

Sorov nodded vaguely, but he had recovered his composure. He dusted down his coat and raised his chin, looking off towards the horizon.

'No,' said Glutt as a storm whipped up in his eyes. The needle's eye was gone. The needle was gone. There was nothing left but madness. It blazed through him. The new flesh forming beneath his muscles burned, furious and unbreakable.

The booms grew louder. Splashes of silver flicked across the clouds. It might have been a natural storm if not for the ominous rhythm of the hammer blows – the footsteps of a colossus, marching towards them. As the detonations came closer, the noise grew unbearable, mingling with the storm in Glutt's head.

Sorov reached into his coat for a hip flask. He drank with his eyes closed, savouring it, then held the flask out to them. 'Gentlemen,' he said, his words almost lost beneath the approaching apocalypse.

Federak snatched the flask and took several hungry swigs, unable to match the lieutenant's calm demeanour, cowering and moaning as he drank.

Sorov took the flask back and handed it to Glutt. 'You are heroes,' he said as Glutt took the flask in his trembling fingers, spilling some of the contents down his chin as he drank. 'And no hero dies unnoticed.' Sorov looked up at the tearing heavens.

A river of flame washed down the valley like gold from a furnace, too bright to watch, incinerating fortifications and bunkers and turning the air to liquid. Sorov was little more than a silhouette by now, but until the very end he held himself with dignity, straight-backed and proud.

In the final seconds, as Federak started to scream and sob, Sorov raised his hand in a salute.

The blast hit.

Glutt howled. Not in fear, but in fury. It was unthinkable that a man like Sorov could be betrayed. Against all the odds, Sorov had led them to victory. Maybe Commander Ortegal could murder the entire regiment, but not Sorov. Not like this.

The force of the bombs rushed through Glutt, melting and evaporating his flesh, but rather than killing him, they fuelled his rage, transmuting him into a pillar of warp fire – lifting him up, still howling, into the tornado and making him one with the storm.

The galaxy could not work this way. The universe could not be so unfair.

As the planet died around him, Glutt recalled his moment of contact with the power that transformed Governor Narbo: that strange, mirrored view of life, so unlike anything he had seen before.

The rock boiled from beneath his feet and Glutt sank into darkness. As he fell, he sensed something flicker at the back of his thoughts – a new consciousness, born from the ashes of his faith.

He reached out, taking it by the hand.

1

A void ship cut through the night, painting artless, lazy spirals through a tide of shattered hulls – looping and falling, reeling like a drunk, spilling fire from its prow. Again and again it battled to find a route. Breaking against the swell. Dancing through the wrecks. Refusing to die.

Draik watched the display for several minutes, leaning casually against a twisted girder and taking long, languid drags from his lho-holder. *Such hope,* he thought. He knew the ship's odds but willed her on all the same. She was a rogue trader by her colours, skimming through the skeleton frames of dead leviathans, burning a furious path towards him.

Draik climbed through an access hatch and up onto a gantry. He could see most of Precipice from here. It looked like just another ugly wreck, drifting through the wandering stars, but this collision of mooring spars and walkways had drawn a feeding frenzy. Ships from every corner of the galaxy were huddled at its anchorage points, scorched and hungry, their captains all busy chasing the same alluring nightmare. Looming over the ships was the Dromeplatz, a mangled, bloody eye glaring down at its congregation of landers and skiffs.

Lights flared overhead as the rogue trader's ship clipped a drifting fuselage. It maintained its trajectory for a few more seconds, then dissolved into a thunderhead, embers and smoke raining down on Precipice, howling over the void screen like a ghost.

'We are a voracious breed, Isola,' he said, shaking his head in wonder. His attaché was on one of the lower gantries, dragging herself up towards him with a string of darkly muttered oaths. He reached down, offering her his hand.

Further down, beneath Isola's scrambling limbs, was the main route through the Skeins – a jury-rigged transitway, welded together from the superstructures of flayed ships. The road was crowded with debris, mechanical and human, all robed in darkness. The glow-globes and lumen-strips had been smashed long ago, so the only light came from the distant glare of the Dromeplatz, a ceaseless sunset, rippling on the horizon and turning the Skeins into a carmine hell. The air beneath the void screen was tormented by engine fumes and recycling turbines. It stung the eyes, burned the throat and drowned everything in a thick, toxic fug. Precipice was a forest of salvaged spires, smouldering and ephemeral, like a half-remembered fire.

'Thank you,' said Isola, climbing up beside him on the gantry. Once she had caught her breath she shook her head and said, 'Captain, we've been here for seven hours. Is this the best use of your remaining time? We're scheduled to leave within the week – unless there is some concrete progress.' She studied the sweltering scene below. Isola had a broad, boyish face, wide-set eyes and neat, slicked-back black hair.

She wore a meticulously pressed uniform and a habitual frown of disapproval.

Draik removed one of his gauntlets and massaged his long, lean snarl of a face. He looked out through the void screen, staring at the phantasm responsible for all this avarice. Beyond Precipice's jumble of crooked walkways and brume-shrouded ships, the revolutions of the heavens had ceased, consumed by a wall of nothing. There were few who could hold its gaze. The Unfathomable. The Abyss. The Deep. The Blackstone Fortress.

Draik stared into the monolithic dark, trying to discern something solid – something real. His eyes slipped across angles and shadows, unable to find purchase, glimpsing hints and suggestions but nothing he could recall for more than an instant. The Blackstone glared back, malign and unknowable. Mocking him. The star fort was the size of a small planet, with Precipice as its ramshackle moon, but even those brave souls clinging to Precipice would never claim to understand the Blackstone. Countless rumours had crossed the Western Reaches – enticing tales of the treasures to be found in its depths. But those reckless few who survived its mantle of debris clouds soon found that the mystery only deepened. The Blackstone guarded its secrets well.

Draik put his gauntlet back on and slapped the girder, sending up clouds of rust. 'Gaulon said to look here, in the Skeins.'

'Gaulon was a drunk and a liar.'

'But not a fool. He knew I'd come looking for him if he lied.'

Isola shook her head. There was a small cogitator slung under her arm – a copper box covered in rows of teeth-like keys. She rattled her fingers over them and the device hummed into life. Needles trembled over luminous dials, valves hummed and mechanisms chittered. She stared at the displays. 'We've covered the whole district, captain. *Twice*.'

Draik waved his lho-holder at the Skeins, gilding the dark with embers. 'People don't come here to be found.'

'Captain, we've been on Precipice for three months. We have far exceeded our remit.' Isola's expression softened a little. 'I admit, it seemed as though you were getting close to something, but what do you really have to show? We've pushed too much into this venture. His lordship's instructions were clear – return to the Curensis Cluster and finish our negotiations with the Tann-Karr. There's a fortune waiting for us in that system. It's time to go. We can forget about Precipice. The Blackstone Fortress is not the only prize in the galaxy.'

Draik said nothing, staring out through the operculum again, his human eye reflecting the void screen's warps and eddies while his augmetic eye flashed red, catching the glow of the Dromeplatz.

Isola looked exasperated. 'Even if you could solve this mystery, there's no guarantee it would change your situation.'

Draik looked at Isola as he took another drag from his lho-stick. Officially, she was *his* attaché, but they both understood her role: she was there to keep him on track, and to report to the family if he strayed. Her loyalty was to House Draik first, its errant son second. She was rigid, punctilious and unswervingly honest. Draik liked her.

'I'm on to something, Isola.'

'You found a name. That's not the same as finding an answer.'

'The Ascuris Vault. All we need is a way in.'

Isola sighed and turned off the cogitator. 'We have our

orders, captain. I sent missives to his lordship explaining that we're already preparing to head back to the *Draikstar.*'

Draik gripped a girder until his knuckles were white.

'We lost five men in that last attempt,' said Isola. 'And left empty-handed. There was no sign we were getting close to the vault.'

He stared at her. 'This time I have something, Isola, I *know* it.'

She closed her eyes in despair. 'How many times have you said that?'

Draik was about to reply when he heard an unexpected sound. He held up a hand for silence.

Raucous laughter echoed up from the shadows.

'Not everyone is hiding,' said Draik.

He gripped a handrail and slid down it onto a lower gantry, dropping into a crouch and staring through the pipework, drawing the rapier that hung at his belt.

There were men swaggering down the transitway, kicking rubbish and bellowing with laughter. Even through the rolling smog, Draik could see how dishevelled and filthy they were. They were shouting and belching as they approached, waving machetes and pistols.

He grabbed a dangling cable and slid down to street level for a better view. A long, rangy shape was scrabbling ahead of them, limping and low to the ground. Some kind of injured animal. They were hurling junk at it, jeering and snorting as it tried to drag itself away.

'Captain,' warned Isola from up on the gantry, but she was too late. Draik had already walked out to face them.

The gang halted. Their laughter faded and they backed away, weapons raised, as Draik strode towards them through the crimson gloom.

'What's this?' growled a man with a mohawk, frowning and swinging his head from side to side, like a dog on a scent.

Despite the gruffness of the man's voice, it was clear Draik had unnerved him. Draik marched through the rubble, imperious and grim, examining the men down the length of his long, regal nose. He grimaced at their filthy rags, as though studying a grub that had crawled from his breakfast. The lights of the Dromeplatz flashed along his rapier and glinted in his augmetic eye. Draik was clearly not from the Skeins. He was dressed in a luxurious military dress coat trimmed with gold piping. His starched breeches were immaculate, and his cuffs were embroidered with fine silver thread. But Draik would have cut an aristocratic figure even in rags. He had the face of an Imperial statue: leonine, flinty and proud, with a hard, sword-slash mouth and a thick waxed moustache.

'Captain Draik,' he said with a stiff bow.

The gang stared at him for a moment, surprised by his clipped, formal manner of speech. Then they burst into laughter.

'It's Guilliman 'is bloody self,' snorted the man with the mohawk, marching across the road and squaring up to Draik. He was massive; a round-shouldered ape, a foot taller than Draik and clutching a ratchet as long as his arm that he had sharpened into a mace.

'Don't let that clicker go,' the brute snapped, waving his weapon at the animal that was still trying to crawl down the transitway. His men leapt to obey, kicking it into a burnt-out cargo crate.

'Captain Draik, you say?' He stepped closer, pressing his oil-splattered chest against the Imperial eagle on Draik's cuirass, staining the gleaming plate.

Draik stepped back and wiped the cuirass clean. 'I didn't catch your name.'

'The Emperor,' grinned the man, eliciting a round of sniggers from the rest of the gang.

'Delighted. I'm after a pilot. Someone who knows how to reach the Dragon's Teeth.'

'Dragon's Teeth? There *ain't* no Dragon's Teeth.'

The man looked at his lackeys and they stopped tormenting the animal to grin back at him. 'Which idiot told you they was real? No one's ever seen 'em. They ain't a thing.'

The animal in the cargo hold snarled and lunged forwards, trying to break free, clicking and snorting until the gang attacked it with renewed violence, driving it back with a flurry of kicks.

'What have you got there?' asked Draik, peering through the gloom. The thermocoupling in his ocular implant clicked, focusing on the crate. The animal was thrashing from side to side and its heat signature was hard to discern. It was larger than a man, though; he could see that much. And it looked to be bipedal, but with backwards jointed legs and claws in place of feet.

'A man-eater,' said the brute with the mohawk. 'Don't worry. We'll kill it. Just having some fun. It's a hunt.'

The other men sniggered and Draik's distaste grew. They looked like a manifestation of every disreputable sight he had witnessed over the last seven hours. His hand slipped involuntarily to the handle of his power sword.

'Captain,' said Isola behind him, sensing the approach of trouble.

Draik was not in the habit of displaying emotion in front of the lower orders, but he was tired and frustrated. He could not entirely keep his disdain from his voice. 'Do your hunts often involve outnumbered, wounded, unarmed prey?'

The man's expression hardened as he saw Draik's hand resting on the sword. 'We hunt whatever we like.' He gripped his mace in both hands and drew back his shoulders. His face was a mess: scarred, misshapen and clogged with filth, but his eyes glittered as he studied the gilded pistol at Draik's belt.

Draik raised an eyebrow and lifted his sword, adopting a loose-limbed en garde position. He knew he should leave these low-lives to their vile amusement, but Isola's words were still echoing round his head. *It's time to go.* Anger and frustration quickened his pulse. A wolfish snarl spread across his face.

'Grax,' said the man. 'Put a hole in 'im.'

A man with a laspistol backed away from the thrashing animal and pointed his gun at Draik.

Draik shook his head, turned lightly on his heel and ran down the transitway towards him.

Grax fired, lighting up the junkyard with a las-blast.

Draik dodged the shot and it burned through the air, hitting nothing.

Grax whirled around, cursing, training his gun on the shadows.

Draik swung back into view, clutching the same cable that he had used to reach the transitway. His rapier flashed cobalt as it slid through Grax's shoulder, causing the man to drop the pistol and stagger backwards, howling in pain and clutching his wound.

More shots blazed through the shadows, surrounding Draik in a cloud of shrapnel as he looped through the air. He loosed the cable and somersaulted over their heads, slicing his rapier back and forth and landing in the centre of the mob, filling the air with blue contrails.

The men staggered, clutching wounds, spouting blood and crying out in confusion.

The man with the mohawk charged, bellowing and drawing back his mace.

Draik waited calmly, sword arm raised, his rapier hanging loosely from his grip. At the last minute, he threw a feint. The man fell for the ruse, lunging in one direction as Draik sidestepped the other way and jabbed his sword in and out of his throat.

The man whirled around, preparing to attack again, unaware of his wound. He marched towards Draik and tried to speak, but his words emerged as a bloody cough. He staggered, confused, trying to catch the blood rushing down his chest.

Draik lowered his sword and stepped back, giving another stiff bow as the man dropped heavily to his knees, gasping for breath.

Draik sensed movement to his left and leapt back, dodging another shot. He twisted and pounced, rounding on his attacker with a graceful twirl, thrusting his rapier into the man's chest with a flash of blue sparks.

There was another howl of gunfire, but this time it was Isola. She had followed Draik out into the centre of the transitway and silenced another man with a shot to the head.

Draik strode back towards their leader. He was supine, sprawled on his back with an ashen face, surrounded by blood. Draik put an end to his hunting days. He looked around for any other attackers. Everyone was either dead or dragging themselves away, stifling groans as they slipped back into the darkness. Draik cleaned his blade and slid it back into its scabbard, surveying his handiwork.

His blood cooled as he met Isola's eye. She did not have to

say anything. Her expression was enough: this was beneath him.

'Take me back to the *Vanguard*,' he said, frustrated with himself. 'I need some clean air and good brandy.'

'Wait!'

The voice came from behind them and they whirled around, pistols raised.

The animal had emerged from the crate and stepped out into the light.

The alien was humanoid, but taller and leaner than a man. His head was long, tapered and avian, with a tall crest of spines and a wide, beak-like jaw. His skin was barbed and as thick as flak armour, but it had been slashed by dozens of blows.

'A kroot?' asked Isola, squinting through the gloom.

Draik nodded. He kept his pistol raised but did not fire, allowing the alien to approach.

'You saved me,' the alien said. He spoke good Gothic, enunciating the words more clearly than the men Draik had just killed. His throat could not entirely abandon his racial heritage though, accompanying the words with a musical jumble of clicks and whistles.

'Still to be decided,' said Draik, keeping his gun pointed at the creature's head.

The kroot staggered to one side then leant across the crate to steady himself.

Draik stepped closer, keeping his gun raised.

The alien clacked his beak a few times, as though crunching food. 'You seek the Dragon's Teeth. I heard you. Over near the crossvault. You came to Precipice to raid the Blackstone, like everyone else. But you need a pilot. You want to reach the Ascuris Vault.'

Draik lowered his gun in surprise. 'How do you know I'm looking for the Ascuris Vault? I didn't mention that to anyone out here.'

'Why else choose that route? The Dragon's Teeth are impassable. Only a fool would try. Or someone who needs the Ascuris Vault. You do not look like a fool.'

'You seem very knowledgeable on the subject.'

'I have been through the Dragon's Teeth.'

Draik frowned. Perhaps he was not the only one who had guessed the importance of the Ascuris Vault. 'Why?'

'I was employed. By a priest called Taddeus. The vault is holy.'

The kroot crouched down and opened the mouth of one the corpses. As Draik watched in disgust, the alien plucked something from his jacket and placed it in the corpse's mouth, whispering as he did so.

'You sought the vault for religious reasons,' prompted Draik.

The kroot shook his head, looking around for another corpse. 'Not me. I did not know of it.'

The creature was frustratingly distracted, but Draik persevered. 'The priests, then, they sought the vault for religious reasons?'

'Taddeus has visions.' The kroot hurried over to another dead body and placed something in its mouth, whispering again.

'You saw the vault?'

The kroot shook his head, still fiddling with the thing he had placed in the corpse's mouth, prodding it then licking his claws, like a chef testing seasoning. 'The priests became odd. Then died. They found no vault. Taddeus got back. But he was insane to begin with.'

The kroot finished his ritual and walked back over to Draik.

He stared at the dead bodies and let out another burst of clicking sounds. 'They do not eat kroot meat and yet they would kill me. It makes no sense.' He looked directly at Draik. 'I will help. I can help you reach the vault. And keep you alive.'

'*You're* the pilot who passed through the Teeth?'

'No, but I can lead you to her.'

'And what will you want in return?' Survival on Precipice meant dealing with species Draik would usually kill on sight. Precipice's brutal, frontiersman law had created a strange, fragile egality that Draik had not witnessed anywhere else. But, whatever the rules of Precipice, Draik could barely hide his distaste at talking to the alien. The creature was barbaric. His hide was covered in ritual scars and tattoos, and rattled with bone fetishes. As he looked closer, Draik saw dozens of tiny cages dangling from the kroot's arms. They were filled with mutilated insects – beetles and flies that had legs and wings removed but were still alive, whirring angrily in their cages as he moved. These were the things he had been putting in the corpses.

'I must repay the debt.' The kroot glanced at the shadow hanging over them. 'The Blackstone brought us together. Do not question its plans.'

Draik looked out into the blackness. 'There are many things in there, kroot, but a plan is not one of them.'

'My name is Grekh.'

'Grekh,' said Draik, lowering his pistol. 'I'm Captain Janus Draik. This is my attaché, Isola.'

Grekh did not reply. He leant against an outlet pipe, trying to catch his breath, seeming to be in pain.

'Isola,' said Draik. 'Pain suppressors.'

Grekh shook his head and waved Isola away. He rattled through the cages strapped to his arms and removed one of the struggling insects. Then he popped it in his beak and closed his eyes for a moment.

After few deep breaths, Grekh stood upright. He looked down at Draik and Isola, teetering on long, gangly bird legs. His eyes were blank and unreadable.

'No one has reached the Ascuris Vault,' said Grekh. 'It is madness to try. But the priest believes in it. He has waking dreams. And if madness is what you seek, I can get you there. I can take you to the pilot.'

'My trade contact, Tor Gaulon, told us the pilot was somewhere here, in the Skeins.'

Grekh shook his head. 'The pilot is a deserter. Audus. She's not here. Your Navy has a price on her head. Her crime was serious. The Skeins aren't safe for her now. But I can find her. We must to go to the Helmsman.'

'A deserter?' Draik frowned. 'We were headed to the Helmsman anyway, I suppose. A short interview can't do much harm. You may accompany us as far as the Helmsman, Grekh. And if you can back up your claims with an actual pilot, I'll pay you a reward.'

Grekh shook his head. 'My reward is to come with you.'

'Where?'

'Through the Teeth. Into the Unfathomable. To the Ascuris Vault.'

Draik laughed, shocked by the creature's presumption.

Grekh retained the same earnest, confident tone. 'There is a debt. Swear to take me. I will lead you to the pilot and I will save your life.'

Isola could not hide her outrage. 'Are you trying to give Captain Draik an order?'

Draik dismissed her concerns with a wave. 'If he fails to give us anything of value in the Helmsman, we can part company then.'

'Swear the oath,' said Grekh in the same flat, abrupt tone.

Draik ignored the creature's crude manners and considered the offer. It was extremely unlikely that the alien would get him to the Ascuris Vault. And if Grekh really could achieve such a feat, enduring the alien's company would be a small price to pay. He nodded.

'Very well. If you find us passage to the Ascuris Vault, I swear, as a scion of the most venerable House Draik, that you will accompany me as my personal retainer.'

Grekh grunted and led the way back down the transitway, walking in a strange, swaying gait.

As they followed, Isola saw a gleam in Draik's eye and shook her head. 'Voracious indeed,' she muttered.

2

Gatto was the first to see the truth. The Blackstone Fortress was not a prize to fight over; it was not a treasure to be ransacked. It was an open grave – a snare designed to catch only the bravest and the most idiotic. Precipice had yet to be built when Gatto arrived. There was no place to dock in those days. No place to pray. Only a headlong plunge into the unknown. He made dozens of attempts to breach the fortress, as desperate as all those who followed, losing a little more of his body with every attempt until he finally accepted defeat. Few since had shown such wisdom, but Gatto had realised that there are more ways than one to find a fortune. As a rapacious horde followed in his wake, crowding the fast-growing port with their ships and dreams, Gatto saw how to feed on the hunger that devoured him – how to save his sanity, even when it was too late to save his flesh.

The Emporium of Fools, as Gatto preferred to call the Helmsman, was a circular hall built around a single, stolen shard of the fortress – an ominous hexagonal slab of pitch, bolted to the heart of the Helmsman's lounges and staterooms. It was the cruellest taunt Gatto could think of, made all the crueller with every sip of his absurdly expensive liquor. It sat there, tantalising, untouched by the bustle and din. Silent and alien. Half of Gatto's patrons would never fly again, trapped in the limbo of Precipice – their ships lost, their crews dead and only enough money left to pickle themselves before the uncaring shard. No one had ever been able to mark it or even discern its nature, but humanity always finds a way to leave its dirty fingerprint. Gatto had covered the shard's lower half with pict captures. Hundreds of them. Strange, haunting portraits of the dead. Whenever one of his patrons failed to return from the fortress, he pinned their portrait to the black monolith, taking perverse glee in the fact that another fool had met the fate he dodged.

Gatto's bar was built around the shard and Gatto was built into the bar. His iron lung was as big as a coffin and roughly the same shape, mangled together from the same rusty salvage as the walls. His robotic arms were in constant motion – dozens of them, whirling back and forth, anticipating the needs of every drinker who slumped towards him, sloshing cups and hurling food in a fluid ballet of lunges and flips. There was a circular, glass-fronted hatch in the centre of his iron lung, displaying his withered organs. They were suspended in grey milk, dark and ugly like a cluster of charred fruit. Gatto's head was the only part of his body still fully intact, but it more than made up for the lack of anything else. As Grekh led Draik through the crowd, Gatto was in full flow, screaming at the room – a casket of vented hate, spitting red-cheeked vitriol at everyone and no one.

Draik grimaced as the Helmsman attacked his senses. It was

deafening. An unsavoury, scandalous explosion of life. The circular room was a warren of alcoves and booths and the air was thronged with Gatto's pets – skinless void-creatures he called bloodbirds. They were not true birds, but huge, leathery moths, fluttering around the room in their hundreds, larger than a man's hand and slick with crimson tar. They had thick, grimy lenses sewn into their heads that rattled and whirred as they flew, focusing on the lurid scenes below. As Draik tried to follow Grekh through the crush of yelling bodies, he had to swat them away. The bloodbirds screeched indignantly at him, but even that could not compete with the sounds of squalid revelry. The pictures on the shard were a constant reminder of what lay in store for most of Gatto's patrons, so no one was drinking to relax. They had come to crush their fear. To fuel their hunger.

The room was sparsely lit, the humid darkness bisected by thin columns of light that shone harshly on a few faces but left everything else hidden in murk. As he followed Grekh, Draik caught snapshots of crazed, adrenaline-fuelled drunks, bellowing at each other, leering and gemmed with sweat. Some human, some not, but all radiating the same thought: *I* will be the one. *I* will scale this peak. *I* will conquer the dark.

'Gatto!' cried Grekh as they forced their way to the bar.

Gatto's iron lung was mounted on runners and he was currently rattling towards the far end of the bar, screaming as he threw trays of food at a group of hulking, glowering abhumans.

'Gatto will be no help,' shouted Isola. She was standing beside Draik, but the Helmsman was so loud that she struggled to make herself heard. 'He never stops yelling long enough to hear anything.'

'He knows everything,' said Grekh. He waved at the

bloodbirds. 'They record things. They see everyone who comes in here. And *everyone* comes in here.'

Draik studied the shadows flitting overhead, wondering if Grekh could be right. The kroot seemed peculiar, even by the standards of an alien. He reminded Draik of similar characters he had encountered on Precipice – fervid, humourless types who spoke like everything was a prayer. A particular kind of mysticism preyed on those who survived several trips into the fortress. A solemn, quiet religiosity. It was as though the strangeness of the fortress attached itself to them, adding its shadow to theirs, muddying their thoughts with its riddles. The locals called them devotees, using the word with a mixture of derision and fear.

A noise came from a few feet down the bar – a tidal roar of oaths and howls, accompanied by the sound of shattering cups.

The crowd pressed against Draik, causing him to stagger as a large shape loomed through the shadows. His instinct was to draw his pistol, but he gripped the bar instead. Precipice's laws forbade the use of firearms in any of its drinking halls or markets. Gunfights broke out, of course, but it could be an expensive business if the proctors got involved. Draik understood the logic. Precipice was more than a simple way station; it was a fragile alliance – a tense truce between smugglers, traders and privateers from every race and creed in the galaxy. These were dangerous souls. In any other situation, they would have gunned each other down without hesitation. On Precipice they forged allegiances and struck deals, united by their eagerness to profit from the Blackstone, but violence was never far away. The first captains to lash their ships together over the Blackstone Fortress saw how quickly such a lawless state would collapse, so they called themselves the proctors and enforced brutal, simple governance. The rules were easy to understand: step out of line and the proctors would execute you, seize whatever you had taken from the Blackstone and then deny ever hearing your name. The law was so simple it worked – most of the time, at least. As the commotion next to the bar grew more violent, Draik steadied himself, straining to see the cause.

A bear waded into the throng, standing on its hind legs and roaring, spraying saliva over the drinkers who were howling and reeling away from it, trying to claw their way back from the bar.

It was more machine than animal, implanted with a junkyard of pumps and flywheels and shackled to the end of the bar. A dozen feet from where Draik was standing, the chains snapped it to a halt. Its rusting lower jaw was stained crimson and there was a man at its feet, screaming and laughing as he slipped in his own blood trying to escape. Hands grabbed the man and hauled him to safety as the bear lurched from side to side, lashing at anyone nearby, bellowing and straining against its chains.

'Bosa!' howled Gatto, his head spinning on top of his iron lung to glare back down the bar.

The bear dropped onto all fours and lowered its head but kept pulling at the chains, straining its massive shoulders and causing the hydraulics in its legs to hiss and pop. Gatto rattled down the length of the bar, apoplectic. As he rushed along his track, he hurled cups and plates and lashed the bar with his metal arms, filling the air with spilled drinks and shattered crockery.

'Rug!' he screamed, reminding the bear of his ultimate sanction.

Bosa held its nerve until Gatto had almost reached the end of the bar, then lurched sullenly back into the shadows, rattling its chains one last time as it padded back into the one corner of the Helmsman that always remained empty. A wave of drunken laughter washed through the room along with cries of 'Rug!'

'Gatto!' cried Grekh as the iron lung rattled back the way it had come, passing right in front of them.

Gatto caught sight of the kroot and halted. Behind him his multitudinous limbs snaked across rows of bottles, filled a cup and banged it down, then he bellowed a stream of obscenities into Grekh's face. Gatto's features were gaunt, swarthy and fixed in a constant snarl. He glared at Grekh, his mouth hung open, spittle hanging from his chin.

'Information,' said Grekh.

The noise around the bar continued unabated, but Gatto fell quiet for a moment, a mischievous look in his eyes. He rolled his casket closer to Grekh and tilted it until their faces were almost touching. Even then, he chose to yell.

'You're going back in?'

Grekh nodded.

Gatto laughed. It was a mean, filthy sound. He nodded to the base of the shard behind him, and the portraits taped across it. 'I thought you might escape me, Grekh. I thought you had more brains than the others.' He noticed Draik and Isola. 'These two as well?'

'If we can find Audus.'

'Audus?' Gatto looked disappointed. 'Too late. She has a hefty price on her head. And there are too many bounty hunters here for a prize like that to go unnoticed.' He poured drinks for Isola and Draik. 'Keep trying, though.' He nodded at the portraits stuck to the shard. 'Make yourself famous.'

'Who took her?' asked Grekh.

Gatto's face turned purple. 'Am I your stinking mother? Do I look like a *friend*, you feathered sack of excrement?'

Draik calmly sipped his drink, eyeing Gatto's rage-knotted

face over the rim of the cup. He grimaced at the taste and put the cup down, leaning over the bar until he was in range of Gatto's spittle. 'I don't think we've ever been introduced. Captain Janus Draik of House Draik.'

Gatto sneered at his delicately embroidered dress coat and the intricate workmanship of his weapons.

'I bet a princess like you has some money.'

Draik nodded, revealing an impressive collection of proctor tokens.

They had barely emerged from his coat before one of Gatto's rubber limbs snaked through the pools of beer and whipped them out of sight. Gatto leant closer to Draik, his bloodshot eyes focusing for a moment.

'Grusel Bullosus took her. She didn't go happily though. She's a maniac. Things got messy.' He grinned. 'She'll be dead by now.' He paused to howl another string of obscenities at Grekh, then rattled off back down the bar.

Grekh clicked his beak again, as though trying to swallow something. Then he rummaged through the caskets hung around his chest, peering into each one and whispering to it, conversing with the tormented insects. He singled one out and tapped its cage with his long, bony talons.

'She's still alive,' he said, raising his voice over the din. 'Bullosus would not kill her. And I know where Bullosus' ship is.' He finished his drink, slapped down some proctor tokens and pushed away from the bar. 'We can get her back. Bullosus is greedy and you have money.'

'Wait,' demanded Draik, grabbing hold of Grekh's arm, then immediately regretting it as dozens of tiny cages shattered beneath his fingers. They were flimsy things, made of wooden splinters and locks of hair, and as they broke they stained his gloves with crushed insects.

Grekh scraped up the remnants of the insects and ate them. He seemed to forget where he was, closing his eyes as he chewed, savouring every morsel.

'I have my own pilot,' said Draik, struggling to hold his place as raucous laughter broke out behind him, causing the crowd to stagger and press against him. He was starting to remember why he avoided the Helmsman. 'This Audus just needs to supply me with directions. In fact, if you were part of the original mission, why can't you just tell me the way yourself?'

Grekh continued eating for a moment longer, then shook his head, rattling his mane of quills. 'You need Audus.' He looked again at the pulped insects on his arm.

Isola shook her head. 'Captain. Why listen to this ridiculous creature? And would you really let some renegade fly the *Vanguard*?'

Draik took out a handkerchief and wiped the dead insects from his glove. 'I'll judge Audus' character when I meet her.' He nodded at Grekh, who was already barging through the crowds to the exit. 'And he may be perfectly sound according to the mores of his own race.'

At the back of the room, someone started playing a fiddle, adding a grating, discordant screech to the general cacophony of laughter, fighting and whirring moths.

Isola tried to answer Draik, but the racket drowned her out and all she could do was follow as Draik made his way back through the crowds of reeling drinkers. Terrible as the music was, people were trying to dance it, so the way back out was even more of a battle than the way in had been.

They had almost reached the door when another group arrived at the Helmsman and swooped into the tightly packed main bar. They were humans but they looked as out of place as Draik, trailing a storm of voluminous robes. They were as tall and slender as Grekh, but where he lurched and hopped, they sliced proudly through the throng with their chins raised, gliding into the Helmsman like an elegant yacht cutting effortlessly through the tide. They all wore masks, and the leader sported an impressive helmet that contained his whole head and was crested with six blade-like antennae, making it look like a stylised star. He was clearly a nobleman, swinging a gilded cane topped by a gem the size of a fist. The filigree on his chest armour displayed an ancient Terran family crest.

Draik stumbled to a halt, shocked to see someone from his own strata of society. The leader of the group was striding at such a pace that, when Draik paused, the two men collided and the noble's cane clattered across the floor.

The rest of the group surrounded him and drew pistols, training them on Draik.

The music faltered.

Grekh waded back through the crowd and interposed himself between Draik and the noble with a threatening snarl.

The Helmsman fell quiet. Even Gatto ceased his ranting to watch the exchange, waiting to decide who was most deserving of his bile.

'Stand down!' said Draik to Grekh, irritated that he had to reveal his connection to such a beast in front of a Terran noble.

Grekh hesitated, then stepped back to Draik's side. A small circle had opened around them and Draik had enough room to bow.

'Captain Draik of House Draik, at your service,' he said, waving Isola to the noble's cane.

She snatched it from the floor and handed it back.

For a few awkward moments, the noble did not move or reply; he just stood there, staring at Draik.

'Helmont Corval,' he said finally, his voice reverberating through the mouth grille of his helmet. 'Emissary of House Corval.'

'I did not anticipate meeting a gentleman in such surroundings,' said Draik.

'Nor I,' replied Corval. 'An unexpected pleasure. Please, you must call on me when you have a chance.' He handed Draik a beautifully embossed calling card displaying his name and coat of arms. 'My ship is the *Omnipotence.* We are moored to the spar called the Celsumgate. I am newly arrived from the Cainus Subsector. I have heard fascinating rumours about this anomaly but I have yet to discuss it with–'

'We must go,' snapped Grekh, stooping so that his stubby beak was directly in front of Draik's face.

Corval stepped back, clearly repulsed by the alien.

Draik glared at Grekh and then gave Corval another bow. 'I have urgent business to attend to but I would be delighted to talk more when I have time.'

Corval seemed at a loss for words again, but he returned Draik's bow.

Draik waved Grekh on and they made for the door, escaping the crush of bodies and stepping out into the blood-red fog.

'Where is this pilot?' said Draik, quickly losing his patience with Grekh.

Grekh headed down the walkway, passing beneath a vast archway. The structure was hundreds of feet tall and oddly beautiful, like the buttress of a grand cathedral, but it was actually the casing of a turbine, torn from the engine of a long-forgotten ship. Grekh weaved through the arch and hopped onto a girder, before loping off in another direction.

3

Draik took a drag from his lho-holder as he followed Grekh into Precipice's forest of cooling ducts, heat shields, cargo bays and bulkheads. It was an ugly scene – hundreds of ships and docking stations, stacked precariously and threaded with rivers of smog, smouldering slowly in the blood-glow of the Dromeplatz. Precipice was divided into four loosely defined districts: Flotsam in the north, Lagan in the east, Jetsum in the south and Derelict to the west, with Dromeplatz as a central hub, the only route from one district to another. The whole sweltering mess bristled with hundreds of embarkation points locked to the three main mooring spars – Eliumgate, Celsumgate and Orbisgate – and hunched menacingly beneath the spherical void screen was the buttress of a long-forgotten frigate, laden with weapons batteries and lance turrets, some of which were allegedly still operational. What began as a simple trading post had become a township of sorts, a gaudy powder keg fuelled by the hot, sluggish air trapped beneath the void screen. Even to a seasoned traveller like Draik, it was an unusual sight, but he was not really looking at it. All he could picture was his father's face when he heard that his errant son had mastered a Blackstone Fortress. What would the duke say then?

Most of Precipice's mooring spars radiated from the central axis like outstretched arms grasping helplessly at the void, but the Orbisgate circled the whole eastern quarter of the station – the region known as Lagan. It was a crooked sphere of gantries and anchorage points. Blinking landing lights dragged it in and out of view and clouds of landers and shuttles whirled around its ports, giving the Orbisgate the appearance of an angry wasps' nest, swarming with desperate industry.

Grekh led Draik and Isola along one of the broader walkways, towards a hulking bulldog of a ship. It was hunched at the end of a mooring point, as dented and buckled as every other ship that battled its way through Precipice's junkyard corona.

There was a guard standing on either side of the landing ramp and they looked like human manifestations of the shuttle they were tasked with protecting – scowling, ogrish brutes gripping battered lascarbines. As Grekh led Draik and Isola up towards the hatch, they all heard the sound of banging coming from inside the ship, along with muffled curses and shouts. Draik was about to speak when Grekh strode in front of him and addressed one of the guards.

'We need Grusel Bullosus.'

The guard's face was blank. Draik nodded his head in a slight bow.

'Let me introduce myself. Captain Draik of House Draik. I have business here with a pilot called Audus.'

The guard's expression remained the same.

Draik enunciated his next words with care. 'There is a pilot called Audus on this ship. I need to speak to her.'

The guard finally glanced at Draik. Then he turned away and spoke into a comms-link beside the hatch.

'Grusel. Someone's here. Says he's Captain Draik. He's asking after someone called Audus.'

There was a moment's pause, then the vox crackled into life.

'Draik?' There was another pause, then the voice came again, breathy with avarice. *'The* Terran? *Wait.'*

A few minutes later the hatch whooshed open to reveal what looked like an explosion in an arms factory. There were weapons everywhere: locked to the walls, stacked in heaps, hanging in crates from the ceiling and scattered across the deck. It was a fantastic collection. Some were weapons Draik could recognise, but many were clearly of alien manufacture. Standing in the midst of all this weaponry, leaning on the doorframe as he tried to catch his breath, was a pale, blubbery heap of a man. He was topless and his grey folds of flab were glistening with sweat. His head looked like an egg, pale and hairless, nestling in a ruff of double chins, and his face appeared oddly shrunken, cowering in the middle of his jowly head. He had the wide-eyed look of the perpetually baffled. At the sight of Draik, the man stood upright, carrying his weight easily on a huge frame. Draik guessed he must be nearly seven foot tall. There was oil splashed across his pallid chest and he was clutching what looked like a piece of construction equipment – a rivet gun or a steam hammer. There was blood dripping from the casing.

He stared at Draik, slack-jawed, taking in the well-tailored uniform and gold braiding. 'Yeah?' His voice was breathy and hoarse, little more than a whisper, but he was gripping the rivet gun like he was about to crush it.

'Grusel Bullosus?' said Draik.

'Yeah.'

'I need a few moments alone with your guest, a pilot by the name of Audus.'

'No,' said Grekh. 'Not just talking. You need her–'

Draik silenced him with a glare.

Bullosus stared at Draik. He still seemed unable to close his mouth, but he saw what Draik was carrying.

'Proctor credits?'

Draik nodded.

The landing ramp juddered as Bullosus stomped out onto it. 'How many?'

Draik flashed him an impressive spread of tokens.

Bullosus stared. '*How* many?'

The bounty hunter was not quite as dim as he appeared. Draik doubled the number of tokens. Bullosus stared at them for a few seconds longer, silently mouthing numbers as he counted. Then he nodded.

'Two minutes.' He turned and thudded back into the ship, waving them on board with his blood-splattered gun.

They passed mounds of ammo cases and piles of firearms in the companionway before climbing down a stairwell into the hold. They paused at a door as Bullosus entered a security code. His fingers rattled quickly over dozens of digits, but Draik's augmetic eye recorded the code, just in case it was needed later. As they stood at the door, Draik heard singing coming from the other side – a haunting melody, completely incongruous with the ship's brutal-looking interior.

The blast door whooshed aside and they entered the hold. The room was a long, low-ceilinged rectangle, lined with rows of thick, reinforced doors, all bolted shut. It was harshly lit and the walls were splattered with blood, giving the place the appearance of a slaughterhouse. There were more weapons scattered across a workbench, along with shackles and restraining harnesses. In the centre of the room, two guards were packing crates, lascarbines slung over their backs.

In the corner of the room there was a mound of xenos body parts – heads, mostly, presumably taken from the Blackstone as hunting trophies that could be sold to nobles too lazy or cowardly to kill their own. The Blackstone was infested with all manner of strange beasts and Draik could only recognise one of the specimens Bullosus had collected. It looked like the head of an enormous insect, with huge, lethal-looking mandibles and a thick, pitted carapace. As he studied it, Draik recalled the name 'ambull' from xenology texts he had pored over as a child. Perched on top of this strange menagerie was a spherical cage, and in the cage was a living creature – a strange-looking amphibian. Draik hesitated, taken aback by the peculiar nature of the thing. It looked like a bloated, leathery toad but it had a small, perfectly human face. This grotesque animal was the source of the music. Its face was earnest with concentration as it sang and the music was eerily beautiful, more like a choir than a single voice.

The two guards stood up at the sound of the opening door and grabbed their guns, pointing them at Draik and the others.

Bullosus ignored them and led Draik to a doorway at the far end of the room. As he walked past the other doors, Draik heard the sound of muffled cries and banging.

Bullosus tapped in another security code – again, recorded discreetly by Draik – and the door dropped into the floor, revealing the cell behind. It was little more than box, barely big enough to hold the woman chained inside it. Audus was cuffed to the wall, slumped against her restraints, her head hanging down against her chest. She was wearing a bulky Imperial Navy flight suit, but even without it she would have been almost as large as Bullosus – not fat, like he was, but broad and powerfully built. Draik could imagine how hard Bullosus must have had to work to take her down.

'Is she dead?' asked Draik.

Bullosus shook his head. He still had the same slack-jawed expression on his face but there was a trace of excitement in his voice as he replied. 'I'm not letting this one die. Too valuable.' He grabbed her by the throat and pushed her back.

As Audus' head lolled to the side, Draik saw a gunshot wound in the chest pocket of her flight suit. He frowned at Bullosus.

Bullosus shook his head. 'I tag 'em, that's all.' Before Draik could protest, Bullosus slapped her, hard, across the face.

Audus was covered in bruises and lesions but she stirred, muttering gibberish as she stood up. She had strong, classical features and her eyes were cool and steady, locking on Bullosus with no trace of fear.

She strained against her bonds but could only move her hands a few inches from the filthy wall. Then she noticed Draik and the others watching from the doorway and frowned. She tried to speak but her mouth was full of something. She spat a dark gobbet of blood on the floor and glared at Draik, her eyes burning.

'I hope I'm worth the money.'

Bullosus stepped out of the cell so Draik could see Audus more clearly. 'He just wants to talk to you.'

'Grekh?' Audus' eyes widened as she saw the kroot. 'You're alive?'

Grekh nodded, but gave no other sign he knew her, busy looking with interest at a gun mounted on the wall. It was a rifle, with long, scythe-like blades strapped to the stock and barrel. It had been left unsecured. Draik gave the kroot a warning glance.

'Talk?' said Audus, turning her glare on Draik. 'You'd better be quick. Fatboy has plans for me. I'm valuable, believe it or not.'

Draik nodded. 'I can be brief. I need passage through the Dragon's Teeth. This kroot tells me–'

'Hey!' cried Bullosus as Grekh grabbed the rifle and slammed it, butt-first, into the bounty hunter's face.

Things moved fast after that.

Bullosus crashed to the floor, dropping his gun, and before he could rise Grekh turned and fired at Audus, filling the room with noise and light.

Draik cursed. Isola had been right – he should never have trusted the alien. He whipped his splinter pistol out and pointed it at Grekh.

The wall behind him exploded into shrapnel as the guards opened fire. Draik dropped into a crouch and returned fire, sending a guard flipping back through the air, clutching a hole in his throat. Isola took the other one down with her lasgun and there was a brief pause as Draik, Isola and Grekh looked at each other through the gun smoke, clutching their weapons. The amphibian in the cage stopped singing to stare at them.

Audus leaped from her cell, launching herself at Bullosus, who had just climbed to his feet. Her weight bowled him over and they rolled across the floor, laying wild punches on each other as they smashed through the table and scattered weapons. The manacles at Audus' wrists were smouldering and Draik realised his mistake – Grekh had not shot her; he had blasted her restraints off.

'You can't get past the teeth without her,' explained Grekh as Draik pointed his pistol at him.

Footsteps clattered overhead.

'More guards,' said Isola, training her gun on the open door. 'Now we'll have to explain all this to the proctors.'

'Bullosus can't go to the proctors,' said Grekh, waving at the guns. 'This is all stolen from Precipice. So are his captives.'

Draik held up his splinter pistol. 'I can use low-grade toxins. Let me do the–'

More shots filled the air as the other two guards stormed into the room, guns barking.

Draik ducked into the cell to dodge the blasts. When he emerged the guards were dead, holes smouldering in their jackets where Grekh had shot them.

'No more killing!' he cried as Audus punched Bullosus to the floor and reached for one of the guns hanging on the wall.

She ignored him, but Isola was close enough to smash the weapon from her grip and send it flying across the room. Audus howled, lifted the metal workbench off the floor and smashed it over Bullosus' head. Bullosus crumpled and lay still, blood rushing from his ears and nose.

Draik strode across the room, grabbed Audus and threw her through the doorway onto the stairs. She bounced back onto her feet but came face-to-muzzle with Draik's pistol.

'Let me kill him,' she said quietly, her eyes straining.

Draik said nothing, keeping the gun pointing at her. Audus cursed and dived at him, giving Draik no option. He fired, sending her crashing to the floor with a splinter in her chest.

Finally there was quiet. Audus was sprawled at the bottom

of the steps and Bullosus and his crew were lying in a fast-growing lake of blood. The caged singer was still silent, staring at the mess.

'Time to go,' said Grekh, lifting Audus onto his shoulder with surprising ease.

Draik looked at the other cell doors, cursing his better instincts. 'We can't leave them to starve, whatever they are.'

Isola dropped to one knee and put a hand on Bullosus' neck. 'He's alive,' she said. 'Someone will have heard all those gunshots. And when they arrive they will be keen to know how Bullosus came by his cargo. No one will starve.'

Draik nodded, then glared at Grekh. 'I never ordered you to start freeing people.'

'Ordered?' Grekh shook his head. 'I am not a servant.' He sounded confused rather than angry.

Draik felt like silencing the kroot in the same way he had silenced the pilot, but he waved him back up the steps. 'We'll talk on the *Vanguard*.'

The *Vanguard* loomed over Precipice with a disdainful air, like a noble bird of prey perched at the centre of a stinking scrapyard, far too proud and elegant for such ill-favoured surroundings. Like everything in the Draik fleet it was sleek, lethal and gilded with Terran heraldry. It looked like the smaller, leaner cousin of an Imperial warship, with a long, graceful prow and hulking, Aradus-class plasma engines. It was only a shuttle – Draik had been forced to abandon his void ship, the *Draikstar*, on the far side of the debris cloud – but it was still a far more impressive sight than most of the vessels moored to Precipice. It was heavily armed and large enough to carry hundreds of servitors, crewmen and attachés. Usually, Draik would feel a sense of relief as he returned to this bastion of civilisation, but as they carried

Audus up the landing ramp he was cursing under his breath.

'She's dying,' he muttered, glancing at Isola in consternation. 'I can't understand it.'

He had expected Audus to be coming round by now but, as they rushed her into the *Vanguard*'s commerce lounge, her heart rate was slowing at an alarming rate.

He placed her on a couch and stared at her in confusion.

Isola and Grekh followed him into the lounge and he waved his other attachés and crewmen away. Grekh was muttering to one of his caged insects, edgy and twitching, clicking his beak repeatedly. Isola began rummaging through the walnut-panelled cabinets that lined the room. The lounge was beautifully appointed, like everything else on the shuttle, with plush, deep carpets and a vaulted ceiling decorated with bas-relief images of Terran beasts. But it was poorly stocked compared to the full-size commerce lounge on the *Draikstar*. 'Combat stimms?' muttered Isola as she rifled through star charts and metal-clasped books.

Draik hunched over Audus, monitoring her vital functions with his cybernetic eye. Data scrolled over the lens of his monocle – a blizzard of runes and chemical formulae. 'The reaction should not have been this severe. Bullosus must have drugged her. And whatever he used must have reacted with the neurotoxin I used to stun her.'

Grekh gripped his rifle, as though he could shoot the drugs out of her system. 'If she dies, I have failed you.'

Isola attached a medicae device to Audus' chest and it began chiming.

She shook her head and stared the cupboards. 'We have nothing left. Nothing for neurotoxins, at least.'

'Return to Bullosus' ship,' said Grekh.

'What?' said Isola.

'Find the weapon he used on her. Put it in a cool place. Her wounds will become less inflamed.'

Isola looked at Draik with a raised eyebrow. Grekh had been making lots of similarly bizarre suggestions since Audus started to fade.

Then Grekh noticed the splinter pistol at Draik's belt. 'Or *your* weapon.' He stepped towards Draik, reaching out for the gun.

Draik gripped the gun's handle, but before he could say anything, the chiming of the medicae device became a long, drawn-out whine.

'Throne!' muttered Draik, slapping the couch in frustration.

Isola rushed over and examined the device on Audus' chest. She shook her head. 'No pulse.' She crouched next to Draik. 'We should not be found with a dead deserter on a House Draik ship.'

Draik shook his head, still staring at the corpse, unable to accept he had let this chance slip through his fingers.

'You tried everything,' said Isola. 'This was not meant to be. It's time for us–'

'It is meant to be!' Grekh looked around the lounge. 'It is the Blackstone's plan. Bring her back. Revive her. Restart her heart. You must–'

'The Blackstone is a star fort,' snapped Draik. He knew it was far more than that – incredibly vast, partially inhabited and full of ancient archeotech, for a start – but the kroot's endless mythologising was grating on him. 'It does not have *plans*.' Then something Grekh had said resonated with him. 'Restart.' Draik rocked back onto his feet and stood, staring into the middle distance. 'Restart, restart, restart.'

He clicked his fingers, rushed across the room and began

flinging open all the cupboards and tossing objects through the air. A bewildering collection of arcana was soon scattered across the floor: ancient-looking timepieces, plant-stuffed terrariums, gun barrels, fragments of mouldering tapestry, books on etiquette and display cases full of medals.

'Where is it?' said Draik as he emptied a bag of numbered skulls onto the floor.

'What?' asked Isola, whipping drawers out and emptying them.

'The axial interrupter we took from the Corliss Sector,' muttered Draik.

Isola shook her head, frowning at him, still rifling through the piles of objects.

'This!' said Draik, emptying a crate of finger bones and holding up a battered old leather strap as if it were a trophy. It looked like a wide belt, but it was trailing bundles of wires and studded with dials and switches. There were needle-tipped prongs running along its length, and as Draik flicked a switch the prongs crackled with electric current.

'That's for restarting plasma cells,' said Isola, eyeing him warily.

Draik rushed back to the dead pilot on his couch, turned a dial and flicked the switch again. This time it sparked with such force that fingers of electricity arced between the prongs, burning so brightly that Draik could hardly look at it.

'Wait!' cried Grekh, with more emotion in his voice than Draik had heard before.

'She's already dead,' Draik pointed out.

Grekh fell quiet and backed away but Draik hesitated. Dead or not, there was something ungallant about what he was about to do. Then he shook his head. Without Audus he would leave Precipice with nothing. He wrapped the belt around the pilot's wrist, forced the prongs into her veins, fastened the clasps, flicked a switch and then stepped back.

There was a hiss of burning skin and the smell of cooking meat filled the room. As the device bucked and flickered with electric charge, the seconds stretched out and Draik pictured himself as the other two must see him, hunched over a corpse, burning a hole in its arm. The whole scene was extremely undignified. He was about to deactivate the strap when Audus sat up with a howl, knocking Draik back across the room. He crashed into Isola and they slammed into one of the cabinets.

Audus continued howling as she leapt to her feet, smoke trailing from her wrist, her eyes rolling wildly.

'Bullosus!' she cried, grabbing Grekh by the throat and slamming him against the wall. Sparks were shimmering across her face and flashing in her mouth until Draik rushed forwards and turned the device off.

She froze. 'Grekh?' She sounded dazed, her hand still locked around the alien's throat. She let go and looked around at the commerce lounge, taking in the subdued, hidden lighting and the fearsome hunting trophies mounted on the walls.

'What is this?' she asked, looking at Draik and Isola.

'Sit down,' said Draik, taking her by the arm and removing the strap. 'You've just–'

Audus shoved him away, nearly falling, then managing to steady herself. She stared at the strap. 'What's going on?'

'Bullosus' drugs reacted with a splinter I fired into you,' said Draik. 'You were temporarily insensible.'

'You shot me?'

'You were attacking me. But my shot should not have had such a serious effect.'

Audus touched the burn marks on her wrist, staring at him.

'You need a drink,' said Draik, pouring brandy into a crystal tumbler and offering it to her.

Audus ignored him. She massaged the stubble on her shaved head and winced. 'Why did you break me out of there?' She glared at Grekh. 'Did you bring him to me? Why?'

Draik waved to the couches, gesturing for everyone to sit. Isola and Grekh took a seat, but Audus remained standing, swaying slightly and looking warily at the door, as though expecting Bullosus to appear with shackles in his hands.

'You need to rest,' said Draik.

Audus glared at him and there was a moment of awkward silence, broken only by the occasional crackle of sparks flickering across Audus' jumpsuit.

'I have a proposition,' said Draik, sipping the brandy as if nothing untoward had happened. 'I am planning another attempt on the Blackstone and I have a very specific route in mind.' He nodded at Grekh. 'Your acquaintance here tells me you are uniquely equipped to advise me.'

Audus looked around the room, seemingly trying to gauge if she was hallucinating or not, then she strode over the drinks cabinet and poured herself a shot with a trembling hand.

'You've got the wrong person.' She was still massaging her head and grimacing. 'I'm done with this shitty place. I'm out of here.'

She finished her drink and looked at the animal heads that decorated the walls. 'Are you going to show me out of this zoo, or do I need to start breaking things?'

'Where will you go?' asked Draik, speaking quietly, still sipping the brandy. His augmetic eye hummed as it focused on her face.

'As far from Precipice as possible,' she said, heading to the door.

'You must have a great deal of sway with the proctors,' said Draik. 'Not many people can get off this station, not without giving them a substantial payment. But you are presumably so trusted, they will let you leave for free.' He finished the drink. 'And pay for your place on a ship too.'

'You must have your own pilot,' she said, her eyes narrowed. 'What do you need me for?'

'To get through the Teeth,' said Grekh.

Audus laughed. 'The Dragon's Teeth?' Her tone was derisive, but Draik noticed she was no longer looking at the door. Something had sparked in her eyes.

'Tell me how to fly through the Dragon's Teeth,' he said, 'and I'll make you so rich you'll have no problems leaving Precipice.'

Audus headed back to the drinks cabinet and refilled her glass. Her hand was steadier this time. 'Why risk such a dangerous route? The Blackstone will kill you soon enough. Why hurry the inevitable?'

Draik shrugged. 'I can transfer the credits as soon as I land on the fortress. My survival, or failure to survive, will be of no consequence to you.'

She sipped the brandy thoughtfully. 'You're trying to reach the place those priests were babbling about? The obscure vault?'

'The Ascuris Vault.'

'Whatever. Why do you want to go there? Are you one of those babbling devotees?' She glanced at Grekh. 'Like him.' She raised an eyebrow. 'Does the Blackstone *talk* to you?'

'I have business there.'

Audus dropped onto the couch then gasped in pain and

placed a hand over her chest. After a while her grimace faded and she relaxed again. 'No, you're not chasing visions like those other idiots, are you?' She looked admiringly at the wealth scattered around the room. 'You're chasing something else.' She stroked the brocades that dangled from the arm of the couch. 'I'm not interested in being your employee, Mr...'

'*Captain* Draik,' said Isola.

Audus glared at her and continued. 'But if you tell me why you're willing to risk so much to reach this vault, I might consider a partnership.'

Draik struggled to keep his expression neutral. 'I have important reasons for finding the vault. Important for the wider Imperium, not just for my–' He cut himself short, shaking his head. 'It doesn't matter why I need to go there. What option do you have but to help me? You're trapped on Precipice until a bounty hunter puts you back in a cupboard. You're deluded if you think you can just fly out of here.'

'I'll take my chances.'

Draik glared at Grekh. 'Is she *really* the only pilot who can do this?'

'I'm the only one,' said Audus.

Draik shook his head. There was an infuriating lack of naivety in Precipice. Common and discourteous they might be, but the people here had only reached the Blackstone Fortress because they were shrewd enough to spot every opportunity. Draik felt as though he had landed in a world in which everyone was a little too much like him.

'Show me what you're after,' she said. 'What's so important that you'd lower yourself to conversing with the likes of me?'

Draik paced around the lounge, muscles rippling across his clenched jaw. 'This is more important than you realise.'

Isola shook her head, a warning in her eyes.

'What use will our research be if we have to leave?' said Draik. He came back to the couch, sat down and looked at Grekh. 'I belong to a certain school of thought. It's old fashioned, perhaps, but I believe that a man's word should mean something. I admit, I doubted you'd find me a pilot, but you proved me wrong and I will not renege on my oath. If we manage to land on the Blackstone, you may join my party.' He turned to Audus. 'Clearly, I am not in the habit of working with deserters.'

Audus' face darkened and she was about to argue, but before she could speak Draik held up a hand and continued.

'However, I must weigh up two evils. Associating with a possible criminal – I do not profess to know the veracity of the claims against you – or leaving Precipice without completing the task I set myself, which I believe could have a significant effect on the war against the Great Enemy. If you truly are able to steer the *Vanguard* past the Dragon's Teeth, then I will offer you a place in this expedition.' He lowered his voice, speaking very precisely. 'However. If either of you betray the confidence I am placing in you, or reveal the details of our arrangement with any other party, I will consider you enemies of the Imperium and,' he touched the handle of his rapier, 'deal with you accordingly.'

Audus tried to speak but he held up his hand again.

'I will need confirmation from you both, in writing, that you have understood the binding nature of our agreement.'

Audus poured herself another drink. She looked at the scrolls and papers Isola had scattered on the floor. 'Rogue traders. How you people love contracts.' She shrugged. 'Whatever. I'll sign. And I'm not greedy. Fifty per cent of whatever proceeds this expedition generates.'

Draik gave her a bemused smile. 'For flying me in?'

'For being your partner.'

Draik had to applaud her gall. And the truth was, he doubted there would be any proceeds to split. His plan was to share whatever information he found with the authorities on Terra. His prize would be of another nature. There was, however, a principle at stake.

'*Ten* per cent for each of you,' he said, holding up a hand as she prepared to reply. 'Janus Draik is not in the habit of haggling. Such an undignified way to approach matters. You may accept my offer or we may part company. It is entirely your prerogative. I feel it is only fair to warn you, however, that your friend Bullosus will be waking up around now, and, from what I hear, he is not the only intermediary contracted by the Imperial Navy to locate you.'

Audus raised an eyebrow and nodded, looking at Isola. 'Ten per cent. You heard the man.'

Isola was pale with anger, but she nodded to an auto-quill in the corner of the room. It trundled across the room and spat vellum from its chest.

'Standard terms,' said Isola, her voice brittle and icy.

The servitor's bundle of digits rattled over the scrolls, inking them with script and stamping them with juicy gobbets of hot wax. Isola snatched them up, pored over the clauses and handed them to Draik.

Draik took a quill from the machine and signed the contracts without looking at the text, then handed them to Grekh and Audus.

Grekh seemed unsure what to do, but finally scratched a symbol and handed a copy back to Isola. Audus took longer, staring at the text and sneering. Then she signed and gave a copy to Isola, stashing the other one in a deep pocket.

Draik nodded to Isola. 'Show them.'

She hesitated.

'Isola,' said Draik. 'Your captain has just given you an order.'

They both knew their relationship was subtler than captain and subordinate, but Isola could not defy such a blatant command. She cleared the table, placing the books and papers on the floor, then ran her finger over a rune engraved in the glass.

The lights in the chamber died as a hololith leapt from the table – a spiral of loops and nodes, like a genetic helix made of shimmering, static-slashed light, hovering a foot above the glass. It rotated, slowly, and the light waxed and waned, washing over the faces of Draik and the others as they leant closer.

Draik was still holding the strap he had used to revive Audus, and he pointed it at some of the intersections.

'Linear motors. Crystalline chambers that cross the whole Blackstone Fortress. The Precipice locals call them maglevs. If you've been on the Blackstone then you will have used one of these to reach your destination. Their design is baffling, obviously. They employ a form of magnetic propulsion to hurl transport chambers along ever-changing routes.' As Draik pointed at the various loops, they flowed and reformed constantly, creating new, increasingly complex variations. 'We can navigate them to a certain extent. The controls are easy enough to decipher. But the trips are always one-way and often not to where you intended.'

'Pretty,' said Audus, tracing her finger over the projection.

'Lethal,' said Draik.

Audus nodded. 'They're random. They spit you out wherever they like.'

'They do not *like* or *dislike*,' said Draik, irritated by the suggestion of a personality. 'But they're certainly unpredictable.

If you find a location that holds a clue to the fortress' past, or its workings, you can rest assured that you'll never get there again. All these expeditions and deaths and we're still no closer understanding the Blackstone.'

Audus narrowed her eyes. 'It's a treasure trove. Relics. Pieces of archeotech. What else do you need to know?' She was watching Draik closely.

'Those boors in the Helmsman lack ambition,' he said. 'They're happy to risk everything for a few fragments of alien weaponry.' He stared back at her. 'But it was not avarice that brought me to the Western Reaches.' He waved at the finery surrounding them. 'House Draik is not in need of funds.' He shrugged. 'I admit, Isola and I have accumulated some intriguing finds. When we first set off from Precipice we followed the same routes as every other wide-eyed adventurer.' He nodded to the rows of heads mounted on the walls. They were as eclectic a mix as the creatures heaped in Bullosus' hold: leering, monstrous horrors of every size and form. 'I've hunted species on the Blackstone that I have never seen mentioned in *any* scientific texts – and the Draik archives are extensive.' He waved through an archway to a companionway lined with cargo crates. 'And you're right – we have discovered technology so ancient and peculiar that a single piece could occupy an adept of the Cult Mechanicus for decades.' He shook his head as he considered everything they had seen. 'The Blackstone is unique. One could trawl its depths for a lifetime and barely glimpse a fraction of its mysteries. A brave man could certainly make himself rich in there.'

'But you want more.'

'I want control,' he said as the hololith flashed in his eye. 'I want to *claim* it. Think what that would mean for the Imperium. Power beyond anything in our arsenal. If I could hand that to Terra they could turn it on the Great Enemy.' Draik's words became more impassioned as he tapped a book on the table – a crumbling, gilt-edged relic called *Ravensburg's Treatise on the Gothic War.* 'From what I can gather, the Imperial Navy have harnessed similar star forts in the past with incredible results. I intend to give them the means to control this one.'

'And the Ascuris Vault?' asked Audus.

Draik pointed at the nodes in the hololith. 'Every one of these points is linked. I tracked signals from every one we found and they all look towards the Ascuris Vault. It acts almost like the Astronomican – guiding the transport chambers through the fortress.'

'You don't know that for sure.'

'Isola can show you our calculations. There's no question that the chambers link to the vault – every single one we encountered.'

Audus was nodding. 'So, if you could reach the vault, you might find a way to control the movements of the other chambers. You might make the place less of an impenetrable labyrinth – make it easier to navigate.'

'Perhaps. And perhaps, if the Ascuris Vault is the nexus of the transportation chambers, it might control other things. It may be the command bridge of the whole space station.'

Audus laughed. 'You think you're going to fly that thing to Terra.'

'All I know is that the Ascuris Vault is the obstacle that has stymied every attempt to understand the fortress.'

'And the Dragon's Teeth?' asked Audus. 'Why there? Why that particular docking point?'

'We have roughly located the vault, based on the signals we tracked from the other chambers, and the only way to get close is through the Dragon's Teeth.'

'Even then we may be sent off track by this,' said Isola, nodding to the shifting spiral of routes in the hololith.

'The Dragon's Teeth will place us very close to the vault,' said Draik. 'We will have a good chance of reaching it before we become lost.'

Audus laughed again. 'I've never heard so many ifs, buts and maybes. You're as insane as Taddeus.'

'Taddeus?'

'The last lunatic who tried.'

'Oh, the priest.' Draik shook his head, remembering who Grekh and Audus had travelled with last time. 'This is no holy crusade.'

'Then what is it? What *are* you chasing?' Audus leant across the table, bathing her shaven skull in glowing vectors. She was studying Draik with renewed interest. 'You say you're not as desperate as all the other wretches in Precipice. So what's driving you to take such risks?'

'I have just explained what success could mean for the Imperium.'

'No, it's more than that. I can see it in your face. This is personal. What does success mean for *you*?'

Isola snapped off the hololith and the lights rose again. 'The captain has told you everything you need to know. You have signed the contracts. How soon can you be ready to leave?'

'We'll need Taddeus,' said Audus. 'I can get you past the Dragon's Teeth, but you'll be dead ten minutes later. Unless you take the priest.'

'This is not a Ministorum crusade,' said Draik. 'Why is a priest so essential?'

'Look,' said Audus. 'You can't imagine how happy I'd be to never see Taddeus again. Even by the standards of this place, he's repulsive. I've had my fill of violent prophecies and bloody visions, but Taddeus *knows* things. When we tried to reach the vault last time, he knew every turn of the route.' She looked irritated by the admission. 'Something was leading him. I'm not saying it was spiritual, or that the God-Emperor was really talking to him, but he definitely knew where to go.'

'Your mission failed,' said Isola. She looked at Grekh. 'That's what you said, didn't you? The priests failed to find the vault?'

'The humans...' Grekh looked at Audus and hesitated. 'The humans became confused.'

'Insane,' said Audus. 'Tell them the truth, Grekh. We went insane. We all did. I saw...' Her words trailed off and she looked awkward, shaking her head. 'The Blackstone is more than nodes and chambers.'

'Is that why you ended up in the Skeins?' asked Draik.

She shook her head, then nodded, then shrugged. 'I can't remember how I ended up in the Skeins. I'm not even sure how we got off the fortress.' She looked at Grekh. 'But *you're* unchanged. And you seemed unchanged then.'

He twitched his head, causing his quills to rattle. 'I am not like you.'

Draik topped up Audus' glass. 'How did the fortress affect you? What did you see?'

She stared into the drink. 'The past.' It was clear she did not want to elaborate.

Grekh nodded. 'To reach the vault you need the priest.'

Draik hesitated. He needed to claim the Blackstone in the name of House Draik, not present it to some deranged Ministorum zealots who would seize it for the Ecclesiarchy. 'What does he want with the vault?'

'He doesn't want the vault,' said Grekh. 'He wants something hidden there. A holy relic.'

Draik nodded, pleased. It sounded as though the priest could lead the way to the vault, take whatever relics he liked and leave Draik to claim the real prize.

Isola leant over to him. 'Even if the priest can reach the vault, he won't be able to protect you from the madness Audus just described.'

Draik stood and began pacing around the room. He waved the axial interrupter vaguely in the air as he circled the couches. 'Think, Isola. Our new colleagues are both prepared to risk their lives by going back through the Dragon's Teeth, as long as we have this priest, Taddeus, in our party. Why would they do that if Taddeus does not really have some way of navigating the fortress?'

'Captain,' said Isola, 'you never struck me as a follower of holy men.'

He gave her a wry smile. 'He's an Adeptus Ministorum preacher and I'm as devout as you are, Isola. We must all be grateful we have the light of the Ministorum to lead us in such dark times.' His tone became more serious. 'And, if I heard our pilot correctly, this Taddeus had almost reached the Ascuris Vault when they were forced to turn back.' He stopped before Isola. 'Almost reached it, Isola. Do you see? Whether it was his faith that got him there or some secret he didn't share with the others, he clearly knows *something*. The pieces are falling together.' He nodded at Audus. 'We have a pilot who can fly us to the correct docking point.' He looked at Grekh with a slight bow. 'And a fighter who has sworn to keep me alive. And now a priest who can lead us to the vault itself, until we are–'

'Until we're so insane we can't go any further?' interrupted Isola, looking at Audus. 'Is that right?'

Audus sank back into the couch, massaging her wrist, wincing at the burn marks. She nodded. 'It's a fair point. How can we shield ourselves from madness?'

'Are you insane now?' asked Draik.

Audus laughed. 'That's a matter of perspective.' She shrugged. 'The confusion I felt on the Blackstone has gone.'

'It was specifically linked to the fortress? It only affected you on the Blackstone?'

'I suppose so, yes. In fact, we were all fine until Taddeus said we were near the vault.'

'Then it's a localised effect, not true mental illness. The Blackstone was projecting thoughts into your minds, protecting the vault. We need a psychic shield. There must be someone in this place who can help us...' His words trailed off. He turned to Isola with a triumphant expression.

'What?' she asked.

'Do you still have Corval's card?'

'Corval?'

'The Terran noble. The man we met in the Helmsman.'

She took it from her pocket and looked at it, still frowning.

'Look at the family crest,' said Draik.

She shrugged, then nodded, comprehension dawning in her eyes.

'What is it?' snapped Audus, reaching over and snatching the card.

'House Corval,' said Draik, 'is a Navigator house.'

'So?'

Isola managed to keep her expression as flat and impassive as ever, but Draik noticed how eagerly she took the card back. 'Psykers,' she said.

Draik nodded. 'If the Blackstone projected madness into your minds, then House Corval may be able to help. The

Navigator houses have ways to shield their minds from the dangers of the warp.'

'But we're not talking about the warp,' said Audus.

'They know how to protect minds,' said Draik. He took the card from Isola.

Isola shook her head. 'You're not thinking straight, captain. We don't even know this Corval. You're risking so much.' She glanced at the others, clearly uncomfortable having to talk in front of them. 'I *know* what this means to you, but we don't know any of these people.' She placed a hand on his arm. 'Can I talk to you alone, captain?'

Draik shrugged off her grip, smoothed down his uniform and took a deep breath. No one in the room, not even Isola, could understand what this meant to him. 'Corval is clearly a man of refined character. And I would hope he recognised the same in me. I'm sure he'll be willing to offer advice.'

Isola was about to protest again when he glared at her. 'Ready the remaining men, Isola. Grekh and Audus will take me to Taddeus.' He frowned, looking at Grekh. 'Do you know where to find the priest?'

Grekh nodded. 'He's not allowed to move his ship. The proctors won't let him leave.'

'Of course not,' laughed Audus. 'If Taddeus leaves here raving about visions and relics, every ship on the Western Fringe will come looking. The proctors are already worried they're losing control of the place.'

'Where is he?' asked Draik.

'An Ecclesiarchy barge,' said Grekh. 'The *Clarion*. Moored to Eliumgate.'

'Good,' said Draik. 'And the Corval vessel is moored to the Celsumgate.' He turned to Isola. 'I'll go with these two to the priest and, assuming that meeting goes well, I will then ask Corval's advice on the madness that Audus described.'

Isola saluted, but hesitated at the doorway, looking back at him.

Draik held her gaze, making it clear that the time for discussion had passed. She nodded and left, crying out commands as she marched down a companionway towards the stern of the ship, flanked by a scrum of rattling servitors.

Audus had stood up and Draik looked at his new companions. Grekh had the crude-looking rifle he took from Bullosus' ship but Audus was unarmed. He strode into the next room and grabbed a laspistol, handing it to her as he walked back into the lounge.

She stumbled as she took it and Draik noticed how terrible she looked – bruised, gaunt and pale and still wincing every time she touched her chest.

'Forgive my manners,' he said. 'This wretched place lowers one's standards. You need to eat. And rest.' He called Isola back in. 'Audus will remain here. See if there's anything edible left in the galley. And make sure she has some rest.' He grabbed a bottle from one of the cabinets, the syrupy, amber contents flashing as he handed it to Audus. 'This amasec is reasonable. Better than the vinegar Gatto sells, at least.'

He patted down his dress coat, checking his pistol and rapier were in place and that his uniform was uncreased. 'We'll return within the hour.'

4

Draik and Grekh left the *Vanguard* and hurried out beneath the junk-strewn gantries of Precipice, immediately enveloped by a tide of fumes, heat and noise. They had barely taken a few steps when something detonated over their heads. Draik ducked instinctively, pointing his splinter pistol at the stars. Then he relaxed and holstered the gun. It was just another ship exploding across the void screen – another desperate captain, failing to breach the debris cloud. It was happening almost daily now. Far more often than when Draik first arrived. The proctors had done all they could to stop word spreading but who could keep such a prize secret? And for every ten ships that failed to make it through the debris cloud, one succeeded, demanding a place at an ever-more crowded feast.

The walkways surrounding the *Vanguard* were thronged with new arrivals and they had to weave amongst swaggering giants and bustling, knee-high crowds. Not for the first time, Draik found himself marvelling at the unifying power of greed. Races and creeds walked past him with a singular purpose, forgetting centuries of enmity as they spilled from their ships and rushed towards the Dromeplatz. There was a bewildering variety of species: the usual colourful mix of hominids – humans and abhumans born beneath a host of different suns – alongside loping, avian monsters like Grekh and glistening, serpentine creatures that slid across the ruined metal, singing in a low, mournful drone that made Draik's skull ache. Slender figures, swathed in cloaks, rushed through the shifting dark, moving with liquid, inhuman grace: aeldari. Even half-hidden, they made his skin crawl. Sylphic, ethereal and cruel in ways Draik could barely fathom.

As Draik veered away from the aeldari he collided with a huge slab of armour plating and almost dropped his pistol. At first he thought he had stumbled into a piece of salvage – an abandoned bulkhead, perhaps, or a cooling tower – but then the enormous shape turned and looked down at him. It was a metal automaton – an ancient Adeptus Mechanicus war machine, with an assault cannon in place of one arm and a power claw in place of the other. He shook his head, surprised, yet again, by the strange inhabitants of Precipice. The automaton was eight or nine feet tall and it did not follow the design of any Mechanicus machinery he had ever encountered before. The thing had to be a mindless drone, but as it stared down at him through a narrow, horizontal lens in its helmet, it almost seemed annoyed with him. He laughed at the absurdity of the idea and rushed on.

They continued fighting their way through the crush until the south gate of the Dromeplatz reared up before them, a soaring arch of fuselage, skirted by a tidal crush of arguing traders and exhausted crewmen. There were several trading auditoria scattered around Precipice but the Dromeplatz was by far the largest. It was built on several levels and so large that it housed dozens of anchorage points, enabling smaller craft to dock directly to its upper reaches and unload cargo straight into the marketplace. It was dome-shaped, built in crude imitation of Imperial architecture, and it was the crimson heart of the whole station, burning red with the glow of three enormous combustion chambers housed beneath its floor. From Draik's perspective, as he approached the south gate, the Dromeplatz looked like a red flame, reflected in the vast, ineffable pupil of the Blackstone Fortress.

As they forced their way inside, the noise and heat soared, enveloping them in a sweaty riot of sound and colour. As always, Draik had to pause to take in the insanity of the place before he could press on. The crews that survived a mission to the Blackstone returned with an exotic mixture of cargoes, and most of it ended up in the Dromeplatz. The wonderful and the sublime quickly devolved into the measurable and saleable – commodities to be pawed at and haggled over before being scattered across Precipice. It was a frenzied scene but Draik had recently begun to wonder if all this industry and furious bartering actually achieved anything. The sellers clutched their proctor tokens and the buyers stashed their purchases, but none of them ever left; they were all trapped in the merciless pull of the Blackstone, hoarding their finds until they made that final, fatal trip to the fortress and lost everything they had won. Precipice was half mania and half torpor – for every new captain that docked, another failed to return, cluttering the mooring spars with silent, rusting sepulchres.

Once he had acclimatised to the tumult, Draik led Grekh into the crowd. They were swallowed up in a cacophony of screeches and howls. The stalls were heaped with xenotech and holy relics, but also crates of animals – bizarre, unclassifiable beasts. One of the mysteries of the Blackstone was how such creatures found a way to survive in its cold, lightless chasms. But survive they did, and many of them could be sold for huge sums to collectors. Draik saw a box of singing amphibian creatures, like the one he had seen in Bullosus' hold. Towering over them, its head bowed, was an enormous canine. It was thirty or forty feet tall and utterly black, merging with the shadows, only its burning red eyes revealing the shape of its vulpine snout.

The upper levels of the Dromeplatz had been built from huge sections of rocket boosters and fuel tanks, salvaged from the debris cloud; even these distant balconies were crowded with stalls and traders, swelling precariously across the narrow walkways that stretched from liftport to liftport.

Traders swarmed around Draik, drawn by his elegant attire, spotting a man of wealth. 'We're not here to buy!' he cried, waving them away and pressing on through the centre of the atrium. 'Let me through!'

'Drukhari!' hissed someone, prodding at Draik's splinter pistol and offering an insulting price for the weapon.

Draik looked down to see a pair of grinning, familiar faces – ratlings, only three or four feet tall, but with gaunt, scarred faces and the battered wargear of Astra Militarum Auxilla veterans. Draik had dealt with them before and found them to be even less trustworthy than most of Precipice's inhabitants.

'Hands off, Raus!' barked Draik, gripping the gun and scowling at the one who had touched his pistol.

They backed away, sniggering, but before Draik could take any more steps a mass of emaciated wretches crowded around him, barring his progress and proffering their pitiful wares.

Grekh gripped his rifle in both hands, but Draik shook his head. 'Do *not* start another fight.'

He fished a token from inside his jacket, then, when he was sure all the abhumans were watching, he flipped it through the air, sending it spinning back towards the south gate.

There was a stampede. Dozens of them bolted after the coin, leaving Draik's way clear.

He strode on, picking up as much speed as he could so that, when the crowds pressed back in on him, he was able to shoulder them aside and keep moving towards the north gate.

He did not pause to look at any of the trading posts, knowing how distracting they could be, and in just a few minutes he had nearly reached the exit. Like its southern counterpart, the north gate was a graceful arch of engine casing and, half hidden as it was by the fumes, it looked worthy of a place in the most beautiful Terran palace.

'Draik!' yelled someone from the other side of the auditorium.

He stopped and looked back.

Draik cursed as he saw the lumpen, porridge-like features of Grusel Bullosus. The bounty hunter was on the far side of the hall, separated from Draik by the crowds but using his massive bulk to barge through the crush.

'I don't have time for this,' snapped Draik, looking back at the north gate. They were minutes away from leaving the Dromeplatz, but not if he had to stop and fight an enraged bounty hunter.

Heat washed over the side of his face, accompanied by the brittle clap of a firing mechanism.

He whirled around in time to see Bullosus topple back into the crowd, clutching his arm, spouting a crimson geyser as he fell from sight.

Grekh's rifle was pressed to his shoulder, still smoking.

'Grekh!' snapped Draik as the din in the hall slipped up a tone. Precipice was always on the cusp of anarchy. Only the proctors' threats of summary execution maintained a fragile peace. The sound of gunfire in the Dromeplatz was enough to trigger a storm of curses and accusations.

Draik watched helplessly as the scene descended into chaos. Insults were answered with punches, and punches escalated into flashing knives. It took less than a minute for the first shots to ring out, followed by the crash of overturned stalls. The colossal canine reared on its haunches and dislodged some of the suspended walkways, sending bodies and gantries hurtling through the air to smash on the flailing crowds below. One of the falling gantries crashed onto a pile of crates and unleashed a flock of winged eels. The eels exploded into flight, filling the air with noise and movement as they thrashed against the side of the dome, confused by the crystalline walls and screaming as they struggled to escape the crossfire. A stray shot hit some fuel drums and a plump blossom of flame rolled across the deck plating, igniting clothes, skin and hair.

Grekh made an awkward attempt to mimic the bow he had seen Draik perform.

Draik stared at Grekh in disbelief as flames crossed the hall.

For a moment he was too stunned to move, then a familiar sound rang out through the din, snapping Draik into action: the clanging, tuneless bells of the proctors' heavies. He focused his augmetic eye on the walkway beyond the south gate. Sure enough, there was already a wall of metal thundering towards the Dromeplatz.

He took one last, despairing look at the carnage Grekh had triggered, then shook his head and raced towards the north gate, with Grekh bounding after him. The way was now clear. Everyone not involved directly in the brawl had spotted a chance to loot the abandoned stalls and rushed back to see what they could lift.

Draik and Grekh passed beneath the arch and out onto the walkway.

Draik cursed as he saw that there was a wall of metal approaching the Dromeplatz from this direction too. The wall was actually the interlocking slab-shields of bullgryns – the proctor's hulking, meat-headed enforcers. Colossal abhumans, ten feet tall and so heavily muscled that they wore thick plate armour salvaged from tanks and personnel carriers. The walkway shuddered under the impact of iron-shod boots. As they reached the gate, the bullgryns loaded their guns – wrist-mounted assault cannons, more suited to downing aircraft than halting a fight.

All along the walkway, people were diving for cover or sprinting back towards the Dromeplatz.

Draik looked around and saw a support strut just a few feet from the edge of the walkway. 'Follow me!' he barked, before taking a running jump at the strut.

It jolted under his weight, but held firm, and he began clambering up it just as the bullgryns opened fire on the crowds below. Screams rang out, followed by the boom of exploding fuel tanks and the snap of breaking lift cables. Draik climbed higher, relieved to note that the gunfire was targeted on the gates rather than on him. Grekh was a few feet below, climbing easily up the strut, but Draik was so furious with the creature that he felt like booting him away and letting him fall to the distant void screen.

The bullgryns pummelled their way into the Dromeplatz and the sound of fighting grew louder as the abhumans tried to regain control.

'Quick!' snapped Draik, nodding back down the way the enforcers had come. 'Before they ask who fired the first shot.'

They dropped back onto the walkway and raced away from the Dromeplatz, heading for the next mooring spar. When they were a safe distance from the fighting, Draik pulled Grekh beneath the loading ramp of a freight hauler and glared at him.

'What in the name of the Emperor were you thinking?'

Grekh looked blankly at him.

'You can't start firing that thing whenever you like,' growled Draik. 'You could have killed us both.'

'We are unharmed,' replied Grekh.

'And everyone else? Are they unharmed? How long have you been here? You must know what happens if someone opens fire.'

'I thought–'

'You thought nothing,' snapped Draik. 'Think yourself lucky that the word of a Draik is unbreakable. Otherwise I would leave you to the proctors and let you explain how you're going to pay for the damage you've just caused.'

Grekh stared at him.

Draik groaned in exasperation. 'Let me do the thinking.'

Grekh remained silent, so Draik whirled around and leapt back up onto the walkway.

'Which is the *Clarion*?' he asked as they passed prow after prow. Before Grekh could answer, Draik waved him to silence, spotting the unmistakable spires and finials of an Ecclesiarchy transport barge.

Draik cursed as he saw a group of bullgryns waiting at the foot of the landing ramp.

'The proctors won't let him leave,' said Grekh.

Draik was about to approach them, with no clear idea what

he would say, when a deafening explosion rocked through the Dromeplatz. The situation was clearly getting worse.

The bullgryns outside the *Clarion* hesitated for a moment, then thudded off down the walkway towards the Dromeplatz, readying their weapons.

Draik laughed and looked at Grekh. 'Perhaps you're more useful than I realised. Wait out here,' he said as he approached the landing ramp. 'And come to warn me if you see those guards coming back.'

'The priest is dangerous,' said Grekh, following him up the ramp, gripping his rifle.

'More dangerous than you?'

Grekh continued following him up the ramp, seeming not to have heard.

Draik stopped and stared at Grekh, then shook his head. 'Very well. But no shooting. Understand?'

Grekh nodded.

The doorway was built like the grand portico of a temple and the colonnades were covered in intricate reliefs – images of tortured, screaming souls, their arms thrown up in agony and despair, consumed by flames. All of them were clutching at their faces and had ragged, empty sockets where their eyes should have been. At the centre of this gruesome scene was a priest, seated in a throne carried by dozens of crook-backed wretches who were also eyeless and howling in pain. Only the priest on the throne could see and his vision burned like a sun on a star chart, an elaborate halo of delicate lines that spread around the doorway, fuelling the flames and blinding the wretched multitudes.

'Taddeus,' said Grekh.

'Is that what Taddeus looks like?' asked Draik. 'With the…?' He touched the mural.

'No. This is his vision. This is why he came here. He'll find that fire in the Ascuris Vault.' Grekh was about to say more, then hesitated and shook his head. 'Ask him to explain.'

The door whooshed upwards and left Draik face to face with a shaven-headed, emaciated-looking woman, dressed in the filthy robes of a zealot and pointing a large, two-handed flamer at him. Her eyes were bloodshot and seemed too large for her sunken eye sockets, straining and blinking furiously as through trying to escape from her skull.

'You-you are…' she stammered, her head flicking to one side as she spoke. 'Trespassing. Th-this is the property of the Holy Synod of Acheron and a sanctum of the Adeptus Ministorum.'

The woman was not looking directly at Draik, but rather at a point just above his left shoulder. Every few seconds, her gaze would briefly flick towards his and, in those brief moments of contact, Draik sensed a dangerous lack of reason. Her finger was trembling over the trigger of her flamer and the pilot light was hissing quietly before the muzzle. Draik heard Grekh shifting uncomfortably behind him, struggling to refrain from grabbing his rifle.

The woman noticed Grekh and frowned in recognition.

Draik spoke in what he hoped were emollient tones. 'I have learned that your master and I have a shared interest. It is important that I see him.'

The woman's lip trembled. She looked on the verge of either laughing or crying. 'Shared interest?'

'A location on the Blackstone Fortress. A chamber called the Ascuris Vault.'

The flamer drooped for a moment in her grip and the colour drained from her face. She glanced back over her shoulder.

Draik tried to peer inside the barge, but it was too dark for him to see anything clearly. There was just the vaguest flicker of candlelight washing over the bulkheads, but that was enough for him to see that the walls seemed to be moving somehow, rippling, like liquid.

There was a rattle of heavy armour as more bullgryns clanked past, down the walkway. Even from here, Draik could hear that the proctors had yet to calm the situation. The woman looked at the bullgryns and the crowds around the Dromeplatz. She shook her head, looking even more disturbed. She was clearly a hardened fighter: her limbs were sinewy and covered in scar tissue, and she held herself like a pit brawler, tensed and hunched, ready to strike. But her eyes were those of a cornered animal.

'Vorne,' said Grekh. 'This man knows about the madness. He knows how to resist it.'

This was not entirely true, but Draik felt sure the Navigators would help, so he nodded in agreement.

'Are you really here?' she said, her eyes narrowing as she raised the flamer again, levelling it Draik's chest.

'Am I here?' Draik threw Grekh a sideways glance, hoping the alien might understand the question.

Grekh's face remained impassive.

'I *am* here,' Draik said, turning back to her. 'I'm Captain Draik of House Draik. My ship is the *Draikstar*. You might have–'

'Heresy,' she hissed, her lip trembling again. She looked closely at Draik's dress coat and his gleaming cuirass, sneering and suspicious, as though she expected to see traitors hiding beneath his epaulettes. 'The seeds of the Great Enemy crawl through Precipice, breeding like rats. Old Night is here. Hunting. Feeding. Fed by all the faithless scum who come here.'

Draik nodded, slowly, conscious of her quivering trigger finger. 'Heresy. Of course. I understand. But I am a sanctioned representative of the High Lords of Terra. House Draik's Warrant of Trade was awarded by Lord Saviona of the Senatorum Imperialis and ratified by every member of the High Twelve. When I see your master I will explain–'

'He does not know me,' she interrupted. There was pain in her voice, and when she allowed her gaze to briefly meet Draik's he saw desperation.

'I can help,' he said, keeping his voice soft.

Hope flared in the woman's eyes. She leant out of the doorway and peered at the eagle on Draik's breastplate, examining its two heads. She tapped them, giving them a suspicious look, as though she expected them to speak. She glanced back into the ship a few times and then, with a whispered prayer, she finally stepped aside, waving them in.

Draik had to pause at the threshold until his eyes adjusted to the gloom. The barge's entrance hall was lit by a single candle, drifting overhead on a winged sconce, humming slightly as an anti-grav platform carried it back and forth, revealing glimpses of the rippling walls. The movement Draik had seen from outside came from hundreds of parchment scrolls nailed to the ship's bulkheads. The thin paper strips were covered with lines of tightly packed text and hurriedly stamped wax seals. There were scrolls hanging from the ceiling too and they rustled as Draik walked by, giving him the odd sensation he was moving through a forest.

The woman rushed ahead, looking back repeatedly to stare at them with a mixture of horror and hope. As he followed, Draik had to step carefully over a graveyard of holy texts. Ancient, leather-bound tomes had been torn to shreds and scattered across the floor. It looked like a slaughterhouse of knowledge. As he trod through the heaps, Draik grimaced at the waste. The books were valuable relics, but it looked like a wild beast had savaged them.

Further down the passageway, Draik heard ripping sounds. The massacre was still taking place. Papers rippled through the dark towards him, flashing in the candlelight, pale and ominous.

Vorne paused at the foot of a metal-runged ladder leading up to an access hatch. The hatch was open and the torn pages were drifting down through the hole. 'He's confused,' she said, looking everywhere but at Draik. 'H-he might not make sense.'

Draik nodded and gave Grekh a warning glance, before following Vorne up the ladder.

Taddeus' sanctum must once have looked like a relatively normal room, complete with ceiling-high bookcases, an impressive brass lectern cast in the shape of the Imperial eagle and a circle of wooden chairs. Now it looked like an explosion in a printing press. There were pages everywhere. The bookcases had been torn from the walls and the furniture had been overturned. The lectern was on its side, half buried in the mess, like a listing ship, and the chairs had been smashed into fragments, their arms and legs scattered across the piles of illuminated manuscripts. Hunched at the centre of the clutter, like a feral animal, was Taddeus. He was a solid-looking, portly man, with a ruddy, wrathful face and broad chest. Draik could imagine he must usually cut an impressive figure, but in his current state he looked more like a rabid dog. His cassock was crumpled and stained, and it was clear he had not left the room for some time. He had the same distracted expression on his face as Vorne and he did not even look up as Draik waded through the papers towards him. He was hunched over a book, tracing his finger over its pages and muttering the word 'no' over and over. When he reached the bottom of the page, he ripped it from the book and hurled it into the air, turning his attention to the next page.

Vorne, meanwhile, had crossed to the far side of the room and hunkered down in another corner, watching her master with a fearful expression.

'Your eminence,' said Draik, quietly.

Taddeus paused, but kept his gaze fixed on the book.

The priest held his book a little closer to his face, staring at the pages.

'I am Captain Draik,' said Draik. 'I do not believe I have had the privilege of meeting you before.'

The priest looked up slowly from the book, fixing his eyes on Draik.

'Sceptic,' he said, his voice low and dangerous. 'You think I failed.' Taddeus staggered to his feet and levelled a trembling finger at Draik. Up close, he was a great, swaggering hulk of a man. 'All of you! I can hear you whispering when I sleep. "He's mad!" you say. "His sermons were lies!"' He hurled the book across the room. 'But I am the one sane man in this den of idolaters.' He grabbed another, as yet unruined book and waved it at Draik. 'The answer is in here somewhere. There must be one word – one word that led me astray, and I *will* find it!' Then he looked back at Draik. 'How did you break in?' He scrambled around in the piles of paper until he found a brutal-looking mace, adorned with holy screeds and studded with razor-edged spikes. 'This palace is forbidden to all but the sons and daughters of Holy Synod of Acheron. You are profaning this citadel with your presence. Acamantus!' he cried, wading back and forth through the ruined books. 'Acamantus!'

'Brother Acamantus died,' said Vorne from her gloomy corner of the room. 'He never made it back to Precipice.' She looked tormented by her master's confusion.

'Precipice?' spat Taddeus, glaring at Draik, as though he had spoken. 'What precipice? What are you talking about?' He grasped his tonsured head and clamped his eyes shut, growling and shaking his head, as though trying to dislodge a thought. 'You all conspire to make me forget my purpose but it will not work. The God-Emperor's light is in me. It will burn through whatever deceits you lay across my eyes. Precipice,' he muttered. 'Yes, Precipice!' He glared triumphantly at Draik. 'See? You cannot fool me, rogue trader. I know this is not the temple at Chalcis. This is…'

His eyes clouded over and he shook his head, clearly confused again. He stomped across the room and wrenched open a control panel, tapping at a runeboard until a shield slid back from the ship's hull, flooding the room with red light as the docks outside were revealed. From this angle, only a fragment of the Blackstone was visible, looming ominously over the ships and mooring spars. Taddeus pressed his hands against the armourglass, staring at the scene outside, still growling under his breath. 'The Unfathomable,' he muttered, 'has been fathomed. I have found it. Here in this snake's nest *I* found it. Acamantus!' he snapped, looking over at the hunched figure of Vorne. 'We waited long enough. It is time to reach the vault.'

'I am Vorne,' she said, grimacing and hugging herself, patting her biceps furiously as she rocked back and forth on her haunches.

'Is everything ready?' demanded Taddeus, marching over to her and hauling her to her feet. 'Where are Brothers Cynus and Lacter and the others? We should be boarding the Blackstone by now, not talking to…' He glared at Draik. 'Not talking to traders and thieves.'

'Cynus and Lacter died too,' said Vorne, hanging weakly in his grip. 'All the brothers are gone, your excellency. We're the only ones left. Do you remember?'

'Gone?' Taddeus laughed. Then he let go of Vorne and marched over to the hatch, crying out to the rest of the barge. 'Everyone, up here now! The time is upon us. We have work to do! Great work! The work of the God-Emperor!'

There was no reply. Vorne dropped back onto her knees and began mouthing a prayer, staring at Draik.

After a minute or so, Taddeus backed away from the hatch, looking dazed. He caught sight of Grekh and looked even more puzzled. 'This fiend was in my dreams,' he whispered, pointing his mace at the kroot. 'What sorcery brought you here? You are a figment of my destiny.'

'He is called Grekh, excellency,' said Vorne. 'He was with us when we attempted to reach the vault.'

The priest's eyes cleared, then glistened with tears. He leant against the lectern, colour leaching from his face. Draik could see the hard reality of the priest's situation thudding into him. Taddeus juddered with each new moment of clarity, taking facts like body blows as he emerged from his delirium. As Taddeus crumpled before him, Draik thought of a way he could help – a small omission, rather than an outright lie, that would make his proposition more palatable.

'Your excellency,' said Draik, stepping closer to Taddeus and offering him a hand. 'I have come to offer my help.'

'Help?' Taddeus glared at him. 'What help could a rogue trader offer my holy mission?'

'Your excellency, I am not a cynic. Far from it, I have been humbled by the tales of how close you came to reaching your goal in the Blackstone Fortress.'

'Tales?' Taddeus frowned.

'Yes, your excellency. But I have also heard tragic stories of your reduced circumstances.'

Taddeus glanced around his trashed room and looked embarrassed. He stood up slowly, refusing to take Draik's hand and using the lectern to drag himself back to his full height. 'Reduced circumstances? *Reduced?* How can a man be reduced when he carries the light of the God-Emperor in his fists?'

Draik bowed. 'I merely meant I have heard of the terrible losses you sustained, and…' He pressed his hand across his chest armour. 'If you are ready to complete your mission, I can offer you the full support of House Draik, both financially and in terms of other resources.'

Taddeus looked appalled. He dusted down his cassock and drew back his shoulders. 'House Draik?' He narrowed his eyes.

'One of the oldest Terran dynasties, your excellency. We have traced our origins to–'

'Privateers,' sneered Taddeus. 'I am not so "reduced" I have to consort with hawkers. You have entered a holy place,' he said, nodding at Vorne. 'And you shall be rewarded for your sacrilege.'

Vorne emerged from her corner with her flamer raised. The panic had gone from her face.

Taddeus wore a large, circular relic of some kind on a chain around his neck – it looked like a medallion, but there were rune studs around its circumference. He touched one of them as he glowered at Draik.

The hatch slid back into place with a rattle of locks. Draik and Grekh were trapped.

Taddeus waved at the piles of books. 'I will find my answer soon enough. Somewhere in these texts is the code that will explain to me how I will return to the vault. But until then, the God-Emperor has given me other, equally valuable work to do.' He stepped back, away from Draik, as Vorne came forwards with the flamer.

'Precipice has drawn every kind of miscreant, deviant and non-conformist into its snare,' said Taddeus. 'Or should I say the God-Emperor has drawn them.'

Draik shook his head.

'The fortress is a trap,' explained Taddeus. 'A minority are here for noble purposes, but the rest are slaves to passion and need – weak-willed fodder for the Great Enemy.' He whispered a prayer. 'I did not fail to reach the vault, captain. I am not *reduced*. I have been given time to purge and cleanse.'

All the while Taddeus was speaking, Vorne was circling slowly around Draik, the muzzle of her flamer trained on him. She had reignited the pilot light and he could hear the promethium sloshing in the tanks strapped to her back.

Draik could feel the weight of his rapier against his thigh. Vorne was only a few feet away. He had spent most of his childhood practicing with a foil and he could probably draw his power sword and disable Vorne before she pulled the trigger. But if he wounded Vorne, and she dropped the flamer, the paper-filled room would go up like a furnace. A locked furnace. Besides, he needed Taddeus to guide him to the Ascuris Vault.

As Draik and Vorne circled each other, Taddeus flicked a switch on his mace and sparks of energy flickered across its razor-edged spikes, humming with lethal charge.

Draik scoured the room for something to help him distract

the priests. He needed to buy time. Most priests had a particular interest in a specific facet of the Imperial Creed. Perhaps if he could find out what most interested Taddeus, he could use that to win him over. Most of the pages in the room were too torn to be recognisable but then, as Draik passed behind the lectern, he saw a bookcase that had yet to be emptied. Draik edged closer so he could see the spines. All of the books were religious tracts, as he expected, but they were all focused on Holy Terra, describing the chapels, palaces and cathedra frequently visited by the few pilgrims who managed to reach the sacred heart of the Imperium. Draik looked at the pages near his feet and saw that they were all on the same subject.

Grekh had dropped into a low crouch and he was clawing at the floor, emitting a low snarl, about to pounce.

Draik spoke quickly.

'Have you heard of House Draik, your excellency?' he said.

Taddeus shook his head.

'We are one of the oldest households on Terra,' said Draik. 'Our estates are said to predate parts of the Imperial Palace itself.'

Taddeus' sneer faltered. 'You have been to Terra?'

'Your excellency, I was born within sight of the Imperial Palace.'

Taddeus nodded at Vorne, signalling that she should back down.

He stepped closer to Draik, lowering his mace. 'You *saw* it?'

'Of course. Usually only from the outside. I was rarely given permission to visit.'

Taddeus looked unconvinced. 'Rarely?'

'My father thought it important that all of his children see as much of the Imperial Palace as we could. Even with his influence there was much we could not visit, but I will never forget the parts I did see.'

'What did it look like?'

'I was a child, but I remember some things. The banners, hanging high, their colours flashing through the censer fumes. Statues of saints, rising from the crowds like giants, marching down processional routes. And doors like mountain slopes, so vast, even seen from so far away.' Draik's mind slipped back across the years. He had only mentioned the Imperial Palace to stall the priest, but the memory hit him with surprising force. He could almost feel the great swell of humanity pushing him on – the devout, filthy, bleeding multitudes who had crossed worlds and spent their whole lives with one desperate hope: that they might be one of the select few who survived long enough to see the Eternity Gate, praying that they would witness that holy portal between mankind and its master. Draik had felt buoyed that day, not by the mindless devotion that surrounded him, but by the knowledge that he was different. Faced with the wild-eyed pilgrims, he saw clearly that he, like his father and his father's father before him, would rise from the fold, born to lead and inspire rather than follow. With his father and sister at his side, Draik had known, without doubt, that he was destined for greatness.

Pain gripped him as he felt the keenness of his loss, saw the heights he had fallen from. Caught unawares by the vividness of his memory, he had to look away to hide his emotion.

Taddeus was watching him closely, and at the sight of Draik's pain the venom faded from the priest's eyes. He dropped his mace, rushed forwards and gripped Draik by the arms.

'Emperor preserve you,' he whispered, embracing Draik

in a fierce hug. 'What a fool I am. I see the truth of it now. Even now, all these years later, you are overwhelmed by the rapture.' He shook his head and held Draik at arm's length. 'Forgive me, Captain Draik. I misjudged you. No artifice could create the faith I just saw in your eyes.'

He signalled for Vorne to lower her gun. 'He's one of us, child. I was not seeing things clearly.' He looked pained again, massaging his temples. 'My mind plays tricks on me.' He shook his head. 'You have breathed the same air that moves through the Imperial Palace,' he said in wonderment.

Draik nodded. That much was true. There was no need to disabuse the priest of his other notions.

Taddeus closed his eyes and whispered a prayer, looking reinvigorated. 'This, too, I have foreseen,' he said. The doubt vanished from his eyes and the fervour returned. 'All has been revealed to me. Those who thought I had failed do not understand how the God-Emperor tests His most trusted agents. Each wound only makes me stronger.' He grabbed Draik's arm. 'And now He has sent you. I dreamt that a guide would come, sent from the God-Emperor Himself. And you are he, Captain Draik. I see that now.'

Draik nodded. 'I found the pilot who previously flew you past the Dragon's Teeth, your excellency,' said Draik. 'We can take the same route but this time you will reach the vault – and take whatever you're searching for.'

Taddeus looked troubled at the mention of the pilot. 'Audus? She's not as devout as we are.' He was about to say more when he caught sight of Grekh and scowled. 'You brought the animal too?'

'He has sworn to aid me.'

Taddeus looked doubtful. 'He swore to aid us last time.' He gave Draik a conspiratorial look. 'They eat their kills.'

'Grekh will be my responsibility.'

Taddeus still looked hesitant. 'We…' He clenched his fists, as though he would rather punch something than speak his mind.

'Your excellency,' said Draik. 'Audus and Grekh told me what happened last time – how you became confused.'

'My visions escaped from my mind,' said Taddeus, massaging his great lump of a skull. 'Everyone else could see the past and the future.' He shook his head and whispered a prayer. 'We all became prophets.'

'I've already considered this,' said Draik, placing a hand on Taddeus' arm. 'I have a solution.'

Taddeus looked eagerly at him.

'The proctors' guards are all busy dealing with a problem in the Dromeplatz,' said Draik. 'You're free to leave your ship if you go now. Are you well enough to make the attempt in the next few hours? Do you have any business to attend to?'

'Business?' Taddeus looked appalled by the idea. 'I did not come here to do *business*, captain. I came to do the work of the God-Emperor. Of course we can leave now.'

'Perfect, your excellency. I have one final call to make before we depart. If you can join me at my ship in an hour's time, I should be ready then. If I'm not there when you arrive, my attaché, Isola, will make you comfortable until I return.'

Taddeus grabbed Draik by the shoulder. 'The God-Emperor lit a fire in us, Captain Draik. That is the passion you felt when you first beheld those sacred doors. Our destinies are conjoined.' He glanced at the engravings that surrounded the door. 'The blind shall be made to see.'

The engraving showed the same scene Draik had seen outside the craft – a priest, surrounded by legions of tormented, eyeless wretches. The priest was carried on a grand throne and he, alone, could see. The dazzling, stylised beam radiating from the priest's face was burning through the crowds, igniting skin and hair and filling the skies with plumes of smoke.

'The Eye of Hermius,' said Taddeus, leaning close to Draik and staring intently at him. 'A devout believer like yourself has no doubt heard of it.'

Draik was about to admit he had not, when Taddeus continued, speaking in a tremulous whisper. 'The flames will hear no plea 'til the faithless soul burns free, 'til the truth is burned in thee, 'til the blind have learned to see.'

Vorne lowered her head as he spoke, repeating his words with her eyes closed.

Taddeus opened the loading hatch. 'I will find you in an hour,' he said, shaking Draik's hand. 'We will finish the work that was begun so long ago.'

Draik nodded. Taddeus' rhyme had troubled him. He had heard such prophecies before; often they were the last words of wayward priests who had earned the wrath of their more orthodox brethren. He decided to learn more about Taddeus once he returned to the *Vanguard*. For now, he simply gave the priest a quick bow and led Grekh back down the loading hatch and into the bustling crowds thronging down Eliumgate.

5

Bullosus paused for breath, wiped the blood from his eyes, then staggered on through the crowds. His arm was ruined, flopping pathetically at his side as he fought his way out of the Dromeplatz. The fighting was over, but the cries of the wounded followed him back out onto the walkway. The proctors had only one method of crowd control – a brutal, uncompromising method, but Bullosus could respect that. He knew the rules of Precipice. What he did not respect was a Terran dandy who masqueraded as a gentleman, then murdered his host's guards and stole his property.

He paused, leaning against a girder, his head spinning. There was too much blood rushing from his bicep; he was going to pass out before he reached the skiff. He tore some of his jacket away and made a tourniquet, stemming the flow, then he lurched on, knocking people aside with his swaying, out-of-control bulk.

'Grusel!' cried Lothar as Bullosus collapsed just inside the loading hatch, panting and cursing under his breath.

'You're dead,' grunted Bullosus.

Lothar shook his head as he tried, unsuccessfully, to haul Bullosus to his feet. 'Only stunned. Aurick too.'

Aurick clambered up from the hold and between them Bullosus' brothers managed to help him up.

'My arm,' muttered Bullosus.

They helped him down to the hold and he sprawled across a table. 'Bind it,' he said as the room swam around him.

His brothers looked at the wound and grimaced.

'Now!' yelled Bullosus.

'It's a mess,' muttered Lothar.

Bullosus struggled into a sitting position and looked down at his arm. He had not paused to study it since fleeing the commotion in the Dromeplatz. It was smashed. The shot had hit just below his bicep, pulverising not just the muscle, but the bone too. It would take a skilled chirurgeon and a lot of expensive bionics to make a limb from the pulp spilling across the table.

'Get Orphis,' he grunted. 'He's always in the Helmsman. He knows how to cut.'

'When he's sober,' muttered Lothar. 'I take it you didn't get the pilot back?' he asked, still grimacing.

Bullosus shook his head, still staring at the ruins of his arm.

'What will we do without her?'

Bullosus had been wondering the same thing. The rest of his useless family had debts worthy of a small planet. He had bought them time by swearing to return with Audus. For some reason she was worth more than any other fugitive in the whole sector. If he left Precipice without her, the game was up. His family's creditors were not the kind of men to offer new terms. If they did not hear from him soon, the killing would start. And here he was, one-armed and bleeding to death.

He tried to rise, but his head spun sickeningly and unconsciousness finally took him.

6

'The current situation has been deemed too risky,' said Emissary Corval. He was seated in the salon of his lander, facing Draik down the length of a long, possibly real, oak table. Behind the Navigator was a vast armillary sphere that dominated one end of the room, scattering candlelight across the walls as it moved. It was a beautiful antique – a vast, spherical cage of hoops, turning slowly around a solid gold likeness of Terra. The outer spheres were embroiled in iron serpents, a meandering forest of jointed snakes that clicked and writhed in time to the revolutions of the heavens. Only Terra was free of their taint, polished and pure, gleaming through the whorls and intersections, crowned by a nimbus of diamonds.

Grekh and Draik had reached the *Omnipotence* without incident. When they left Taddeus, the fighting in the Drome-platz was finally dying down and Precipice had returned to its usual state of tense lethargy. Draik had insisted Grekh wait outside and he was now alone with Corval, apart from a few liveried servants who were bustling around the table, clearing away silverware and crystal with silent, well-drilled efficiency.

'The High Lords are divided, of course,' continued Corval, 'over whose jurisdiction the problem falls under. The Grand Provost Marshal and the Fabricator General almost came to blows, apparently. No one can quite agree what the Blackstone is, so no one can decide who is responsible for it. My information is now out of date, naturally. From what I heard when we translated back into real space, the debates rumble on, but I believe it will be a matter of months, at most, before Precipice is dismantled. There is too much at stake for this problem to languish in the usual bureaucracy. Chaos warbands are massing all across the Western Reaches and the one thing everyone can agree on is that we can't let the Blackstone fall into enemy hands. Lord Commander Guilliman has been too busy to knock heads together, but he means to address the next assembly of the Senatorum Imperialis and I doubt he will be interested in listening to petitions or debating points of law. My instinct is that he will side with the Fabricator General. Guilliman's interest will be purely martial, obviously – is the Blackstone a hammer to crush the Great Enemy or not? The quickest way he can answer that question is to turn the site over to a Mechanicus explorator fleet. And the Martian priesthood will have little time for the rabble that are currently gathered in Precipice. They will require a tabula rasa before they begin their work, and they will happily create one with fire.'

Corval was still wearing his ornate helmet and his voice was a distorted growl, but to Draik it was a balm. After weeks of listening to the Precipice's savages it felt good to hear an educated fellow countryman. He had explained, on arrival, that he had little time to spare, but Corval had refused to talk business on an empty stomach, insisting that Draik join him for supper. Eating, for Corval, was a peculiar ritual in which his servants shielded his face with a silk handkerchief while passing him tiny morsels of food with a bewildering array of cutlery. The food was exquisite, and cooked in the Terran style, every mouthful reminding Draik of his home, making the meal both a delight and a torment. Corval was a member of several clubs and societies Draik had attended as a youth and they had spent nearly an hour exchanging anecdotes. It was only now, as the food was cleared away, that Corval had turned the conversation to the Blackstone Fortress.

Draik sipped his wine and considered Corval's words. 'You're very well informed. Few have such detailed knowledge regarding the dealings of the High Lords. House Corval must be well connected.'

Corval shrugged. 'Ours is one of the oldest Terran families, Captain Draik, but I would be lying to say we have the ear of the High Lords.' A note of humour entered his voice. 'But we have connections of others sorts – people with ways of gathering information that is not usually shared with the general populace.'

Draik nodded and smiled to show he understood. Almost anything could be learned on Terra through the right combination of bribes and threats.

'It would sadden me to see Precipice destroyed,' he said, thinking back over what Corval had said.

'Really?'

Draik shrugged. 'It sounds ridiculous, I know. These people are lowborn and vulgar, but by the Emperor they're dogged. They're both the worst and the best of humanity, emissary. Uncultured and uncouth, yes, but utterly without fear.'

Corval nodded. 'Your concern for the lower orders does you credit.'

'Either way, I hope to give the High Lords something else to consider before they discuss the Blackstone with the Lord Commander.'

Corval nodded, slowly. 'Indeed. I guessed as much when I saw you in the Helmsman.' He laughed. 'I hope you understand, I would not usually frequent such a dreadful establishment. I wanted to learn some concrete facts about the Blackstone and, from what I can gather, the Helmsman is the only place on Precipice where captains gather in large numbers. I've heard so many intriguing rumours en route to the Western Reaches but I was hoping to find someone reliable. Someone I could trust to tell me what the Blackstone *really* is. All I've found so far are petty larcenists with no interest in the Blackstone's true significance.' He leant over the table. 'But you didn't come here looking for pocket change, did you, captain? What have you learned? I sense you have loftier ambitions than the rest of these crooks. I would consider it an honour if House Corval can assist you.'

'You're a gentleman of the old school, Emissary Corval. As I knew you would be.'

Corval sat back in his chair. Candlelight flashed across the trio of eye-lenses at the centre of his star-shaped helmet, giving Draik the disconcerting sensation that he was seeing the Navigator's inhuman, third eye. Draik knew that all Navigators had this specific, sanctioned mutation – an eye nestling in their forehead, able to peer into the madness of the warp – but if Draik were to truly see it, the eye would send him irrevocably insane, perhaps even kill him. He coughed and turned his gaze elsewhere.

'I have made several journeys to the Blackstone,' said Draik.

'It has been a costly business, in more ways than one, but I have come to think that I can do more here than simply treasure hunt. During my last attempt, I uncovered what I believe may be the crux of the whole mystery – a central chamber to which all the others are merely attendants, locked in orbit, as it were. I spoke to some poor, damned souls, too badly injured to make their way back to Precipice, and the deeper I travelled, the more consistent their stories became. I heard several mentions of a hidden chamber called the Ascuris Vault. One of them even did me a sketch.' He showed Corval a small piece of paper with a spherical grid scrawled on it. 'This was drawn by an informant of mine, a man by the name of Tor Gaulon. He's dead now, but he swore to me he had seen this place with his own eyes. When I consulted my notes from previous expeditions, I found that his description of the vault exactly matches the signals transmitted from the Blackstone's transportation chambers. If we can–'

'Forgive me, captain, I'm lost. Are you saying this Ascuris Vault is the "brain" of the Blackstone?'

'Perfectly put, Emissary Corval. But let me explain why that's so important. Travel through the Blackstone is dangerous in the extreme, as you will learn if you decide to venture inside. The place is crawling with aliens – aggressive, carnivorous species, many of which I have never encountered before, and the Blackstone's architecture itself is hazardous, reforming and reacting even as one tries to climb from one location to another. But those problems are nothing compared to the difficulty of using its transportation system. The fortress is traversed by the use of maglev chambers. They're fascinating creations of alien manufacture, but they're impossible to steer with any consistency. They move from one place to another, but their routes soon become random and, after depositing you far from your intended destination, they become inert. That's why the fortress is so perplexing. And the Blackstone's defences are triggered by movement – in the same way alien bodies trigger an immune system, so simply staying in one place is not an option. The result is that parties of explorers race around the place like lunatics, sometimes stumbling across valuable finds, but more often becoming lost and never returning. But I believe the Ascuris Vault is the solution to this problem. I think it's the central point on which all the other maglev chambers hinge. The fulcrum, as it were. If I can reach it, I believe I will have come closer than anyone before to understanding the nature of the fortress.'

'And what then, captain? Do you mean to contact Commander Ortegal? I believe he is the officer in charge of this subsector.'

Draik sipped his wine again. 'No. I intend to return to Terra myself, with whatever I have learned in the Ascuris Vault. I mean to present my findings to the High Lords in person.'

Corval was silent for a moment. Then he nodded. 'I see. May I ask why? Ortegal is a dullard but he's a well-meaning dullard. Do you doubt him?'

'Not at all.' Draik sipped his wine again.

'But you would rather the news came from you?'

'From House Draik, yes.'

'Ah, of course. I understand. Yours is a mercantile dynasty. A find such as this will be a great boon.'

'There will be no impropriety. I will inform Commander Ortegal and send reports to Terra before I leave Precipice. But I will explain my findings in person.'

'Fascinating,' said Corval, rising from his chair and crossing the room with such soft steps that he seemed to glide. Draik noticed again how impossibly slender he was. Navigators were often ravaged by the arduous nature of their calling, tormented by years of guiding ships through the lunacy of the warp. Where others could avert their gaze, Navigators stared, unblinking, finding rhythms in the frenzy, finding a path in the blindness. As a result, they had evolved into something altered – a new class of human – but few outside of their own dynastic families could claim to understand the true nature of the Navigator breed.

Corval paused at a cabinet and fiddled with what Draik presumed was another astronomical instrument. It was a metal cylinder, punched with tiny holes in a pattern he could not decipher. Corval flicked a switch on its side and the cylinder started to turn, slowly, glinting in the firelight like the armillary sphere at the end of the table. Rather than illustrating the movements of the stars, however, the cylinder flooded the room with music – a faint, crackling recording of a choir, their voices raised in tribute to the unknowable beauty of the galaxy, the melody spiralling like the orbits of the spheres.

The Navigator swayed his hand in time to the hymn, lost in thought for a moment. Then he returned to his chair. 'It sounds like you have a clear plan, captain. How may I be of help? Funds? A crew?'

'You are extremely kind, emissary, but no, my need is more complicated than that. I have recruited a pilot who can reach the docking point – a hazardous location the local drunks have labelled the Dragon's Teeth. I also have a guide in the form of a Ministorum preacher by the name of Taddeus. He is…' Draik hesitated, unsure how devout, or not, the Navigator might be. 'He is pursuing an agenda of his own, but he is able to lead me to the Ascuris Vault. I also have what remains of my household guard. My problem is of a more psychological nature.'

'Now you *have* intrigued me,' said Corval, looking up from the phonograph.

'The priest, Taddeus, warned me that the final approaches to the Ascuris Vault are protected by a particular weapon – a kind of mental projection that confuses anyone trying to reach the vault. I spoke to members of his party and they are reluctant to explain in detail, but the Blackstone has a way of distorting perception, so that the past becomes jumbled with the present. The end result is fatal. The priest's party turned on each other. It sounds to me like some kind of telepathic psychosis.'

'Telepathic psychosis? And that made you think of me?' The Navigator sounded amused.

Draik smiled. 'Your work requires you to shield your mind from the dangers of the empyrean, does it not? You have to protect yourself.'

'Indeed, captain. The dangers we face are as much spiritual as psychological, but we can ignore the semantics. Essentially, yes, you are right.' Corval tapped his helmet. 'This may look ridiculous, but it's a powerful relic. Its original name is unpronounceable, even for me, but my archivists refer to it as a cerebrum cowl. It amplifies my second sight, enabling me to follow the Emperor's light even in the darkest corners of warp space.' He nodded to the serpents on the armillary sphere. 'But it also wards me against the beings that call those corners home. Such devices are rare and incredibly valuable – and their workings are arcane in the extreme, but it may be that I could find you something simple enough to be of help. It would be hard, though.' He drummed his fingers on the table and shook his head. 'No, that would be no use, even if it were possible. In the time it would take to have a device sent here, you might have missed your opportunity. Precipice's days are numbered, I'm sure of it.'

Draik was about to speak when Corval held up a finger and continued talking. 'But there is a way. Yes. Now that I think of it, it is actually a more appropriate solution. If you will indulge me, captain, I would be honoured to accompany you myself. My cerebrum cowl, allied to my experience of navigating the immaterium, should enable me to protect your party from whatever delusions the Blackstone tries to throw at you.'

'I would not have presumed to ask that you accompany me in person.'

Corval waved a dismissive hand. 'I came here to see the Blackstone. And now I shall see it in the company of a friend.'

'I'm afraid time is of the essence, though,' said Draik. 'My plan is to leave in a matter of hours.'

'And I have no intention of delaying you. Let me know the time and place.' Corval laughed. 'Having experienced the Helmsman in all its glory, I do not think this boneyard holds much else in the way of interest for me. The sooner we begin the better.'

They finished their drinks and Draik prepared to leave, bracing himself for the degradation outside. Before he said goodbye, he paused to admire the armillary sphere one last time. As he looked closer he noticed a detail that had eluded him earlier. Not all of the serpents were arrayed around the outer rings. The sphere representing Terra was resplendent – like the jewel-encrusted finial of a royal sceptre, polished to such a sheen that it seemed luminous. But hidden in the filigree, coiled around the spires of the Imperial Palace, was a serpent – smaller than the others, but moving with purpose, venom glinting on its teeth.

7

The *Vanguard* clanged and hummed as Draik stormed down its companionways, wondering if he had forgotten anything. The roar of the plasma engines vibrated up through the deck, rattling the gilt-framed canvases that lined the bulkheads and shaking servitors that were trundling through the gloom, trying to seal cargo holds and airlocks in preparation for their departure.

'Is everyone else ready?' he said, glancing back at Isola.

She was making notes on her cogitator as she struggled to keep up with him, but she nodded. 'The two priests are here and they have joined Audus and Grekh on the bridge. They're waiting for you there. Emissary Corval is the last to arrive.'

Draik nodded, pleased. Now that the rioting in the Drome-platz had died down, the proctors would be trying to discover who was responsible. If he had been seen leaving Taddeus' ship, it was quite possible their bullgryns would arrive at the *Vanguard* and start asking questions. Or someone may have even seen him with Grekh when the kroot fired the shot that caused all the trouble. Paying off the proctors was never a problem for a man of his means, but he had no time for negotiations and haggling. He was desperate to be gone.

'I'll see to Corval,' he said. 'You make sure there's no trouble on the bridge. They all know each other, but I don't get the impression there's any love lost between Audus and the priests.'

Isola nodded and headed off in another direction as Draik continued toward the *Vanguard*'s main loading ramp.

The doors were already open and the Navigator was waiting on the walkway outside, watching the crowds bustling past.

'Emissary Corval.' Draik rushed down the ramp and grabbed his hand. 'I cannot tell you what a relief it is to have a like-minded companion with me on this expedition.'

'I'm excited to come,' laughed Corval, looking out through the void screen at the colossus hanging over Precipice. 'Excited to see the Blackstone, despite all your warnings.'

Draik nodded and waved him up the ramp. 'It's a unique place. Hazardous, certainly, but beautiful in its own way.' As he closed the door behind them, Draik hesitated. 'You've come alone? No servants? No guards?'

Corval laughed and tapped the pistol at his belt. 'I'm able to look after myself, captain.'

Draik shrugged and waved him on. 'The others are already on the bridge.'

As they hurried through the rumbling *Vanguard*, Corval stopped and tapped one of the paintings. 'Is this a Catali?' he said, sounding shocked.

Despite his impatience to leave, Draik could not help pausing and looking back in surprise. Catali's work was an acquired taste and it had been decades since he met someone else who had even heard of the artist.

'You know his work?'

Corval stared at the painting. His expression was hidden behind his mask, but his voice betrayed his emotion. 'I do,' he said, his words hushed.

The painting was only loosely sketched, but drawn with such skill that every mark seemed to carry meaning. It showed a proud Terran noble. He was at prayer in a ruined temple, kneeling, his head resting on a sword as moonlight washed over his imposing features. The mood was sombre and full of pathos.

'I've collected his work for as long as I can remember,' said Draik, waving at some of his other pictures. All of them showed similarly poignant scenes: stately, imposing aristocrats at prayer, lost in thought.

'How well he captures our burden,' muttered Corval. His voice sounded odd – quite unlike his previous, confident tones. 'See how bowed and humbled they all look. Crushed by duty, but never defeated by it, determined not to relinquish their responsibilities, determined not to fail.'

There was something in Corval's words that threw Draik back into the past, reminding him of what he was fighting for – of his determination to return home.

Corval had turned from the painting and was watching Draik in silence. He seemed on the verge of asking a question. Then he shook his head and laughed. 'Forgive me, captain. You're in a rush and here I am wasting time, revealing my poor knowledge of art. Lead on!'

Corval's laugh did not ring true. Draik sensed that he was hiding something – a sadness. The Navigator clearly carried a burden of his own.

He was about to ask Corval why he had come to Precipice when the *Vanguard*'s thrusters roared and Draik had to steady himself against the wall.

'Captain,' came Isola's voice from speakers overhead. 'Everything is ready.'

Draik nodded and hurried on down the companionway. 'We must talk of this again, emissary,' he said, glancing back.

Corval nodded, but gave no reply, still staring at the paintings as they headed towards the bridge. He looked hesitant and unsure, like a man who had seen a ghost.

8

The Blackstone rushed towards them, voltaic and grim, choking the darkness and silencing everyone on the bridge of the *Vanguard*. Draik had been this close many times before, but familiarity did nothing to lessen the shock. There was no familiarity, in fact. Every time he returned, the horror was new, the menace more explicit. Explosions flitted across the surface, caused by failed approaches and colliding debris, splashing light over a baffling jumble of polyhedrons. Draik tried to discern a pattern, tracing the planes and vertices, but with every fitful burst of light the shapes became more confused – shapes without shape, each more bewildering than the last.

'Five degrees starboard,' said Audus. She spoke softly, but her words jarred in the heavy silence that had fallen over the bridge.

Draik's pilot responded and the primary thrusters roared, the sound vibrating up through the deck plating and causing Draik's amasec to slosh in its glass. He finished the drink and studied his companions. The Western Reaches had robbed him of most prejudices – such luxuries would be laughable in a place like Precipice. Even so, this was an unusual group. Corval was at his side, his thoughts unreadable, hidden behind his helmet. At Draik's other side was Isola, studying the hololithic star chart that hovered in the middle of the bridge. An attaché and a Navigator, perfectly respectful companions for a rogue trader – but not so the others. Taddeus the Purifier was seated at the back of the bridge, mouthing silent prayers. His florid features were beaded with sweat and he was not even looking at the Blackstone. There was a book open on his lap, a hand-written journal, the pages rife with lurid apocalypses and coin-eyed corpses. His sweat was pattering on the gaudy vellum, landing with a gentle, persistent tap. Beside him was his disciple, Pious Vorne, her fists locked tightly around her flamer and her eyes closed in prayer. There were a few officers of the Draik Household Guard scattered around the bridge, but none of them were standing anywhere near Grekh. The kroot was hunched in his seat, straining against his harness like a captured animal. It was hard to know if the Blackstone unnerved him as much as everyone else because his eyes were hidden. Almost as soon as they left Precipice, Grekh had reached into his sack and taken out a bloodbird – one of the dripping, crimson moths that Gatto kept in the Helmsman. The creature was still alive, and fluttering weakly, but Grekh had strapped it to his face so that the creature's wings obscured his eyes. Every now and then, Grekh would place a hand on his stomach and mutter something in his own language, but he had said nothing else since takeoff.

Audus was leaning over Draik's pilot, watching his every move until the time came for her to take the controls. Isola had offered her new clothes, but she had insisted on wearing her filthy old Navy flight suit, with its bulky pouches, air sockets and hastily removed insignia. The laspistol Draik had given her was now strapped to her leg and she had also acquired a combat knife while he had been away. Draik was keen to know her story. Grekh had called her a deserter and Gatto claimed the Imperial Navy had put a price on her head, but Draik felt there was something more to her than that. In Bullosus' hold she had shown no sign of fear or panic. There was no trace of cowardice in Audus. So why was she on the run? He resolved to quiz her when there was time, but for now, he had noticed that she seemed excited about something, leaning over the controls and muttering to the pilot.

He crossed the bridge to stand beside her.

She tapped the viewscreen, pointing out a cluster of runes. 'Here,' she said, sounding slightly dazed. 'The Dragon's Teeth.'

'You sound surprised.'

Audus shrugged. 'This place is insane. You know that. I hoped I would find it, but I was never sure. And we've reached it much faster than I expected.'

Isola eyed her suspiciously. 'And navigating through the Teeth? Is it merely a *hope* that you can manage that?'

Audus scowled at her. 'This is good news. We could have circled the fortress for weeks before hitting the right track. How long have we been out here? An hour or two?'

'Four hours and thirty-five minutes,' replied Isola.

Audus was no longer listening. 'Move,' she said to the pilot. 'I'll take her from here. You don't want to be responsible for what happens when we reach the Teeth.'

The pilot looked at Draik, who nodded.

Audus shuffled in her seat, familiarising herself with the displays and controls and nudging the ship into a new approach trajectory, teasing another roar from the *Vanguard*'s engines.

Draik, Corval and Isola all walked past her and looked up at the bridge's oculus, dwarfed by the huge dome of armourglass. The hull was surrounded by a corona of flame as debris collided with the ship's void shield but, after a few minutes, they saw something definite amongst all the obscurity. A colonnade. Two parallel rows of spires, hanging in the void, leading towards the Blackstone.

'Fascinating,' said Corval.

'These are the Dragon's Teeth?' asked Draik, without looking back at Audus.

She nodded, still fiddling with the *Vanguard*'s controls. 'Strap in. There's a *lot* of crap to fly through before I can really scare you.'

Draik and the others had barely had the chance to find seats and fasten their safety harnesses when Audus banked hard, hurling the *Vanguard* past the elegant bones of an aeldari void ship, its hull picked clean by salvage crews, leaving just a framework of ribs and spars.

Almost immediately, Audus rolled the *Vanguard* in the opposite direction as another leviathan surged towards them – a rusting hulk, so blasted and warped it was impossible to recognise.

The bridge of the *Vanguard* was lined with tall alcoves, each of which housed a hard-wired servitor – semi-human wretches, mindless beyond the very specific navigational tasks allotted to them. Most were little more than a head and an exposed spinal column, welded into a nest of bionics, surrounded by a jumble of iron limbs that clattered across control panels as the servitors made adjustments and calculations. As Audus wrenched the *Vanguard* from port to starboard, steering it with increasing violence, the servitors chanted hymns, soothing the ship's machine-spirit with droning plainsong, verse and answer echoing up into the barrel-vaulted ceiling.

Draik was not interested in the wrecks or Audus' impressive manoeuvres, but he leant forwards in his seat, fascinated by the approaching landmark. He could tell from the drifting remnants of ships surrounding it that the colonnade was vast. The columns looked like narrow, inverted pyramids – canines bereft of a mouth or the pilings of a pier. They began hundreds of miles from the Blackstone and terminated at its surface, framing an area of shadow that Draik knew was a docking point.

'It does not seem a particularly challenging approach,' said Corval.

Before Draik could reply, Audus looked back over her shoulder. 'Wait and see.'

As they neared the first of the spires, Draik saw how tightly packed they were. There would be no way to fly through the sides of the colonnade – they would have to go straight down its centre, like an honour guard at a funerary procession. Even so, he had to agree with Corval. It would not be hard to glide down the centre of the colonnade – even for a shuttle as large as the *Vanguard*. In fact, it was one of the easier approaches he had seen. He glanced at Grekh, wondering if the creature had tricked him. Was it really essential to bring Audus along, or did Grekh invent a reason for Draik to rescue his friend? The kroot was still wearing his fluttering, bloodbird mask. It seemed unlikely he would have friends.

Audus laughed. 'Looks like we're not the only ones with a death wish.'

Draik looked back out through the oculus and his augmetic

eye zoomed in on a flash of silver, flickering at the entrance to the colonnade.

'Xenos,' he said. The craft was dwarfed by the monolithic stone towers, but Draik recognised its looping, organic curves. 'Aeldari.'

Audus adjusted her trajectory, giving them time to watch as the alien ship glided towards the Dragon's Teeth.

'Now you'll see what you're paying me for,' she said, settling back in her chair.

The bridge fell silent as they watched the scene unfold. The distant ship passed the first of the vast talons without incident, but then, a few minutes later, the two lines of rocks began to sway and drift out of position, like parading soldiers dazed by the sun and falling out of step. It created a ripple of movement that rolled away from the aeldari ship, as though the craft had disturbed the surface of an invisible pool. At first, the rocks seemed to be moving at random, but Draik slowly began to discern a pattern – complex and baffling, but a pattern all the same. The spurs of rock rolled and drifted, but never collided, moving past each other like partners in a dance. It was an incredible sight. The rocks were the height of mountains, but they glided between each other with easy, seamless grace.

The aeldari ship held its course for a while, racing down the avenue of claws, but soon the pendulum swings of the rocks caused it to veer and bank. The closer the ship came to the Blackstone, the more violently the rocks swayed, rushing towards each other and turning on end.

The aeldari pilot was clearly skilled. The speck of silver weaved between the tumbling rocks with an acrobatic series of loops and dives and Audus leant forwards in her seat to watch. 'Damn. They know their stuff. I think they might...'

Her words trailed off as the rocks whirled amongst each other in a bewildering flurry. The ship hit one and detonated. There was a brief petal of flame, then the embers scattered to the void.

One by one, the rocks slowed and fell back into position. After a few minutes, the wreckage of the ship had vanished and the drifting colonnade looked like it had not moved for millennia.

Isola turned to Draik. 'This is madness,' captain. Even by the standards of the Blackstone.'

Draik looked at Audus. '*Is* it madness?'

'Of course,' she laughed.

'She got us through before,' said Grekh, his words muffled by his fleshy mask.

Taddeus stared at Isola, outraged. 'Everything is as I have foretold.'

Draik was still holding Audus' gaze.

'Look,' she said. 'I wouldn't have come if I didn't think this was doable.'

Draik was a skilled duellist and marksman and more widely read than anyone he knew, but it was his aptitude as a judge of character that kept him alive. Audus was hiding something. She was full of flippant comments and nonchalant sarcasm, but it was a smokescreen. When Draik looked in her eyes he saw hunger – the same hunger that had driven him to risk everything going back to the Blackstone. She needed this as much as he did.

Her cocksure gaze faltered as she sensed Draik peering into her thoughts. That moment of doubt was enough for him. She was no fool. And she was not insane.

He nodded. 'Take us to the Blackstone.'

She looked at him a moment longer, as though wanting to

refute something he had not even said. Then she muttered and turned back to the controls. 'Two degrees starboard.'

The cathedral-sized ship turned slowly to face the stone colonnade. The rocks drew the eye inescapably towards the confounding surface of the fortress, a tenebrous jumble of plains and peaks.

'Primary thrusters two and three.' Her gaze locked on the avenue rising up ahead of them. As they drifted closer, the rocks took on a surreal aspect, their vast size distorting perspective as they leant over the *Vanguard*.

'Engage,' she said, and the ship hurtled forwards between the first two rocks. This close, it was impossible to imagine such goliaths mobile, but as the *Vanguard* sped on, Draik quickly saw movement. The towers leant away from the ship as though repelled, then rolled back, pendulum-like, gathering momentum.

Audus whistled tunelessly as she gripped the controls and steered the vessel manually, trying a few gentle rolls. The mind-wiped servitors fidgeted, rattling in their alcoves, muttering binaric code and adjusting brass-plated cogitators.

Audus looped and rolled the *Vanguard* as though it were no bigger than a fighter. Her whistling became less tuneful and more forced, but there was no other sign she was under stress. As her manoeuvres became more daring she became more relaxed, settling her broad shoulders back into the command chair and controlling the ship with a single hand.

The stones turned faster. Soon, it looked like the *Vanguard* was hurtling through an avalanche, tossed on the tides of an earthquake, riding the crest of a basalt thunderhead, but still Audus looked calm. The whistle faded, but her lips remained in the same position, needlessly pursed, her expression forgotten as she focused every thought on the dance.

As he watched her, a strange thought occurred to Draik. The titans whirling around them were moving in a familiar pattern. He had seen this dance before.

He leant forwards against his restraint, staring at the maelstrom.

No, not a dance, he realised, a different kind of art. *The* art. The stones were duelling. Positions and thrusts, thrusts and parries, parries and returns. A dazzling display of the skills Draik learned as a youth. His hand moved in time, almost involuntarily, and he mouthed terms his father drove into him on the point of a blade. Prime. Seconde. Carte. Tierce. Quinte. Turn to the side. Legs straight. Head up. Thrust. Disengage. Thrust. Parry.

'What is this?' he whispered, with a rising sense of alarm. Was he losing his mind? Was this the madness Audus had spoken of? He looked around the bridge and saw that the others were unchanged. Grekh was hidden behind the bloody creature on his face. Taddeus was reading his journal, not even looking at the lunacy of Audus' manoeuvres. Isola was scowling, but it was her usual scowl. Pious Vorne looked deranged, her eyes rolling feverishly in sunken sockets, but that was how she had appeared when she first admitted him to Taddeus' barge. The house guard who had remained on the bridge were watching Audus with awed expressions, but none of them showed any sign of confusion.

He looked back out of the oculus. 'Prime. Seconde. Carte,' he muttered. 'Parry. Disengage.' There was no doubt. The stones' movement followed the principles he had learned at the academies on Terra. 'Impossible,' he muttered, but he could almost picture his father's stern, impassive face, breaking into an unexpected smile, pleased as Draik surprised him with his skill, learning the positions and techniques that only an older swordsman would usually attempt. Just like on the Ecclesiarchy barge, when he had spoken of the Imperial Palace, Draik found himself unexpectedly jolted into the past, caught unawares by a memory that had been hidden for decades.

The rocks moved so fast their shapes grew blurred and abstract, impossible to discern. As quickly as it came, the memory vanished, but it left Draik with an odd feeling of disquiet, as though the stones knew something about his past that he did not. As though they knew *him*.

'How can she see?' whispered Isola, staring at Audus, not speaking to anyone in particular.

The scene beyond the oculus was a dazzling blur of textures and after-images. Audus' hands moved across the control panel with almost inhuman speed, her expression blank.

Then she exhaled a long-held breath and collapsed back in her seat. The tumult outside vanished, revealing a sheer wall of darkness, scored with hundreds of faint, luminous intersections.

'Emperor be praised,' intoned Taddeus, tracing runes in the air.

Grekh ripped the bloodbird from his face and stashed it back in his bag, staring at the mountainous shape looming over them. For a moment, something flickered in his eyes. A hint of emotion. Draik wondered if he had misjudged the creature. Perhaps there was something more going on in that head than he had imagined.

Draik looked back at the Blackstone, recalling with a grimace the odd sensation that always hit him when he came this close to it. The fortress was made of a black, alien substrate, like a great slab of obsidian. Cold and inert. But every time Draik approached its surface, he had the unpleasant feeling that it was watching him. Looking him directly in the eye. Peering into his soul.

Audus steered the *Vanguard* towards a diamond-shaped fissure in the rock. It would have just been a patch of darkness in the darkness, but the edges were limned with a faint, cold glow, shining from somewhere deep within the fortress.

Audus waved Draik's pilot over and walked away from the controls, looking a little punch-drunk as she flopped into a different seat. 'You can take it from here,' she said. 'You'll see a plateau just inside the vent when you get closer. It works perfectly as a landing platform.'

Draik nodded at her. 'You have earned your share. You can wait on the *Vanguard* if you like, until we need you for the return journey.'

She stared, dazed, looking through him rather than at him. Then she shook her head and focused on his face. 'Wait here? Screw that. You aren't leaving me alone in this place. I'm with you for the duration.'

He nodded. It was probably for the best. They were a small group, and however coarse Audus was, she was an able fighter. Then he remembered the strange thought he'd had while she was navigating the rocks. 'Do you fence?' he asked.

She laughed. 'What?'

He shook his head. 'No matter. Is the atmosphere stable down there?'

She frowned at him, intrigued, then shrugged. 'Yes, same as the rest of this place. There must be an airlock of some kind as we reach the vent, but I've never seen it. I've no idea how they work. You certainly don't see anything closing behind you.'

He nodded. It had been the same each time he docked. The Blackstone was clearly not made by human hands, but the air was breathable, although it did not always behave as one might expect.

As the *Vanguard* plunged into the Blackstone, its thrusters splashed crimson over the fissure's walls, and the resultant jumble of shadows only made the place seem more bewildering. Draik saw enough to know they were alone, though. The plateau Audus had mentioned was about a mile wide, diamond in shape and criss-crossed with the same network of pale lines they had seen on the surface. It was a simple enough job to make the final approach and land the shuttle, and ten minutes later they clattered down the landing ramp into the darkness.

The cold hit first, sugaring their boots with a glitter of frost. Then came the sounds – distant and subterranean, an eerie mixture of rumbles and clangs, muffled and distant, as though heard underwater. They echoed and reverberated, half-heard, speaking of bottomless pits and vast, immeasurable distances. Finally there was the presence, the indefinable sense Draik had recalled during their final approach – the unshakable feeling that the Blackstone was peering into one's soul, a mountainous sentience studying microbe-like invaders.

For a long minute they all stood there, staring into the blackness, paralysed by the strangeness of the place, looking for movement in the shadows, recalling horrors they had seen before. Then Draik strode ahead of the group, the lumen on his pistol stifled by the sombre gloom. He waved the feeble light from left to right, but it only revealed the ground a few feet in either direction. The clatter of his boots echoed up through the blackness, describing a cavernous space. His guards fanned out around him, trying to pierce the darkness with the lumens on their lasguns, but they were as unsuccessful as Draik. Their brass-trimmed uniforms glittered like jewels languishing at the bottom of a well.

Taddeus and Vorne came to stand beside him, followed by Isola, Audus and finally Grekh. They all stared into the nothingness, wonder in their eyes.

'Which way?' Draik asked, turning to Taddeus.

The priest hesitated, hunched forwards, clutching the medallion-like rosarius hung around his neck and muttering something under his breath.

'Your eminence,' said Draik. 'Which way?'

Taddeus nodded and straightened his back, causing his robes to rustle around his prodigious gut. 'A moment, captain,' he said, placing his hand over the relic and closing his eyes. The device responded to his touch. Diodes flickered into life around its edges and there was a series of ratcheting clicks as its mechanism whirred into life. Then he took out his journal and flicked through the pages, jabbing one of his fat fingers at his notes.

'Straight on,' he said, slamming the book and pointing dramatically ahead with his mace. 'For half a mile. Until we reach the far side. This hall leads us to an antechamber. Beyond that lies the maglev.' He glanced at his disciple, Vorne. 'The maglev that will take us to the Ascuris Vault.'

She stared back at him, the light of the relic flashing in her widened eyes. 'Emperor be praised,' she whispered.

'Emperor be praised,' replied Taddeus.

Draik nodded and was about to move on, when he recalled the apocalyptic scenes that filled Taddeus' barge – eyeless, wailing masses, consumed by the flames that radiated from a saintly priest. He glanced at the book hanging from Taddeus' belt and remembered a question he had intended to ask before they left Precipice. 'Your eminence, what do your visions show once you have the eye of...'

'The Eye of Hermius,' whispered Vorne, making the sign of the aquila.

Draik nodded. 'What will happen when you retrieve the Eye of Hermius? What will you do with it?'

Taddeus gripped Draik's shoulder in his large, meaty hand. He leant close, his eyes as wide as Vorne's, his breath coming in quick gasps. 'I will *see*.'

Audus was standing next to the two priests, fiddling with the pistol Draik had given her. At Taddeus' words she smirked.

Taddeus' enraptured grin became a snarl. 'I will see the truth,' he said, sneering at her. 'And I will see every soul that harbours deceit. Every soul that contains beliefs outside the Imperial Creed. I will see the impure, the damned, the faithless, the disloyal.' His full, crimson lips trembled, glistening with spit. 'I will see who should be saved...' He leant close to Audus. 'And who should *burn*.'

She rolled her eyes.

He nodded slowly, stepping closer, trying to cow her with his bulk. 'Even a devout soul such as mine can be tricked. But not Hermius. His vision was clear. Once I see what he saw, I can strike with impunity.' He was breathing quickly, warming to his theme. 'I will complete the work he began all those centuries ago. I will begin a new crusade and–'

'Your excellency,' said Vorne, placing a hand on his arm. 'They won't understand.'

Taddeus gave her a sympathetic smile. 'They must, if they are to endure what lies ahead.'

'Perhaps,' said Draik, 'but not now. Lead us to the maglev. Once we're on our way to the Ascuris Vault you can tell us more.'

He gave Audus a warning glance and she looked away, still smirking.

Draik was about to wave the group on when he remembered

Corval. He thought for a moment that the Navigator might have remained on board the *Vanguard*, but then he noticed him a few feet behind the others – a pillar of darkness, motionless, barely visible.

'Emissary Corval,' he said. 'Are you ready to begin?'

Corval took a moment to reply, watching the group in silence, then he nodded.

Draik nodded back and strode off in the direction Taddeus had indicated. 'It won't be long before the Blackstone welcomes us back.' His breath trailed behind him as he went, a silver plume, spiralling in the gun lights. 'Keep your weapons ready.'

Most of the group followed him in a loose V formation, but Grekh loped off to his left, hunched over his rifle, his rangy frame pacing in and out of view.

'Stay close,' he said, but Grekh gave no sign he'd heard, staring into the void along the barrel of his rifle.

As they hurried across the vast space the feeling of being watched grew stronger and the noises grew louder. Some sounded like huge pipes rattling against metal, others like mournful choirs, alien and incoherent, rising to a crescendo. Draik heard, quite clearly, the unmistakable sound of a lasgun firing repeated, desperate bursts before being suddenly silenced. Then he heard screams – human, perhaps, but too distorted by distance for him to be sure.

They had only crossed half the distance when the strangeness of the Blackstone started to assert itself.

At first, Draik thought he had merely slipped. He was striding ahead of the group, scouring the shadows for signs of movement, when his feet suddenly slid from beneath him. He landed, painfully, on his side, hitting the cold, unforgiving floor. He tried to rise, but started sliding to the left, drawn by an invisible force.

'Gravity shift,' he cried out. 'Grips.'

Anyone who had travelled through the Blackstone knew the mercurial nature of its physics. Nothing was fixed. Nothing was permanent. Nothing could be trusted.

As Draik slid across the floor with increasing speed, he felt no panic. He had been through this several times. He holstered his pistol and calmly unclasped grappling hooks from his belt, swinging them into the grooves that crossed the floor. The hooks sank into the gaps with a loud clang. For a moment he dangled there, hanging from the hooks as his mind adjusted to the new physics. The floor was now a wall and the new floor was somewhere far beneath him, perhaps miles below.

The others had all come prepared. Most carried hooks of their own and, at Draik's warning, they jammed them into the wall to avoid plummeting down the sheer drop. Corval had something more refined, a pair of maglocks in the palms of his gauntlets, and he moved with spider-like ease across the rock face.

'Keep going?' asked Draik, looking back for Taddeus. With his pistol holstered he was now in almost complete darkness, but the rosarius beneath Taddeus' chin radiated pale light, and the priest's jocund features bobbed towards him out of the blackness, like a severed head.

Taddeus grunted and puffed as he hauled his bulk across the wall, but he nodded. 'The gravity shifts again when we reach the antechamber. If everything is as it was last time.'

'Unlikely,' muttered Audus, earning herself a glare from the priest.

The going became painfully slow as they clambered across the side of the crevasse, lunging and swinging their hooks into the narrow channels.

At one point, Isola cursed and scrambled furiously as one of her hooks plunged into the void. Draik was about to head back and help when one of the guards reached out and handed her another. Even in the faint light of Taddeus' rosarius, Draik could see her annoyance at being the only one who had struggled. He stayed silent and carried on climbing. By this point his shoulders were burning with the pain of holding himself aloft.

'Almost there,' said Taddeus, as though sensing his pain. 'A few more minutes and you'll see the entrance.'

Draik nodded and continued swinging across the polished stone, his knuckles skinned from bashing across the wall. A few minutes later, he saw a pale ghost up ahead – a horizontal strip of grey that spurred out from the wall – an area of lighter dark. He realised it was a doorway, just seen side-on due to his current angle.

As he neared the aperture, he began to discern shapes in the chamber beyond – angles and inclines, similar to those he'd seen on the surface, and built on an equally daunting scale. He was about to ask Taddeus if this looked like the right place, when pain knifed through one of his hands.

He looked up and saw that he had sliced one of his grappling hooks through the side of his gauntlet, cutting away some skin. He could feel blood trickling down his wrist and into his sleeve. He cursed his clumsiness. Blood-slick hands would not be able to grip as well as he needed. He wiped the side of his hand on the wall, trying to stem the flow. As he passed his hand over the surface, some of the blood sank into one of the narrow channels that criss-crossed the wall.

As his blood disappeared into the groove, it caused a reaction. What he had taken to be rock blistered into dozens of little black plates, like flakes of iron ore. However many times

Draik came to the Blackstone, it always showed him something new. He watched, fascinated, as the flakes shifted and clicked, locking together in a neat, tessellating pattern. The pattern took on three dimensions, becoming pyramidal, like a geometric puzzle carried on dozens of glinting, chitinous legs. It moved with mechanical stiffness, like a clockwork automaton, and there was something almost comedic about how it skittered across the smooth black wall.

Then it fastened itself to the back of his gauntlet and began feeding. Draik gasped in surprise as fresh pain knifed through his hand. He could not see any face or mouth, but blood and shreds of leather began rushing from his hand.

He loosed his grip from the wall and slammed the thing, backhanded, against the rock. Rather than falling or fleeing, it locked its legs even more tightly around his gauntlet and started vibrating, like a motor, scattering more blood into the air.

'Damn you,' he muttered, gripping the wall again.

As the pain grew, he realised the thing was about to cut through his tendons. He could never hold his weight one-handed. He looked down to see if there was a ledge but it was like trying to see through oil. He tried to wedge his feet into some of the channels in the wall, but it was useless; the grips of his boots were far too thick to find purchase. This absurd little device might stop him before he even reached the maglev chamber.

He looked back to the others, but they were too far away to help.

Keeping his damaged hand on the wall, he grabbed his pistol with his other hand and fired into the pyramid's shell. It shattered like glass, filling the air with coal-like shards that flipped away, tinkling down into the abyss.

Draik muttered a curse as he saw the mess it had made of his hand. There were dozens of tears through his gauntlet and broken skin beneath, glistening and bloody. The tendons were intact, though, and his hand still worked. He was about to continue on his way, when he noticed that the wall beneath him was rippling, apparently affected by the blood he had spilled, moving like fallen leaves caught in the breeze – flaking and rising, becoming a shifting mass. As he scrambled further across the wall, he saw that the shards were forming into pyramids, hundreds of them, identical to the one that had just shredded his hand.

'Move!' he yelled. Most of the group were still several minutes from the portal.

Draik reached the opening and stepped inside, finding to his relief that gravity had returned to its original direction and he could stand.

He looked back in time to see a blinding explosion of light.

Heat ripped through the frigid air. He staggered back, shielding his face, engulfed by the stink of burning promethium.

When the glare faded, he was faced with the surreal sight of the others clambering across the same surface he was standing on, hauling themselves furiously towards him, their legs dangling uselessly a few inches in the air. The wall was alight with dozens of fires. Vorne dragged herself towards Draik gripping her flamer one-handed, its muzzle still glowing and dripping fuel. Her mouth was a determined snarl, and as she climbed through the doorway she spat prayers at the burning shapes behind.

The others quickly followed, turning to look back at the inferno she had created. The blaze was fierce. Bright enough to finally shed some light across the chamber they had just crossed. Every inch of wall and floor was in motion, clicking, tumbling and forming a sea of black pyramids – thousands of them, some as small as the one that had attacked Draik but others as big as canids. The larger ones were as featureless as the smaller ones – just black pyramids carried on a jumble of multi-jointed legs. They were all moving towards the doorway, a flood of angles and thrashing limbs. As Draik bound his injured hand the walls began rising and reforming, shedding tides of pyramids as they took on a new shape.

'Can we close this?' he asked, looking up at the portal they had just clambered through. It was rhombus-shaped – a skewed diamond, over a hundred feet tall. Draik could see no markings anywhere around its frame, nor any sign of a door.

The ocean of geometric shapes was clattering and rolling towards them with increasing speed, gaining momentum, like a wave rushing towards a beach. The distant, half-heard chorus was climbing ever higher, more like screams than music, merging with the metallic, echoing booms.

Vorne lifted her flamer and targeted the approaching wave, but she looked absurd – it was like pointing a gun at an avalanche.

Draik looked at Taddeus. 'Does it close?'

Taddeus shook his head, flicking through the pages of his book. 'This isn't right. This didn't happen last time we came.'

Audus laughed. 'You're looking it up in a book? This is the Blackstone. *Nothing* happens like last time.'

Vorne glared at her, keeping her burner pointed at the approaching storm. 'Address His Excellency with respect.'

Audus scowled, but before she could reply, Draik nodded to the darkness that lay in the opposite direction. 'Then we keep moving,' he said. 'How far to the maglev chamber?'

'This antechamber is smaller than the room we just passed through,' said Taddeus. He was sweating despite the cold, and he dabbed his eyes with his sleeve. 'If gravity remains stable, and we run, five minutes or so.'

Isola had drawn her pistol and was pointing it at the carpet of scuttling pyramids. 'We could never stop them all.'

Draik nodded. 'Then we run.' He looked at Taddeus. 'Which way?'

The priest was momentarily hypnotised by the sight of the previous chamber collapsing and rushing towards them, then he nodded and raced off into the darkness. 'Follow!' he bellowed. 'The God-Emperor is with us!'

They ran, keeping close to Taddeus, using the lumens on their scopes but only managing to reveal glimpses of what lay ahead. The chamber seemed almost identical to the last – sheer, black rock lined with a tracery of geometric designs – but the floor sloped away to the left, meaning they had to run at an awkward angle. There was no sign of the triangular machines, but Draik guessed it was only a matter of time.

Finally, for the first time since they arrived, Draik saw a light source. Taddeus became a rippling silhouette, his robes fluttering against a rising, pale glow. It was like a dawn – cold and grey-blue, creeping over the horizon ahead of them. It revealed a flat, featureless plain. Taddeus was making for something – some landmark Draik had yet to spot.

They all ducked as a deafening smash rang out. It came from behind them – the sound of a thousand plates crashing on rock. Draik kept running but looked back over his shoulder to see the pyramids flooding through the portal – a tumbling, glinting landslide of angular shapes. They spilled onto the floor of the antechamber and sped after them, their spindly legs clinking across the stone like a hailstorm.

Some of the group paused, looking back, horrified.

'Keep going!' cried Draik. 'There are none up ahead.'

As he looked back at Taddeus, he saw the point the priest was racing towards. It was like a facet of enormous crystal – a hexagon of light that deepened the darkness around it. Taddeus was entirely silhouetted now, but Draik could tell he had stopped.

'This is it!' cried the priest.

Draik raced to his side.

'Why have you stopped?' he demanded, trying to haul the priest forwards.

The machines were thundering towards them, gaining speed, only minutes away.

'Wait!' muttered Taddeus, rifling through the pages of the book.

A few of the guards arrived but Draik waved them on towards the light source.

The rest of the group caught up, and gathered round Draik and Taddeus.

'Excellency,' gasped Pious Vorne. 'This is it!' She waved at the light ahead. 'I remember it clearly.'

The guards were still racing towards the shape, but the rest of the group hesitated, seeing the doubt in the priest's face.

'They're almost on us,' said Corval, his metallic voice echoing oddly through the gloom.

'Yes!' cried the priest, running his finger over some text.

'We have to move!' snapped Draik.

'The shadows,' whispered Taddeus, looking up from his journal and watching the silhouetted guards as they raced into the light. They were trailing long shadows as they sprinted but their shadows also reached out before them, as though there were a light behind them too – several lights, in fact, because the shadows ahead of them had fragmented, spreading fingers of darkness across the floor.

'They need to…' Taddeus hesitated.

'What?' demanded Draik as the tide of pyramids roared towards them.

'Damn!' gasped Audus as one of the guards' shadows rose from the ground and enveloped him.

'What is that?' cried Draik, gripping his pistol.

The guard staggered and lurched as the darkness wrapped around him, a black, serpentine coil, lashing around his nose and mouth until he fell to the floor, moaning and punching at the shape, unable to breathe. Another guard fell in the same way, attacked by his shadow. It spread itself across his face and his muffled cries rang out as he struggled to breathe. He tried to rise, but more of the shadows reared up, twisting around his arms and legs, dragging him down. There was an audible crack as his back snapped.

'Halt!' cried Draik to the rest of his guards.

Heat and light exploded behind them as Pious Vorne fired her burner into the pyramid drones. The front wave was just seconds away, and the ground was trembling under their weight. Vorne heaved her burner from side to side, drenching them in flames.

'What do we do?' demanded Draik, grabbing Taddeus by his robes.

'The light is a lie,' whispered the priest, lurching forwards and starting to run in a new direction. 'Close your eyes! The light is a lie! Run to the warmth!'

It sounded like the words of a madman, but there was no time left to do anything else.

'You heard him!' cried Draik, ignoring Isola's incredulous expression.

Draik closed his eye and deactivated the ocular implant that filled his other socket. At first he felt nothing, distracted by the deafening roar of the pyramids behind him. But then, after a few seconds, he felt a warm current on the air. It was nothing like the fierce heat of Vorne's flamer – more like the sticky, humid heat of Precipice. Blind and deafened, he started to run towards it, following the trail of warmth, using it like a beacon. He could still hear the muffled cries of his guard as the shadows crushed the life from him.

Finally, he stumbled to a halt as his legs sank into a thick, viscous substance, knee-high and the temperature of blood.

'You're in,' said Taddeus, grabbing his arm and pulling him deeper into the pool. 'Look.'

Draik opened his eye and saw that he was inside a black prism. It was like being inside a piece of faceted, hollowed-out onyx. The chamber was much smaller than the previous ones – thirty feet wide and filled with rippling, oil-black liquid. It was a maglev chamber. Draik had seen many others in this exact same shape, but none of them had been filled with liquid. The others crashed into the pool, causing a sluggish wave, but no splashes.

'What is this?' muttered Audus, grimacing at the odd way the liquid clung to her flight suit.

'Taddeus!' snapped Draik, looking around for a control panel. 'The controls?'

The priest nodded and looked at Vorne. 'Hold them off.'

As she spewed another gout of flame into the darkness, Draik's guards began firing too, blasting furiously into the heaving mass of black pyramids. Taddeus waded to the back of the chamber, and the others added their shots to the furious barrage – Draik, Isola, Corval and Audus with their pistols and Grekh with his rickety rifle perched on one shoulder, kicking deafening rounds into the wall of burning drones.

It was like firing at a tsunami. The pyramids rolled across the floor and exploded into the chamber. One latched on to Draik's chest, another on to Vorne's neck. Three thudded into Grekh, clattering furiously as they shredded his skin and he staggered backwards, blood spraying from his beak.

There was a loud *clink* as the chamber closed, turning the opening into another polished facet of the prism.

The torrent outside continued, but it crashed uselessly against the surface of the chamber. Draik could not see them through the black crystal, but he could hear them, drumming against the surface and thrashing their limbs. He wrenched the machine from his chest, held it at arm's length and prepared to shoot it. Then he noticed that the pool of oil was now littered with fragments of the pyramid shells. They were melting and sinking from view.

He dropped the drone into the pool. It thrashed its limbs then froze, as though stunned. Then it fragmented as the oil closed over it, scattering pieces of shell across the gloopy liquid. The others followed his lead, flinging their attackers into the pool with a torrent of curses and gasps. Grekh was covered in the things so he plunged beneath the surface, vanishing from view. He rose a second later, free of the machines but also free of oil, which seemed too heavy to cling to his hide.

They all stood there, panting, looking around the chamber, trying to catch their breath. Draik checked them each in turn. Audus was fine; she barely seemed to have broken a sweat. Corval was studying the chamber with interest, clearly unhurt. Isola was bleeding from a wound to her neck and her uniform had been torn on one side, but she seemed fine otherwise. Grekh was busy chewing on something, biting down with his thick, brutal-looking beak. It was a fragment of shell – taken from one of the pyramid devices. As Draik watched, Grekh managed to gulp the fragment down, gagging slightly, before leaning back against the faceted walls with his eyes closed, lost in thought. Next to him were the remaining guards. There were three of his men left, and they were looking at the chamber with undisguised dismay, no doubt unnerved by what had just happened to their comrades outside. Taddeus was still on the far side of the chamber, fiddling with something, so Draik waded through the oil towards him.

The priest was running his hand over the crystal's faces, whispering as he used his other hand to tap the surface with his mace. As Draik watched, one of the facets fell back at his touch, revealing a bowl of oil contained in a recess about halfway up the wall, level with Taddeus' chest. The substance looked identical to the liquid they were standing in, but there was a difference: this was the source of the heat. It radiated from the bowl like animal warmth. There was no mistaking it; the invisible trail they had followed stemmed from this point.

Taddeus was drenched in sweat, his robes clinging to his slabby limbs. He turned to face Draik with a wary expression. 'Caresus? You came all this way, just to visit my humble temple?' He embraced Draik in a damp hug. 'I'm honoured, your excellency. I will have rooms prepared. When you are rested, meet me in the cloisters and I will tell you what I have learned.'

'I'm Captain Draik, your excellency. We're on the Blackstone Fortress.'

Vorne appeared at Taddeus' side and gripped his arm, looking concerned.

Taddeus laughed, then frowned, giving Draik a wary look.

He looked at Vorne, who nodded. 'He's right, excellency,' she said. 'Captain Draik is helping us find the vault. Remember?'

Taddeus' eyes clouded over and, for a second, his suspicious look was replaced by one of fear. Then he shook his head, puffed out his chest and shrugged her off. 'Of course I remember,' he snarled. 'I was just showing the captain the controls.'

He nodded at the pool, about to say more when Draik interrupted him.

'Why did you let them run?'

'Who?'

'My guards. You let them run towards the light, straight into those shadows. Why didn't you stop them?'

Taddeus looked pained. 'Forgive me, captain. My memory…' He clenched his fists, struggling to find the right words. 'Sometimes it plays tricks on me.'

The priest looked ashamed of his failure and Draik's anger faded. He nodded to the bowl of oil. 'How does this work? I've not seen controls like this in any of the other chambers.'

Taddeus nodded, clearly glad to change the subject.

By now the others had gathered round them to watch. Grekh was still crunching noisily on a piece of shell. 'Does it only go to one place?' he asked.

Taddeus made a point of ignoring the kroot and spoke to Draik. 'It leads only to the Ascuris Vault. Place your hand in and see.'

Draik hesitated, considering the enormity of what lay ahead. He was minutes away from proving or disproving his theory.

He plunged his hand into the oil.

9

'Betrayed from birth,' said the voice in the dark. ***'Taught to feel ashamed and hide behind a disguise. And then, when you took off your mask, and showed your worth, what did they do?'***

'Abandon me,' replied Glutt.

Light shimmered in response to his words, a few feet away, tracing the bulbous curve of a glass. The shape was familiar, but the light guttered and died before he could give it a name.

'They betrayed you,' said the voice. There was such sympathy in its tone. Such understanding. He had never heard anything like it.

Daemon. The Imperium's most terrible secret. They existed. They were real. He had looked beyond the needle's eye, and this is what he had found: ether-spawn. He should have been terrified, but nothing in the daemon's words matched the horror faced on Sepus. The willingness of man to abandon man. To turn away as the bombs fell. The willingness to denounce a soul as loyal and noble as Lieutenant Sorov's. That was the true threat. He had long suspected the truth, watching the callous brutality of his superiors, but since Sepus, Glutt had seen with a new clarity. Seen the truth he had always guessed at. The enemy was not without but within, hiding in the feeble hearts of men.

'Commander Ortegal betrayed me,' he said. The name dragged bile into his mouth and the light flared again, revealing more of the glass. This time Glutt saw it clearly. A small still. The daemon called it an alembic.

The daemon. Its name was unpronounceable. The closest he could manage was Fluxus. It had set him adrift in a heady dream. As Sepus fell, Fluxus had carried him up through its burning skies, guiding him, teaching him, helping him harness the nascent power beneath his skin. The daemon had offered him wealth and freedom, but Glutt only asked for one thing: the head of Commander Ortegal.

Whole worlds had flashed beneath Glutt's feet since then, sights beyond imagining. All the daemon asked was that Glutt collect specimens as they travelled: pieces of bark, vials of marsh gas, fragments of bone, flakes of oxidised metal – ingredients to be dropped into the bubbling alembic. All the while, Fluxus promised that the time would come. Soon Glutt would punish Ortegal for his betrayal.

Glutt dragged his gaze from the pale light and looked around. The daemon had shown him places of incredible beauty, but now they were in a void. He was standing on a cold, slate-grey floor, which vanished into shadow a few feet in either direction. There was only him, the voice of the daemon and the alembic. It was a crude-looking thing – a pot-bellied beaker, with a long, snout-like funnel through which he had pushed whatever fragments of teeth and metal

Fluxus requested. It was rattling on the cold floor as the fire grew in its centre.

'Vengeance,' he whispered. The light flared and a shape flickered in the flames. Something tiny and foetal. Glutt reached out and allowed power to rise from his palm, then he hurled light into the shadows. To his surprise, the darkness resisted, pushing back, crushing his light to a pale dome, before extinguishing it completely and returning him to shadow.

In the brief conflagration, he glimpsed figures – gun-toting soldiers, their heads bowed and hooded, their flak jackets torn.

'Who is that?' He felt no fear. Fluxus was calm and Fluxus knew every thing. The strangers could not be a threat.

'Your old regiment,' replied the daemon.

'They're alive?'

'As alive as they ever were.' The daemon hesitated. *'Humans are never much more than hollow shells, Glutt, propelled by senseless biology but never perceiving more than a fraction of the wonders around them. Only a rare few, such as yourself, become something more. I merely preserved a few shells from the flames of Sepus to protect us as we create our weapon. Even in here we are not entirely safe.'*

Glutt considered looking at the men again. He recalled the awkward, unnatural way they had been standing, and imagined them waiting silently all around him in the darkness. Even before the daemon explained it, he had guessed the truth. He had progressed far beyond the lowly creatures he once called brother. His eyes had been opened. His mind awakened. He decided to leave them to the shadows.

'Where *is* here?' he asked, looking back at the alembic. The foetus had developed a large, bubble-like swelling. A face.

Three little eyes, gummed shut like puckered scars. A hint of boneless nose. A wide, smiling mouth.

'A cancrum.' Despite being no bigger than a human hand, the daemon's voice was a rich and humorous, the growl of a benign bear. *'A place to work.'*

Glutt tried again to pierce the dark. He saw the same frozen glimpse of his comrades, their heads still bowed, before the light failed. He dropped to one knee and touched the floor. It was cold, so cold that frost splintered across his glove, glittering and aching through his finger bones.

'Not that,' said Fluxus. *'That's Old Unfathomable. Humans would call it a Blackstone. The cancrum is the shell that's growing around us. We are building a cocoon, so we can hold our place in here for long enough. Old Unfathomable isn't keen on visitors. She would drive us out if she could.'*

The bubble-face rose from the liquid with an audible *pop* and looked up at him. The three scars prised themselves open to reveal coal-black eyes, blinking and tacky with pus.

'The cancrum will keep us safe as we grow your weapon,' said Fluxus. There was another popping sound as more of the daemon emerged from the skin soup. It bubbled and slid into the neck of the alembic, distorting its face into an elongated leer as it squeezed down the narrow channel.

Glutt watched, fascinated as the daemon birthed itself, spewing onto the cold stone floor. It was a fountain of bloodless muscle, rippling and unfolding as it grew. A few minutes later, Fluxus stood swaying before Glutt, stretching its limbs and arching its back as though emerging from a long sleep.

'Who are you?'

'The betrayed,' said Fluxus, the humour fading from its voice. *'Just as you are. The False Emperor turned His back on me long before Commander Ortegal did the same to you.'*

The daemon reached out to Glutt, extending a flabby, pallid limb. ***'But together we will have our revenge.'***

Glutt pictured the face of Lieutenant Sorov, burning in the pyres of Commander Ortegal's treachery. Anger hardened his resolve. He reached out and his hand closed around a soft, slippery claw. 'Tell me what to do,' he said.

Fluxus gripped his hand tighter and the daemon's mouth tore into a wide smile. ***'You have already done it. You carried me here. To a place where no one can hurt us or interfere with our work. You have already achieved something incredible.'***

Glutt shrugged, humbled by the daemon's praise. 'You gave me a whole new form. You saved me and remade me. And you made me strong enough to survive the virus bombs. Smuggling you onto that junk hauler was an easy enough task in comparison.' Glutt was being modest. It had been terrifying travelling on Imperial vessels knowing that he was a host for something utterly forbidden, knowing what he was carrying in his soul, knowing that discovery would result in summary execution. But Fluxus' voice had been there, constantly, reassuring him as he stowed away on ship after ship. The daemon had promised that, if they could just cross the system and reach a thing called a Blackstone Fortress, it would be able to leave Glutt's body and regain physical form, and that they would both be safe.

Fluxus smiled again. ***'You did more than smuggle me on a ship. You got me here, to the very heart of the Blackstone. I think you are already forgetting how hard that was.'***

Glutt frowned, trying to recall the journey but finding that his memories were strangely jumbled. He remembered angular, black machines flooding through the darkness towards him, collapsing as he unleashed waves of growing, unshackled power. He sensed that it had taken incredible amounts of violence to come this far, but hard as he tried, he could only remember fragments.

'Old Unfathomable has muddied your thoughts,' laughed Fluxus. ***'She has a habit of doing that. But trust me, I could never have come this far without you to carry me and hide me.'*** The daemon waddled away, its bloated bulk teetering on cloven hooves as it vanished into the darkness.

Glutt followed. There was no break in the darkness but as their footfalls echoed away he sensed that they were in a vast, empty hall. Eventually, Glutt heard noises. It sounded like the crashing of waves on rocks – a distant, thunderous boom that grew louder as they walked. When they finally reached a wall, the noise was unbearable – a seismic, rolling crash, as though mountains were crashing down around them.

Fluxus pointed to the wall, indicating that Glutt should touch it.

He hesitated. It was the same bristling black armour he had seen beneath Governor Narbo's skin – the shell of a mollusc or the carapace of an insect.

Fluxus gave him a reassuring nod, its three eyes blinking with excitement. ***It's safe,*** said the daemon, speaking directly into his mind so as to be heard over the din.

Glutt touched the wall and it juddered beneath his palm, jolted by the tumult outside.

The cancrum holds, said the daemon. ***We're safe in our cocoon***.

Glutt shook his head, wondering at the violence that was trying to break through to them. +What's out there?+ he thought.

The Blackstone, replied the daemon and, for a moment, its good humour faltered. ***She wants us gone.***

Since the joining of their minds, Glutt saw echoes of the daemon's thoughts. It was afraid of whatever was thrashing against the wall. The idea troubled him. He did not intend to be failed again.

+Commander Ortegal must die,+ he thought, eyeing the daemon suspiciously.

Fluxus jerked and twisted, still in the process of being born. The bird's foot growths at the end of its wrists swelled and cracked into heavy, pitted crab claws. Fluxus nodded, evidently pleased by this new development. ***The cancrum will hold. Old Unfathomable is an affront to nature. She is beyond nature – from beyond the stars – but in this rarefied air, you and I will create wonders.***

In the distance, a flash of emerald flame managed, briefly, to punch through the heavy pall.

Fluxus rushed back the way they had come, leaving the tidal roar of the wall behind.

When they returned to the alembic, its contents were burning so brightly Glutt had to shield his eyes. The liquid had vanished, replaced by a teeming mass of grubs. They looked like worms or pupae, but lit from within like fireflies, their flesh pulsing and shimmering as they coiled around each other inside the glass.

'Quick,' snapped Fluxus. ***'We need one of your comrades.'***

Glutt did as the daemon asked, summoning the Guardsmen over with a thought. The shadows trembled and shifted as they trudged towards him, closing around the alembic in a circle.

As they approached the glass, the light of the worms washed over them, revealing the strange nature of Glutt's regiment. Most of them had hidden their faces behind masks and rebreathers, but some of their eyes were visible, and they were the blue-white eyes of corpses. They moved with a jerking, automaton-like gait and they wheezed as they walked, a thin, bubbling hiss that did not sound like it came from a human throat. They responded to Glutt's unspoken command, but they were no more than puppets, animated by his will.

Glutt peered through the gloom at their uniforms. They were still clad in their standard issue Astra Militarum garb, but the regimental insignia had been obscured or snapped off, replaced by the vile, jagged stars of Chaos.

'Will these things be any use in a battle?'

Fluxus smiled. ***'Their past has died, but their flesh is still strong. See for yourself.'*** It nodded at Glutt's staff.

Glutt leant back and swung the staff, slamming its head into a Guardsman's stomach.

It was like hitting a rotten log. The staff connected with a dull thud and the man's flak jacket oozed black, tar-like liquid, but the Guardsman barely staggered. Nor did he look at Glutt, keeping his cloudy eyes fixed on the shadows.

Still smiling, the daemon nodded at Glutt's pistol.

He drew it and fired, at point-blank range, into the Guardsman's chest. This time the soldier did stagger back a few paces and more of the dark, clotted liquid spattered across the floor, but then he stepped calmly back into place, seemingly oblivious to the hole Glutt had just ripped through his chest.

Glutt's pulse was racing. He fired again and again, causing the soldier to jerk and dance. He pictured all the lying wretches who led him into an unwinnable war and laughed as he fired, sending the soldier staggering away from him.

The whole scene seemed suddenly hilarious. His laughter became hysterical as the pistol kicked and blazed in his hand.

'Stay with me,' said Fluxus, placing a claw on his arm.

Glutt reined in his laughter and lowered the gun, still giggling as he saw that the soldier was still standing. 'With an army like this we will be unstoppable.'

'These troopers are nothing like enough to face Ortegal's whole regiment. We have a few dozen men and he has thousands.' The daemon tapped the alembic with one of its hooves. ***'But once we have perfected our weapon, we will have a better chance.'***

Glutt looked at the luminous grubs, still battling to hold back his laughter. '*How* do we perfect it?'

'We need to test the recipe. Offer one of your men some refreshment.'

Glutt carefully lifted the alembic and shook it until one of the worms tumbled down the spout and into his palm. It moved with furious speed, writhing through his fingers and vanishing into the darkness.

Fluxus' grin froze. Then it shook its head. ***'No matter. Try again.'***

Glutt tipped the glass again and this time he managed to lock the worm in his grip, feeling it thrashing against his palm as it tried to escape.

'Against the chest,' said Fluxus, nodding at the nearest of the Guardsmen.

Glutt pressed the worm against the soldier's bloodstained flak jacket. Black blood sprayed through his fingers as the worm burrowed into the man's chest.

A second later, the guard gasped, expelling a blast of foetid breath as he toppled to the ground.

Glutt raised his staff, summoning light into the eagle at its head. The darkness pressed against it, but there was enough to illuminate the change jolting through the Guardsman.

He thrashed on the floor for a few seconds and then lay still. After a few more seconds, his clothes and armour flattened against the floor, containing nothing but ash.

'*This* is the weapon?' Glutt laughed, looking back at the grubs. 'They're perfect! How many are there?'

'Several hundred. Enough to wipe out half the commander's officers before he dies himself.'

Glutt shook his head, his humour fading. 'No. Not enough. That's not what I meant at all. We have to bring it all down. The whole system. The whole wretched Imperium. It's all a lie. If they're shells then they're rotten shells. Do you understand? Mankind needs to evolve.'

Fluxus leant closer, blinking its trio of eyes.

Glutt continued, sensing that the daemon understood. 'Killing one man at a time won't change anything. We need to *infect*. We need to create a chain reaction that goes far beyond the flesh of a single host.' He nodded at the shadowy figures that surrounded them. 'Not one of them has fallen. Do you see? All we have is a poison. We need a plague. Ortegal said we were a contagion so let's give him contagion. Let him suffer! Let him oversee a sector-wide catastrophe. Let him die in ignominy. In disgrace. Let the whole galaxy hear of his failure. Then I will reveal what I have become and what others like me may become. Then people like me will know that there's hope. That they don't have to feel ashamed of their gifts. That they can rise up. That they can be who they were born to be.'

Fluxus laughed. ***'You are ambitious.'*** Then its face grew serious. ***'But perhaps you have a point. I brought you here for a reason. I had a suspicion you might say something like this. This place is unnatural. We could do things here that would be impossible elsewhere.'*** The daemon looked into the darkness. ***'And I have bought us plenty of time.'***

'Are you sure? That noise we heard... Will the cancrum hold?'

'Of course. The empyrean is in our veins. If we keep bleeding ourselves into the cancrum, the Blackstone will take months to break through it. It is not of this galaxy. It does not understand etheric beings such as us.'

Glutt shook his head, excited by the implication. 'Us?'

'Yes, you too. You cast off your human shell on Sepus. You are more than that now. Take your combat knife. Cut your arm.'

Glutt hesitated, but the daemon's smile overcame his doubts. He drew out his knife and pressed the tip into his forearm. Nothing happened. There was no pain. No blood. He pressed harder and drew the blade up his arm, cutting a line into his skin. It parted to reveal a hard, black shell.

The daemon smiled. 'Evolution.'

Glutt touched the strange, bristly armour. Rather than revulsion, he felt pride. He had always known he was more than human. And now he had proof.

The daemon led him back to the cancrum wall and, following its lead, Glutt pressed his hands onto it.

'Open your thoughts,' said the daemon. *'Let the cancrum into your mind. Let your mind into the cancrum. See how secure we are.'*

Glutt did as he was asked. With the needle's eye forgotten, it was shockingly easy to reach out. His conscience rippled out across the shell, feeling every crevice and burr. There was liquid pulsing through it, a bloodstream, carrying its life force, but this was the blood of gods – heady and potent, shimmering into every corner of the cancrum. The cocoon was as big as a city, miles wide and several feet thick, like the walls of a vast fortress. Fluxus was right. What could break through something so impenetrable? Beyond the wall was the alien. Unfathomable, Fluxus called it, and it was. As Glutt tried to peer into the darkness beyond, his mind turned back on itself, baffled, fractured by thoughts too strange to grapple. He felt the power of the place, pummelling against the daemon's sorcery, immense and full of wrath but unable to break through – as confused by them as they were by it. He smiled. Fluxus was right. They had as much time as they needed to create an apocalypse.

Glutt was about to remove his hand when he sensed something else. The Blackstone hurled more strangeness at him, trying to redirect his thoughts with glimpses of alien landscapes and impossible geology, but he pushed through, sensing duplicity. The Blackstone was trying to trick him.

Fluxus appeared in his mind. ***Where are you going?***

Glutt reached further, beyond the tumult outside the walls. His mind glided through impassable gulfs and bewildering puzzles, homing in on the area that the Blackstone seemed most keen for him to avoid.

'Someone's here,' he muttered.

Where?

'Outside the cancrum. Someone is approaching.'

Impossible.

'I see his soul, Fluxus. A psyker like me. Coming here. He's close.'

Show me. The daemon sounded irritated as it placed a hand on Glutt's eyes.

He felt its presence, disembodied, beside him as he fixed his gaze on the psyker.

You have such power. Fluxus laughed, shocked.

The storm of visions grew more ferocious and Glutt almost lost his grip on his prey, stymied by an influx of thoughts. Hundreds of voices flooded his mind, babbling, screaming and praying. The Blackstone was trying to bury the psyker, hiding it beneath a torrent of other minds. Glutt pressed on, partitioning his mind until a vision swam into focus: a group of travellers inside an obsidian stone.

We must not let them reach us, said Fluxus.

'Why? What harm can they do if even the Blackstone can't drive us out?'

They're coming here with a purpose. That chamber will bring them here. The Blackstone can't comprehend us, but maybe they will. One of them is gifted in the same way you are. We can't risk it. We must send them astray.

'How?'

We're in the heart of the fortress. That's why the Blackstone is so outraged by our presence. We can redirect the chambers from here. I'll teach you how. Glutt saw the daemon's essence, gliding on past the black crystal and scouring the surrounding levels. Then the daemon laughed. *There, that should be enough to make sure they don't come any closer.*

Glutt followed the daemon's gaze and nodded, smiling.

10

Draik tried to free his hand from the oil, but it was locked in place. He instinctively tried to reach in with his other hand, but it bashed against a hard surface. The oil had solidified. His hand was embedded, wrist-deep, in a stone block.

'What is this?' he demanded, looking at Taddeus. 'Did you know this would happen?'

Taddeus held up his hands, smiling. 'Once we reach the vault, your hand will be yours again.'

He was about to reply when Audus cursed.

'Is this rising?' she asked, staring at the inky pool they were all standing in.

Draik looked down and saw that the liquid was already up to his thighs.

'This was all predicted in my writings,' said Taddeus. 'There is nothing to fear. This is the Emperor's will.'

'What is it?' asked Audus. 'Oil?'

'The lifeblood of the fortress,' said Taddeus. 'Who knows what it is. It won't harm you. Put your trust in the Emperor.'

Isola was looking desperately around the chamber for an exit, but every facet was identical – each polished plane reflecting the growing panic within. 'I've never seen this in any other maglev chamber. We'll drown.'

'No,' said Grekh. 'Listen to the priest.'

The group fell quiet as the black liquid rose, washing up over their stomachs and chests. Vorne was the shortest, and they all turned to look at her as the liquid crested her chin and crept towards her lips. She showed no fear, keeping her eyes locked on Taddeus as she whispered a final prayer. Then, the liquid rose over her mouth and nose. For a brief moment, they could see her eyes, staring out above the oil, then it washed over her stubbled scalp and she was gone, no trace of her visible beneath the surface.

Soon after, Draik felt the liquid edging towards his own mouth. He closed his eyes. Every instinct screamed at him that this was wrong, and as the surface rose to his lips he took a final, deep breath and held it. The fluid rippled over his skin, filling his nostrils, pooling in his eye sockets and finally closing over his head.

Draik opened his eyes. To his surprise, he saw, rather than pitch dark, the chamber as it was before. The surface of the liquid was above his head, shimmering and mobile when seen from beneath, like a rippling ceiling, but beneath it nothing had changed. Isola looked back at him, relief in her eyes. Emissary Corval was patting his helmet, checking the joins. Grekh barely seemed to have noticed and Vorne was still mouthing prayers, her eyes locked on Taddeus.

The surface of the liquid rose higher, until it reached the chamber's ceiling, then it vanished.

'What is this? I don't…' Draik hesitated, surprised by the sound of his voice. It was muffled, like a distant echo, and he wondered if, despite appearances, they *were* in liquid. He moved his free arm and felt resistance, as though he were underwater, his muscles straining to move, but when he inhaled his lungs filled with air.

'The atmosphere,' said Taddeus. His voice was deadened and strange, like Draik's, as though coming from another room. 'It's different in some of the chambers down here. Richer. We're in the heart of the fortress.'

'We're there?' Draik shook his head. It had been too easy. Something seemed wrong.

Taddeus smiled and nodded at Draik's hand – the one embedded in the rock.

The rock was liquid again. He pulled it free with ease.

As he did so, one of the wall facets slid away with a muted clang, revealing another chamber. Taddeus stepped from the maglev chamber into the larger room beyond and the rest of the group followed, leaning forwards and walking slowly, as though crossing a seabed.

Taddeus had only taken a few steps when he turned and struggled back towards them, his face pale. He seemed unable to speak, shaking his head as he dragged Pious Vorne out to look. She grimaced and grabbed her scalp, clearly dismayed.

'What is it?' asked Draik, looking past them into the chamber.

It was different from any they had seen so far. Dark, again, but not entirely black this time. There was faint light radiating up through the floor. It was enough to reveal that the chamber was a long, straight gallery. It was fifty feet or so wide and disappeared into the distance. It was constructed from the same black substrate, but there was none of the skewed geometry they had seen before – just a straight, unerring passageway that vanished into the gloom. The ceiling was smooth and unadorned, but the walls were punctuated by hexagonal openings, like windows, every ten feet. They looked out into pure darkness.

'What's wrong?' asked Draik, peering down the corridor. He could see no sign of danger.

Taddeus stared back at him, horrified.

'This is the wrong place,' said Vorne, gripping the preacher's arm and looking around in dismay. 'The maglev has taken us somewhere new.'

'Somewhere I have not seen,' muttered Taddeus, staring at his journal. 'A place outside of my visions.' He glared at the shadows, as though seeking someone to blame. 'We have been misled.'

'Of course it's not the same place,' said Audus from the doorway. 'These things never repeat the same route.'

Taddeus glared at her, gripping his mace. Audus calmly drew her pistol and pointed it at Taddeus, raising an eyebrow. Vorne grabbed her flamer in both hands and took a few steps back, preparing to fill the passageway with fire.

'Wait!' snapped Isola, shoving Vorne's flamer and pointing it at the ceiling.

'Something's down there,' muttered Draik, ignoring the scuffle and looking down the gallery.

The argument went forgotten as they all looked into the darkness. Draik's implant whirred and clicked, trying to focus on the shadows. He glimpsed movement – something humanoid – but then it was gone.

'I saw it too,' whispered Isola. 'A man.'

A sound drifted towards them. The leaden atmosphere muffled it, but to Draik it sounded like breathing, or sniffing; like a predator on the scent of prey.

Audus lowered her pistol, the sneer falling from her face. 'What *is* that?'

They were still staring down the passageway when they heard a dull clunk behind them. The maglev had sealed itself. The only way was forwards.

Draik triggered the lumen on his pistol and stabbed it into the darkness. 'Move,' he said, his voice still muffled. 'Even if we could get back into it, the maglev won't go anywhere now. We can't stay here.'

Taddeus opened his book and began flicking frantically through the pages, shaking his head. 'I have *never* seen this. The chamber should not have brought us here. We've been tricked.' He looked around the group, his eyes settling on Audus. 'Someone has double-crossed us.'

Audus laughed and shook her head in disbelief.

'Or someone here lacks faith,' said Pious Vorne, still gripping her flamer.

'Oh, sure,' said Audus. 'Burn the witch. Everyone loves a show.' She waved her pistol at the walls. 'The Blackstone plays games. That's what it does. You must have noticed.'

'Not with me,' said Taddeus. 'My visions have never led me astray. Every time I–'

Draik held up a hand to silence them. 'We need to move. It's not safe to wait near a maglev. Not safe to wait anywhere, in fact. Whether you know this route or not, your excellency, we have to go.'

'Go where?' Taddeus slammed his book shut and looked around the group. 'Who will lead us? How will we choose a path?' He looked back at the maglev. 'We must find a way to make it return. We must go back to the antechamber and try again.'

'The captain has already explained,' said Emissary Corval,

stepping from the shadows and looming over the group. He tapped his cane on the faceted shell. 'These transportation chambers become inert after each journey. Even if we waited here for days, and survived, this door may not open again for another year – another ten years.'

Isola was still staring into the darkness ahead of them. 'There are turnings,' she said. 'How will we decide which to take if the preacher has never seen this place?'

'I can tell you,' said a voice.

It took Draik a moment to realise it was Grekh.

'Have you been here before?'

Grekh shook his head. He had finished chewing the fragments of shell and was pursuing one of his other peculiar activities. He had crouched down, taken a knife from his bag, and was tracing the blade around the edge of his shadow. The surfaces in the Blackstone seemed to be indestructible, so his knife left no mark on the floor, but he was utterly focused on his task.

'But you know the route?' Draik could not hide his doubt.

Grekh nodded, continuing to trace his shadow.

Draik shook his head and looked back down the passageway. He could feel Isola staring at him, full of doubt. 'We *will* find it,' he said, without looking at her.

Nobody spoke. Apart from Grekh, they were all watching for his lead.

'Your excellency,' he said, turning to Taddeus. 'This atmosphere.' He forced his arm slowly through the dense, heavy air. 'You said it's because we're in the heart of the Blackstone, is that right?'

Hope flashed in the preacher's eyes. 'True.' He looked at Pious Vorne, who nodded eagerly back at him.

'So we can't be too far off course?'

'No.' Taddeus grabbed his rosarius and muttered a prayer. 'That's true. I have spoken to many explorers and only those few who reached the utmost depths experienced this.' He walked over to Draik and gripped his arm. 'The God-Emperor knew what He was doing when He set you on my path, Captain Draik. He knew this moment would come. His light is in you. I see it. Lead the way. Trust your instincts. They will not fail you.'

Draik was not so sure about that, but he knew they had to keep moving. He had seen enough fatalities to know it was not safe to stay where they were. He nodded and began walking down the passageway, hauling his legs through the thick air with all the speed he could manage, pointing his lumen into the shadows. The others followed, weapons raised, with Grekh finally loping after them when he had finished his ritual.

Draik paused at the first hexagonal window and tried to see out, but it was impossible – the darkness was complete.

Isola stepped to his side, her pistol raised. 'Captain,' she whispered, nodding to a distant shape up ahead – a brief flicker of movement in the dark. It was human-sized but seemed unaffected by the torpid air, moving incredibly fast, flickering through the shadows.

As Draik stared into the darkness, the shape vanished. He frowned, wondering if it was just a trick of the light. 'Keep your weapons ready,' he said as they advanced.

They reached a crossroads and Draik halted, looking left and right, no idea which path to take. As the group gathered around him, Grekh jabbed his knife at the left-hand turn.

'Why?' asked Draik. 'What do you know that you're not telling us?'

He saw, again, a hint of emotion in the creature's eyes,

before it vanished and Grekh's expression was blank once more. Draik shook his head, exasperated. He stepped into the left-hand passageway and took a few steps down it, trying to discern any sign of a landmark.

Most of the group stayed in the main passageway, looking doubtful, but Emissary Corval followed Draik and, when they were out of earshot of the others, he leant close, lowering his voice to a whisper.

'Do not trust the kroot. It is not what it claims, captain. I'm not a true telepath, but I can catch glimpses. Whatever it might claim, that creature is not here through any sense of duty. It's keeping something from you. It came here for its own ends.'

Draik looked back at Grekh. The creature had wiped an oily, sweat-like substance from his pitted skin and was daubing it on the polished walls. 'I sense it too,' agreed Draik. 'He's planning something.'

'We're a long way from Terra,' said Corval. 'We need to look out for each other.'

Draik nodded, looking over at the disparate group he had assembled. 'You must think me a fool, emissary. I was in such a rush to get here, I didn't take time to consider the reliability of these people. Religious zealots, xenos beasts, smirking deserters – not the kind of associates I would usually choose.'

Corval held up a hand. 'Normal rules do not apply out here, captain. I would have done exactly the same. There's no logic to this place. Prophecies and visions are as good a guide as anything else. I'm sure we can find a place that triggers Taddeus' memories again. But the alien is a different matter.' A note of distaste entered Corval's voice. 'He watches you constantly. Have you noticed? I don't know what his intentions are, but I'm sure they're not wholesome.'

Grekh was still smearing the tacky substance across the walls, scribbling what looked like runes or territorial markings.

'I swore an oath,' said Draik. 'I told him he could serve me if he got me to the Dragon's Teeth. I will not go back on my word, however vexing it might be.'

'Of course not. Nor would I expect you to. If *we* can't behave with dignity, then who will? It's a gentleman's duty to show the low-born how to behave.' He laughed. 'Whether they heed the lesson or not. Of course you must honour your oath. I'm simply telling you that this creature cannot be trusted. And I intend to watch it closely.'

Draik nodded in thanks, then headed back into the main corridor.

'We carry on,' he said, waving for the others to follow.

Grekh looked up, confused, finally paying attention as they marched away from him. He hurried after them, clicking his beak and looking down the barrel of his rifle at the shadows up ahead.

A few minutes later, Draik halted.

'Wait!' he whispered, holding up a warning hand. Then he edged forwards, drawing his rapier and flicking the activation rune, scattering blue light from the blade. At first, he thought there was a bundle of rags strewn across the corridor but, as he edged closer, he saw the gruesome truth. Some of the mess was torn cloth, but more of it was ripped flesh – skin and organs, shredded in a kill frenzy and hurled in every direction. The floor and walls were glistening with blood and there were gleaming fragments of bone jutting from the carnage, splintered and cracked, crushed by powerful teeth.

As he reached the remains, Draik prodded them with the tip of his sword, flipping back a hood to reveal a ghastly, bloodless face with delicate, elongated features and wide, almond-shaped eyes.

'Xenos,' he muttered.

The others gathered round, grimacing and whispering prayers.

'Another one,' said Isola, pointing her lumen down the corridor. The light could still only reach a few feet, but it revealed a pile of body parts.

They took a few steps towards the next body when Corval halted and muttered in disgust: 'You wretched creature.'

Draik looked back to see that Grekh was hunched over the first corpse, his beak slick with gore as he chomped through the alien's organs, snorting as he wolfed it down.

Draik marched back towards him, repulsed by the sight of Grekh gulping down a freshly slain body. 'Show some dignity.' He tried to wave Grekh away from his glistening feast. 'For Throne's sake. We're not savages.'

Grekh looked up warily, but continued wolfing down the meat.

'Get back,' said Corval, drawing a laspistol and pointing it at the kroot. 'Captain Draik gave you an order.'

The creature backed away, reluctantly, into the shadows, swallowing a final morsel and wiping the back of his claw across his beak. Draik stared at the kroot in disgust, wishing, not for the first time, that he was more sparing with his oaths.

'This one's alive,' called Isola from further down the corridor. She was almost hidden in the darkness, no more than a vague silhouette thrown by the lumen on her gun.

Draik rushed towards her with as much speed as the dense air would allow.

It was another alien, an aeldari, with the same sharp, high-boned features as the first. Isola was on her knees, holding the alien's head off the ground. He was a horrible grey colour and there was blood bubbling from his nostrils. Large pieces of his chest and throat had been torn away, and Draik wondered how he was still managing to breathe. He was clearly moments from death.

Draik had spent a lifetime in the company of alien envoys and ambassadors. Unlike most of his race, he had even formed friendships with beings like the one dying in Isola's arms. He prayed that this survivor had not seen Grekh's grotesque behaviour.

'Can you speak?' he asked, trying the phrase in several aeldari dialects before the alien looked up at him in shock.

'My heart,' replied the alien, reaching for his chest. Unlike the other xenos, this one wore an ornate suit of armour. Aeldari armour was unlike anything manufactured by humans. Draik had seen it deflect all sorts of blows, but it moulded to the aliens' slender bodies like leather – a tight-fitting bodyglove. This one was torn in several places but the alien sighed with relief when his hand closed over a gemstone in the suit's chest-plate.

'Who did this to you?' asked Draik.

The alien tried to speak, then grimaced, arching his back in pain, clamping his eyes shut.

When he recovered, he locked his feverish eyes on Isola. 'Take me with you,' he said, still gripping the stone on his chest. 'Get me out of this place.'

'Can you walk?' asked Isola, trying to lift him.

The alien gasped and slumped in her grip. Fresh blood rushed from his mouth but he was still trying to speak. 'The Talisman of Vaul,' he muttered. 'The promise of a god.' His words became a stream of gibberish.

Isola gave Draik a sideways glance and shook her head.

Draik was about to ask another question when they all heard a sound. It was clear this time, the snorting and sniffing of hounds on a scent. Draik stood, trying to pierce the darkness with the lumen on his pistol, but only revealing more body parts, flung carelessly across the floor.

'We need to go back,' muttered the alien, lying weakly in Isola's grip.

'Not possible,' said Draik, not really speaking to the alien, still staring through the darkness. A few moments later, the alien coughed and slumped in Isola's arms. She held him for a little longer, then shook her head and laid him on the floor.

Draik stared at the corpses. He had seen deaths before on the Blackstone but nothing quite this savage. He marched on, his pistol still pointed before him. 'Keep moving. We have to find another transportation chamber.'

As they headed further down the corridor, the sounds of panting and sniffing grew clearer. They reached another skewed, diamond-shaped aperture and passed through into a large room. The temperature dropped dramatically as they crossed the boundary and Draik almost fell as he rushed forwards, suddenly propelled by a lack of resistance. The atmosphere had returned to normal.

The floor was divided into wide, step-like terraces that led down into the darkness. Draik waved for the others to follow and hurried on. The descent seemed bottomless and the temperature sank even lower, causing Draik's clothes to stiffen with frost. Just when he was wondering if they should turn back and find the route Grekh had suggested, he reached an open space. The others had just gathered around him when a shadow broke free from the rest of the gloom, rushing towards him at incredible speed.

Without thinking, Draik raised his splinter pistol and fired.

The muzzle flash revealed a grey-skinned horror, humanoid and hunched, with long, ape-like arms that were stretched out towards Draik. It carried no weapons, but its body was a rippling mass of muscle. It had a flat, eyeless face, built around a gaping, incisor-crammed mouth and dozens of snorting air holes. The creature staggered as Draik's splinters thudded home, punching into the featureless upper half of its head. By the time it reached him, its momentum had gone. It crumpled to the floor a few feet away, grasping feebly at the splinters embedded in its face.

'Ur-ghuls,' Draik muttered. He had faced these creatures before, many years earlier, while escaping from a xenos torture cruiser. They were determined hunters. Reared to track and kill. If he hadn't managed to steal the splinter pistol he still carried to this day, he never would have discovered how to kill the creatures.

'They're blind!' he cried. 'They hunt by smell. Fire into their faces!'

'More!' cried Grekh, stepping to Draik's side, firing his rifle one-handed from the hip and grabbing a grenade with his other claw.

Dozens of shadowy figures raced towards them, a few falling back as Grekh fired into them.

The kroot's grenade exploded, hurling ur-ghuls through the air and revealing the scale of the attack. There were hordes of the eyeless creatures approaching from every direction, stooped low and bolting towards them on all fours, growling and snorting. Draik fired furiously and drew his rapier. Isola and the others gathered around him, adding more shots to the fray as a drumming din filled the air – the sound of clawed feet pounding across the chamber.

Flames ripped through the darkness as Vorne fired into

the slavering creatures. Several fell back, engulfed in flames, thrashing silently as they tumbled away. None of them screamed. It was like watching pict footage with the sound muted. Vorne's flames lit up the stairs they had just descended and Draik saw that they were swarming with xenos – far more than they could battle through. There was no way back.

'Keep going!' he cried, waving the others on and running deeper into the chamber.

Ur-ghuls rushed towards him. He downed one with a barrage of headshots, then stopped another in the same way, but a third leapt at him, hissing and grasping.

Draik sidestepped and plunged his rapier into its chest.

The creature's hide was thick and unyielding. He drove the blade home but, as the ur-ghul fell, it took Draik with it, his sword trapped in its chest. The thing thrashed beneath him and locked iron-hard hands around his throat, pulling his face towards its gaping mouth.

Then it stiffened as he fired, repeatedly, up through its jaw, shearing the front of its head away. The strength went from its grip and he freed himself, wrenching his blade out as another creature hurtled through the shadows. Draik caught it on the tip of his sword, triggering a burst of power as the rapier punched into the alien's face, spilling sapphire beams from the wound. He pulled the sword free, stepped back and fired into the ur-ghul's mouth, jolting its head back and knocking it from its feet.

There was a flash of light at his side and another ur-ghul flew away from him as Grekh approached, his rifle still smoking.

Draik snatched a moment to look around.

Everyone was firing in different directions, their faces plucked from the dark by muzzle flashes.

'Go!' he cried. 'We need to get out of the open!'

He ran further into the chamber, battling the sense that he might fall into an abyss at any moment. The others rushed after him, but it was ridiculous to run blind. He increased the power supply to his optic implant, driving it towards burn-out. Even with the power amplified, it only revealed a vague glimpse of what lay ahead, but that was enough.

'A ramp!' he cried. 'On the opposite side. It's clear.'

He sprinted across the chamber and rushed up the slope. Halfway up he turned to look back.

The rest of the group were still firing and the darkness around them was seething with ur-ghuls, their eyeless faces lit up by the blasts as they scampered and bounded towards their prey. Draik fired back the way he had come, taking down another two, then he grimaced as one of his guards was dragged from sight, vanishing beneath a wave of thrashing limbs.

Grekh paused, examining the fallen guard, or taking something from him, Draik couldn't be sure which, then he ran on.

Isola pounded up the ramp to his side, gasping as she fired back down into the fray.

Emissary Corval loomed out of the darkness, practically sauntering up the ramp, firing his pistol with calm disinterest. Then came the two priests. Taddeus' power mace was dripping with alien blood and his eyes were wide with religious zeal. Pious Vorne walked backwards up the steps, still spewing a torrent of sputtering flames into the stampede below. Then came Audus and the remainder of Draik's guards.

When he was sure they had everyone, Draik waved them on and they ran up the ramp, firing back over their shoulders as the ur-ghuls scrambled after them. The ur-ghuls clawed frantically over each other, hissing and gasping, but the ramp was too narrow. Draik and the others fired into the bottleneck crush, killing dozens of the frenzied creatures.

Draik was the first to reach the top of the ramp and see what lay beyond.

He staggered to a halt and muttered a curse, his pistol hanging limply in his grip. The next chamber was lit. It was as cavernous as the preceding ones, and the ceiling was a crystal spire, open to the heavens. Starlight flooded down through the panes, illuminating the expanse below – a circular hall, with openings scattered around the circumference. One of the doorways was a maglev chamber. Draik spotted it instantly. It matched the design of others he had seen, with a hexagonal door. He should have been pleased, but it was the other doorways that had caused him to curse. Ur-ghuls were pouring from them in their hundreds. The maglev was on the opposite side of the hall and the ur-ghuls would swamp them before they could get even halfway there.

He looked back to see if there was any chance they could return the way they had come. His guards and the rest of the party were all shooting down the ramp, but the ur-ghuls were gradually making their way up, tumbling from the darkness with frenzied hunger.

Isola looked up at him as she fired. At the sight of his expression, her face darkened. 'More of them?'

He nodded.

The others backed up the slope towards him and saw the starlit chamber and the ur-ghuls rushing into it.

'There's a transportation chamber on the far side,' he said, nodding to the one door not spewing monsters.

As Taddeus reached the top of the ramp his eyes flashed

with excitement. 'I have seen that chamber. We're back on the right route.'

'But we'll never reach it,' said Isola, shaking her head as she watched the ur-ghuls flooding the hall.

'We will,' said Draik, his face rigid with determination. 'If we go now. We could still break through.'

Audus raised an eyebrow. 'Some of us, maybe, but not all of us.'

Draik could feel his chance slipping away and his pulse hammered in his temples. He pictured his father's face as it was the last time they spoke, cold and distant. 'I *will* reach the vault,' he whispered, speaking to someone who would never hear him. He started walking down the ramp into the hall, checking his pistol as he went.

'Wait!' cried Vorne. 'His Eminence is the slowest of the group,' she said, wiping frost from her eyelashes as she strode towards Draik. Behind her, the others were still firing into the ur-ghuls from the previous chamber and she had to raise her voice to be heard. 'He's the Emperor's chosen. You can't leave him to die.'

'If the Emperor chose him, He'll get him to the other side,' snapped Audus, loosing off more shots.

When Vorne received no reply from Draik, she turned back to Taddeus.

'The time has come,' she said. 'I always said I would pay you back for saving my soul.' She tapped the fuel canisters strapped to her back. 'There's enough here to take them all down, or at least kill most and drive away the rest.'

Draik paused and looked back at her. 'But how would you get the tanks in the middle of them without...' His words tailed off as he saw her expression. She was consumed by faith – her eyes were filled with a mixture of determination and passion. He had seen this so many times before in the faces of Ecclesiarchy zealots and it always appalled him. 'No,' he snapped. 'No martyrs.'

Vorne hesitated, glancing at Taddeus. Taddeus said nothing. He just gripped his rosarius and whispered a prayer.

Draik's anger grew. The ur-ghuls were rushing towards the centre of the hall. His chance would soon be gone. But Vorne was now under his aegis. Self-immolation was not how a Draik operated. He thought again of the gruesome scenes carved into the walls of Taddeus' barge. 'What kind of Emperor do you worship?' he muttered, glaring at Taddeus.

Audus stopped shooting for a moment to stare at him, surprised. For the first time since they met, she dropped her cynical sneer and looked serious. 'Well said,' she muttered.

'What now?' demanded Isola, her face ashen as she watched the ur-ghuls gathering below.

'How did you know to avoid this route?' said Draik, turning to Grekh. The question had been scratching at the back of his thoughts since he reached the top of the ramp. He still didn't trust the creature but, whatever the kroot's motivations, he seemed to know a lot about the Blackstone.

Grekh shrugged.

'How can we get across this hall? How can we stop those things?'

'*We* can't,' said Grekh.

'But someone else could?'

Grekh looked at the hall, taking in the narrow doorways, the crystal spire and the vast, empty expanse of floor. 'The Blackstone brought us together.'

Corval shook his head. 'This thing speaks in riddles so it doesn't have to tell the truth.'

Draik was looking in the same direction as Grekh, his eyes

skipping over the featureless floor. No, not featureless, he realised. It was marked by the same network of grooves they had seen in the first chamber. 'Yes,' he said quietly. 'I see it.'

'We can do this,' he said, staring at Vorne. 'All of us.'

Vorne looked at Taddeus, but Taddeus gave her a relaxed smile. 'He carries the God-Emperor's fire. Trust him.'

Vorne's relief was obvious. She valued her life as much as anyone else, but her faith was so strong that she would have sacrificed herself anyway. The idea hit Draik with the force of a revelation. He had witnessed countless acts of martyrdom during his life, but his horror was always lessened by the belief that religious zealots were so faith-drunk they were barely human. Even as a child, he had been inured to the horror of pilgrims dying on the crowded roads to the Imperial Palace, because he thought them lunatics, happy to die for their faith. The idea that Vorne was sane and *still* prepared to sacrifice herself disturbed him.

'What's your plan, captain?' asked Emissary Corval, interrupting his train of thought.

'Run as fast as you can and make for the maglev. I'll deal with the rest.'

'Run as fast as we can?' Vorne's relief was replaced with scorn. 'That's your plan?'

Taddeus placed a hand on her shoulder. 'I have faith in him.'

Vorne looked no less convinced, but she was clearly not in the habit of challenging Taddeus. She nodded and looked back at Draik, a fierce warning in her eyes.

He looked at each of them in turn, then gave the signal to run.

They sprinted across the hall with ur-ghuls approaching from every direction. No one was shooting anymore. Faced with such numbers, it was pointless. When they were about halfway across the hall, and the ur-ghuls were almost on them, Draik slashed his palm open with the edge of his rapier and stopped.

None of the others even noticed his absence, dashing on towards the maglev, but the scent of his blood drove the ur-ghuls into a frenzy and they rushed towards him, snorting and gasping. Draik was quickly surrounded by a circle of ur-ghuls as they forgot about the rest of the group and singled him out, their needle-teeth glistening in anticipation of a feast.

They were seconds from Draik when he dropped to one knee and pressed his bloody palm against one of the intersections on the floor, squeezing the blood through the gap. Then he turned on his heel and sprinted after the others.

Behind him, the floor exploded. Iron-dark shards burst from the ground, clicking and clacking as they snapped together, forming hundreds of pyramids. The ur-ghuls tried to stop, but it was too late. Their momentum threw them into the cyclone of whirling stones, hissing and pinwheeling their gangly arms as they failed to halt. Draik did not stop to look back as he raced towards the maglev.

The others had already reached the chamber and opened the door and, as he ran towards them they looked past him with dazed expressions on their faces. Draik could not see the carnage he had caused, but he could hear it – an explosion of clattering plates, tearing flesh and juddering limbs. He was moments away from the doorway when a heavy shape thudded into him and sent him sprawling onto his side, sliding across the sheer, black floor.

Las-blasts flashed through the air, and he saw, in the corner of his eye, an ur-ghul being torn apart as Isola and the others gave him covering fire. He staggered to his feet and ran on, and was just a few feet from the chamber when more of the creatures slammed into him. Gunfire screamed all around him as the others tried to defend him, kicking ur-ghuls away from him in every direction, but pain exploded in his bicep as one of the creatures sank its teeth into his arm. The creature tore furiously at him and the air turned to blood mist.

Draik rammed his rapier into the ur-ghul's chest, planted his boot in its stomach and kicked it away. He scrambled to his feet and ran in to the chamber as the others fired into the tumult outside.

'Go!' he cried. 'Close the doors! We have to–' He fell silent as he turned and saw what he had done.

The entire hall had erupted into motion. Every surface was fractured and split, creating a storm of oil-black shells. There were thousands of them, spiralling up into the air and crashing down in landslides, all matching the same tessellating, pyramidal design. The ur-ghuls were being torn apart. Hunter had become prey. They tried to flee back to the other doors, but every space they trod on sprouted pyramids. The constructs swarmed over the ur-ghuls like mechanical toys, whirling and juddering as they sliced through their flesh.

Draik was so dazed by the scale of the destruction that it took him a moment to realise that there were still some ur-ghuls trying to follow them into the maglev chamber.

Audus was next to him, spitting curses as she smashed the butt of her pistol into the face of one monster, while on the other side of him Taddeus was pummelling another with his mace, shattering its skull with prayer-fuelled rage. The area around the doorway was heaped with wounded xenos that were still trying to reach their prey.

The main threat was no longer from the aliens, though. The wave of pyramids was spreading out across the hall, and hundreds of the machines were scuttling towards the maglev. In a few seconds they would shred Draik and the others in just the same way they had devoured the ur-ghuls.

'Close the doors!' cried Draik, looking around the chamber for a control mechanism. There were niches in the walls, chest height and filled with the same black liquid as the previous maglev. But this time there were four of them, side by side and identical.

Draik looked at Taddeus, but the priest shook his head.

'I saw this chamber in my visions, but we approached from the other direction.' He stared at the four little alcoves. 'I'm not sure.'

Draik shook his head. 'The doors won't close until we trigger the mechanism.'

'Quick,' said Audus, firing at the approaching host.

'Grekh?' said Draik, noticing that the creature was outside the chamber, hunched over one of the fallen ur-ghuls.

'Throne,' spat Corval. 'What is it doing?'

The mountain of black shells was about to crash into them.

'Grekh!' howled Draik.

The kroot lurched to his feet and loped back towards them, a piece of grey alien flesh in his mouth and blood rushing down his neck. Draik's hand edged towards one of the niches as he saw a chance to leave the grotesque creature behind, but an oath was an oath. He waited until Grekh had leapt into the chamber, still clutching some of the xenos corpse, before he turned to Taddeus.

'Choose one.'

Taddeus stared at the alcoves, still shaking his head. 'I have not seen this, captain.'

'Now!' cried Isola as the pyramids crashed over the final few feet.

'Ask Grekh,' cried Audus. 'He understands this place better than any of you.'

Draik looked at Grekh.

The kroot swallowed some of the still-warm flesh and nodded at the middle alcove.

Draik thrust his hand into the niche.

11

The sun was a memory, ennobling temple walls, illuminating banners, but long estranged from the sky. Pilgrims did not seek Holy Terra for natural illumination, of course; they sought an illumination of the soul. Did they ever find it, wondered Draik, as they breathed their last – crushed beneath oblivious multitudes, reaching for gates that never opened and clouds that never broke. He looked at them crawling through the muck, watching them through a spear-tip window so tall he could not see the apex. The glass was leaded and stained, ablaze with saints and scholars and framed by a casement wrought in the shape of a vast, double-headed eagle.

Draik's father was a few feet away, finalising the commission that would take Draik to the far side of the galaxy. He had already explained that this was not a punishment but an honour, crushing Draik's soul with every lie.

'Captain,' he said. 'Can you hear me?'

Draik frowned. His father never addressed him as captain. There had been a galaxy between them by the time Draik had assumed that title. And the voice was not his father's age-ravaged croak, but a metallic, inhuman burr. As Draik tried to place the voice, a dark tide poured into the streets below, washing over the statuary and engulfing the pilgrims, boiling and rolling, turning the horizon black.

'Captain Draik,' said the voice again as darkness enveloped him.

An icy chill radiated through Draik's coat, throbbing in his bones and reminding him of where he really was.

'The Blackstone.' His speech was clumsy, as though he had just awoken. He opened his eyes but saw only darkness.

'Yes, the Blackstone,' said the voice, sounding pleased. 'Hang on to that thought. The fortress is beguiling you – sending you back into your past. I am Emissary Corval. We have come to the Blackstone seeking its innermost chamber. Do you remember?'

For a moment, the darkness lifted and Draik glimpsed the three lenses of Corval's helmet. Light flashed in the glass, reminding him of candlelight on windowpanes and pushing him back into the past.

'Sound the trumpets,' said his sister as she walked towards him, trailing velvet, ermine and vitriol. 'Bang the drum.' A sea of powdered wigs and coronets parted to let her join him at the window. 'Behold, as Terra's most noble son prepares to sally forth.' She laughed, leaning close, whispering in his ear. 'I won't tell them the truth if you don't.'

He kept his gaze fixed on the crowds beneath the window. If he saw the victorious look in her eye there would be violence, and there had been enough of that.

She sipped her wine and looked at the crowds below, pitiful

and bleeding, no idea of the high-born eyes looking down at them.

'Even those filthy wretches will enjoy the privilege you have been denied, brother. While you breathe your last in some dreadful backwater, they will be here, talking their drivel in the blessed streets of Holy Terra.' She laughed again, looking back into the room, at the distant figure of their father. 'And the irony is that it's breaking his heart. It's killing him to send you away.' Her tone soured. 'Thanks to your stupidity, he will have to make do with me, a mere *daughter*. All your embarrassing breaks with protocol, all those inelegant deals, all those ill-advised duels and then, finally, this – a murder, Janus. A *murder*. What son ever disappointed a father as completely as you have?' She sneered. 'I could weep for him, I really could.'

Draik wanted to argue, to explain, but the candlelight shimmered again and left him facing Emissary Corval. He saw the Blackstone more clearly this time. They had emerged from the maglev into a small, octagonal antechamber with a doorway in each wall. Something was wrong. Audus was curled in a foetal position on the floor, cursing and raging. Pious Vorne was wrestling with Taddeus, who had blood rushing from what looked to be self-inflicted head wounds. As Vorne grappled with the heavyset preacher, he was moaning frantically and trying to reach his eyes with his fingernails. Isola was still inside the maglev chamber, pummelling the faceted walls with her fists as though trying to break through solid rock. Grekh sat quietly, gnawing thoughtfully on a piece of flesh, and Draik's guards were hurling abuse at each other, on the verge of drawing weapons.

He grabbed Corval's arm and climbed to his feet. 'What happened?'

Corval held him until he was steady then turned back to the others. 'This is it – the madness Taddeus warned you of.'

As Corval reached Draik's guards, he placed one hand against the side of his helmet and extended his other hand towards the arguing soldiers.

A tracery of circuits blazed around the Navigator's cowl, flooding energy down his sleeve and causing his gauntlet to pulse with cool inner fire.

'You are with Captain Draik,' said Corval, his voice amplified and strange, resonating through the gloom. 'You are on the Blackstone Fortress.'

The guards ceased their argument, but Corval kept his hand raised and the light grew more powerful, distorting the air with heat haze and causing the men to stagger, clutching their heads.

'Follow the sound of my voice,' said Corval. 'The fortress is trying to confuse you.'

The men became still as Corval approached them, looking around with dazed expressions. He gripped each of them in turn, grabbing their shoulders with his shimmering hand and channelling the light through their uniforms. He stayed with them for a few minutes, until they nodded at him, looking embarrassed but less confused.

Corval moved round the whole group, with the exception of Grekh, repeating the process until everyone was calm. Then they gathered around him in silence. Until that moment, Corval had been a shadowy presence in the group, barely acknowledged by anyone but Draik; now they looked at him as a leader, horrified by whatever memories had gripped them and desperate to avoid slipping back.

'What do we do?' asked Draik, still trying to shake the memory of his sister's vicious laughter.

'Celebrate,' said Corval, with an unusual note of levity. 'According to our spiritual guide,' he nodded at Taddeus, 'this malady only occurs near our goal. We have almost reached the vault.'

Taddeus whispered a prayer and his face turned a worrying shade of purple. He seemed too excited to breathe. 'The blind shall be made to see,' he muttered, gripping his power mace and closing his eyes.

'But what of the...' Isola looked anxiously back at the wall she had just been pummelling.

Corval shook his head. 'I'm shielding us. It was surprisingly easy. Perhaps the Blackstone is not quite as impenetrable as it might seem.'

Draik nodded his head in a slight bow. 'You are modest, emissary. Your skill has made light of a problem that would have crushed a lesser mind. We are all in your debt.'

Corval returned the bow. 'I would suggest a few minutes' rest before we press on to the Ascuris Vault. I know we are eager to reach our goal, but you have all just been through an unusual psychic trauma. There may be aftershocks.'

The fight with the ur-ghuls had left most of the group exhausted, so the Navigator's suggestion was met without argument.

Draik looked at his attaché, who was standing on guard beside him. 'Isola, you too. Take the time...' His words faltered as his gaze fell on Grekh. The kroot still seemed oblivious to everything that had happened, sitting just outside the maglev, gnawing on the bit of meat he had salvaged from the previous chamber. Draik stepped closer, a dreadful realisation washing over him.

He stooped and grabbed the kroot's arm, pulling it closer so he could see what Grekh was holding. The flesh was chewed beyond recognition, just a pulpy mess, but it was still encased in sodden shreds of cloth – torn fragments of a House Draik uniform.

Grekh stopped eating for a moment, staring back at him. The others gathered round to watch the exchange.

Draik remembered seeing Grekh snatch something from the guard who died fleeing from ur-ghuls. 'That's from one of my men?' he said, his voice tight with rage.

Grekh nodded.

Images of glorious Terra were still echoing round Draik's thoughts, scenes of nobility and privilege, and here he was, consorting with a snorting, man-eating savage. Rage jolted through him like a current and he whipped his pistol from its holster, jamming it against the creature's forehead, directly between its blank, impenetrable eyes. His finger settled over the trigger.

There was silence. He could feel the others behind him, waiting to see what he did next.

'He was dead,' said Grekh.

One of the other guards hissed in disbelief and Draik heard the sound of weapons being readied.

He stood in silence for a moment, pressing his gun harder into the kroot's face. Then he stepped back.

'That thing has no place in your company,' said Corval.

'We would never have got here without him,' said Audus, glaring at Corval. She looked pale and shaken from whatever visions had been tormenting her, but she stepped to Grekh's side with a determined scowl. 'You never would have found me without him and he's done nothing but watch our backs since we landed. The kroot just think differently about death, that's all. He didn't *kill* that man. And it's not like we're going to be giving anyone a burial in this place.'

Draik lowered his pistol. Even through his outrage, he could hear the sense in Audus' words. But there was no way he was going to spend another minute with the vile creature.

'Go,' he said, grabbing Grekh by the shoulder and hurling him across the chamber towards one of the doorways. 'Get out of my sight.'

Grekh stood, shaking his head, shreds of meat still hanging in his grip. 'My debt…' he said.

'Is repaid,' snarled Draik, still battling the urge to kill him. He knew the name of the man Grekh was currently digesting. 'Go. Before I change my mind. Audus says you know this place better than any of us. I'm sure you'll find a way out.'

Grekh shook his head, looking at Audus for support.

She was about to speak up again when Draik yelled an order.

'On the count of three,' he said, glancing at his men.

They raised their lasguns and pointed them at the kroot.

'One,' said Draik, raising his pistol.

Grekh gave a last shake of his head, then bounded off through the doorway, vanishing into the darkness.

Draik stood there for a few seconds, his pistol still raised, considering how low he had come, how far he was from where he should be.

'Which way?' he said, turning to Taddeus, his voice still taut. 'Where is the vault?'

Audus was shaking her head and cursing under her breath but the rest of the group relaxed, visibly, to see Grekh gone.

Taddeus beamed at Audus, waving his mace at one of the doorways. 'Take heart. Deliverance is at hand. We don't need rabid xenos creatures to lead the way.' He tapped his journal. 'We are back on the routes I understand. These are the places I have been shown. The God-Emperor's brilliance has found us, even here, in this lightless pit. We're almost there.'

After they had rested and checked their weapons, Taddeus led them down the corridor he had pointed out. It was as dark as all the previous ones, but it was far narrower, so the lumens on their guns were enough to light up the walls and flash in their widened eyes. Every few feet they passed circular openings leading to other passageways, but Taddeus rushed on down the main corridor until it opened out into another large hall.

Draik hesitated at the threshold, confused. It looked like they had emerged in a moonlit forest. As in one of the previous chambers, the ceiling was open to the light of the heavens – a vast, faceted dome of crystal that glittered with the radiance of a thousand stars. The light poured down through the dome and splashed, cold and beautiful, across hundreds of columns. They were not trees, as Draik had at first thought, but rods made of the same black substance as the walls. They varied in height, some hundreds of feet tall and others no higher than a man. High up, they were linked with bough-like crossbars, creating shady, bowered walkways and adding to the sense of a forest. As Draik stepped closer, he saw that the rods were arranged in a pattern – complex, but deliberate and familiar in some way. The chamber fell away on one side, a sheer drop that plunged into a pit, beyond the reach of the starlight. On the other side, beyond the columns, was a broad staircase. Draik's head ached as he followed its meandering, physics-defying course. The steps started normally enough, then veered off at a bizarre angle and looped back, creating an intersection that Draik could not understand, however long he stared at it.

Taddeus had not paused, striding on through the columns

with confidence, making for the distant staircase as the rest of the group hurried after him. Draik was halfway across the room, still trying to decipher the pattern of the columns, when Corval placed a hand on his shoulder.

'Captain,' he said. 'What is it?'

Draik shook his head. He had the same odd feeling he'd had when he watched the Dragon's Teeth move in the same sequence as his childhood training regimes. There was something about the arrangement of these columns that mirrored his past. It was as though the Blackstone were trying to tell him something. He was on the verge of explaining all this to Corval when he realised how absurd it was. He'd sound like one of the fools who became enamoured by the Blackstone's mystery, imbuing it with religious significance and personality.

'There's a pattern here,' he said, without elaborating. 'I can't decipher it.'

Corval nodded, looking around at the featureless poles. 'It might be significant, captain. Your goal is to decipher the workings of this place. These details might point to a wider pattern.'

'True,' muttered Draik, still unwilling to explain that his interest was more obscure.

'Take a moment,' said Corval. 'We're racing through all these rooms at such speed, without pausing to examine their mysteries. We could miss something crucial if we don't stop to look when we have the chance.'

It was true. They were sprinting past wonders that might never be seen by human eyes again. As the others rushed on and began climbing the staircase, Draik stepped closer to one of the columns and Corval wandered off through the stone glade, looking up at the distant ceiling.

'Captain!' Corval waved Draik over towards the edge of the room. 'There's something over here.'

The others had now disappeared from sight, heading on into the next chamber, so Draik moved quickly, not wanting to split the group. He dashed between the columns, starlight flashing on his cuirass as he reached the edge of the chamber.

'What is it?'

Corval was staring into the darkness, his cowl flickering with psychic resonance as he leant out into the void.

'I can't tell. Can your eyepiece penetrate this wretched darkness, captain? Focus it over there. Do you see that?' Corval pointed down into the unseen depths and Draik saw something moving in the shadows. He stepped past the Navigator, fascinated.

'I *do* see something,' he muttered, dropping into a crouch and opening his optical implant's aperture as wide as it would go. Something started to materialise. 'A face,' he gasped as the features swam into view. Again, he sensed that the fortress was dredging his past. The face was familiar. His breath stalled in his throat as he realised what the Blackstone was showing him. 'Numa,' he gasped, his throat dry.

'Numa,' said Corval. The Navigator's voice sounded odd.

Draik leapt to his feet, looking back at Corval. The Navigator had drawn his pistol. It was pointed at Draik's face.

Corval hesitated, just for a second, his hand wavering, then he fired.

The hesitation gave Draik time to dodge, draw and fire, but his shot went wide as Corval's blast ripped through his shoulder, knocking him off his feet and throwing him backwards.

Corval said nothing as Draik fell, silently, into the frigid dark.

12

'She went back in,' said a voice, loud and grating in his ear.

Bullosus woke with a grunt, sitting bolt upright and looking around the hold. He felt stronger, but the pain in his arm was worse. Lothar and Aurick were watching him with grim expressions on their faces.

'Who?' he said. 'Where?'

'Audus,' said Lothar. 'Back into the Blackstone.'

Bullosus pounded his fist on the table, leaving an impressive dent. 'With the Terran?'

'And the priest.'

Bullosus' anger flooded him with vitality. His mother, father, brother and sisters were all facing a death sentence, while that pompous dandy played games on the Blackstone. 'Then we're going back in too.'

Lothar was almost as big and ugly as his elder brother, but fear flashed in his eyes. 'That place will kill us, Grusel.'

Aurick nodded. 'It's not safe.'

Bullosus stared at them both. 'Without Audus, we cannot save them.'

The words hung in the air as all three brothers pictured the faces of their family. Lothar and Aurick nodded, looking ashamed.

'Did you tag her?' asked Lothar.

'In the chest. She'll be easy to track.'

'What about that?' asked Lothar, pointing at his wound.

Bullosus cursed as he remembered the shattered mess that used to be his arm. The chirurgeon had done enough to keep him alive but the arm was useless. Perhaps he was a fool to go back in? Could there be another way? He slumped back onto the table, looking around the gun cases that lined the walls. There was a fortune to be made if he could just live long enough to sell them. He had been dealing weapons since he first crawled out of the festering hive city that spawned him, but he had never seen anything like the relics in Precipice.

His gaze fell on a broad, curved blade that was even more valuable than the guns. A radium scythe. Throne knows how it had ended up in the Blackstone. It could cut through almost anything. If he lived, it would come close to clearing his debt on its own, but the deal was fixed: Audus for the lives of his family.

As he looked at the scythe, an idea occurred to him.

He nodded to the bottle of amasec his brothers had been drinking. They passed it to him and he downed it without pausing for breath, savouring the heat that rushed up through his chest and cleared his thoughts.

Orphis was still in the corner of the hold, cleaning his surgical instruments, a jaundiced, skeletal husk of a man, hunched and trembling as he packed his things away, eager to return to the Helmsman. There was a chainknife hanging on the back of the door.

'Cut me above the elbow,' Bullosus said, glaring at the chirurgeon. 'Hook the radium scythe to my artery.'

Orphis paled.

'Mess it up and I'll kill you,' said Bullosus. It was a calmly stated fact rather than a threat.

Orphis nodded slowly, then grabbed another bottle of amasec and drank almost as much as Bullosus. He took the chainknife and triggered the blade, filling the hold with the rattling din of saw teeth.

As Orphis leant over him, Bullosus held up his working hand, signalling that he should pause.

'Sing,' he demanded, glaring at the squat, amphibian thing in the corner of the room.

As the chainknife's teeth bit into his arm, and the air turned crimson, Bullosus drifted away, carried on the gentle lullaby that spilled from the cage. The tune took him away from the sweat and blood, back through the decades – back to his childhood, when he was too young to know how messed up everything was.

13

Corval stood at the brink of the precipice, waiting for euphoria to arrive. Three decades, keeping himself alive, holding the horrors of his disease at bay, just to achieve this simple end: the death of one man. But where he had expected elation, he found only numbness. The void before him merged with the void in his soul. What does a man do once he achieves his life's ambition? Corval had only ever thought of reaching this point: killing Draik – murdering him where no one could hunt for clues, where no one would question his death. But what now?

To his immense surprise, Corval realised he wanted to live. What a joke. Living. The one thing he could not risk. He placed a hand over his chest, feeling the movement beneath his suit. His skin was bubbling like broth, struggling to contain the vileness beneath. His damnation was almost complete. What life could there be for someone like him?

He took a metal syringe and a small canister from his

robes. He placed them on the floor and unfastened the hauberk of his thick, rubber-clad suit. He paused, looking around, peering into the shadows to make sure the others weren't near, then he pulled open his shirt. His chest was deformed, wrenched out of shape by a large, egg-shaped swelling at the centre of his ribs. Corval muttered an oath as he saw that it was splitting down the middle, revealing an amber-coloured eye with a vertical slit of a pupil. As Corval picked the syringe up from the floor, the eye began to roll, as though trying to escape from his chest. Corval hesitated. He had been through this process every day for years, but this time there was something new. Beneath the eye, a narrow depression had formed over his diaphragm. It looked horribly like a mouth.

He pushed the needle into the eyeball and sucked the fluid into the syringe. Once he had lanced the growth, leaving an empty sac, he injected the golden fluid into the metal canister and placed it back beneath his robes, where it clinked against several others he had filled since landing on the Blackstone. He took a tin of salve from another pocket and rubbed it over the wound. The skin blistered, smoking slightly as his skin melted and reformed, sealing the hole.

He looked at the nascent mouth for a moment, unsure what to do. It was moving, mouthing silent phrases beneath his skin. He could see the beginnings of teeth, strong and healthy, clamping and shifting under his stomach muscles. He took some of the salve and rubbed it over the depression. The skin blistered and thickened, obscuring the mouth a little, but he could still see it trying to speak.

'Not much time,' muttered Corval, fastening his shirt and hiding his disgrace, wondering what to do next.

He had always intended to take his own life straight after

Draik's, hiding his shameful end in some dark, unreachable corner of the Blackstone, but now he had been waylaid by an absurd, childish hope. An idea had been simmering at the back of thoughts since Draik had first described the Ascuris Vault. The Blackstone followed no laws of physics. The histories were clear on the subject. Even time was mutable within the walls of the Blackstone, chemistry and biology the same. Explorers had emerged from the Blackstone changed – not just mentally, but *physically*. If Draik's theory was right, and the Ascuris Vault was the fulcrum of the whole fortress, perhaps it could offer him a chance at redemption? He had tried to crush such thoughts, worried that such absurd fancies might distract him. But now, with Draik dead, what difference did it make? Why not follow Taddeus to the vault? They were so close now. He could suppress his mutations for a little longer. He laughed at the ridiculousness of it, but he ran towards the steps anyway, preparing the lies he would tell the others.

We were attacked. Draik fell. I could not save him.

It would be easily done.

Since Corval had shot Draik there had been a distant rumbling sound echoing round the chamber – a low, grinding moan. He had barely registered it until now, but as he headed back into the stone glade, it grew noticeably louder.

He looked up into the network of beams and saw that one of them was trembling. He had thought they were all smooth and featureless, but this one bore a jagged crater that was glowing faintly around the edges. There was smoke trailing from a spike at its centre. Corval laughed as he realised it was the splinter Draik had fired. He strode on, calling out for the others, trying to sound shocked and upset.

'Help! We've been attacked! Come back!'

There was a loud click as the damaged beam retracted, slid into a column and vanished. The rumbling grew louder.

Corval stumbled to a halt as he saw that several of the poles were now moving, reacting to the fallen beam, repositioning themselves. He shook his head in disbelief as the tremor rippled across the whole chamber, each moving pole causing another one to shift. It looked like a breeze, rippling through crops.

He picked up his pace, sprinting between the columns, but before he got halfway across the chamber they turned and reformed, metamorphosing into completely new angles and shapes. Corval had to dodge and leap as the chamber rebuilt itself, clicking and shifting all around him. Columns rose directly in his path and the noise became horrendous. Through the blizzard of movement, he saw the rest of the group reappear at the top of the staircase, shocked expressions on their faces as they saw him struggling to reach them through such a bewildering scene.

Draik's attaché took a few steps down the staircase, scouring the chamber for a sign of her captain, but she was driven back as new columns sheared up through the steps. The stairs recoiled, as though alive, moving like a mechanical serpent, rearing and twisting, giving Corval the odd sensation that a colossal monster was rearing over him, preparing to strike.

Isola and the others vanished from sight as the whole chamber rotated, spinning on its axis, ratcheting and clicking, responding to the chain reaction Draik's splinter had caused.

'Taddeus!' cried Corval, amplifying his voice over the din. Without the priest he had no guide. He would be lost. Panic gripped him. His hunger for life was stronger than he expected. 'Taddeus!' he howled, lurching across the fragmenting floor.

Corval fell, cartwheeling through the air. He hit a rising column and crashed to the floor, dazed, as the chamber turned around him.

For what seemed like only a moment he lost consciousness, but when he sat up with a gasp, the chamber was still. He climbed to his feet, trying to get his bearings. The chamber was completely transformed. There was no sign of the staircase, the columns had vanished and even the walls had shifted, turning the room into a long, crooked triangle with a doorway at each corner.

Corval shook his head, shocked by the scale of the transformation. How could such a vast structure simply rebuild itself? Even the abyss he had blasted Draik into had vanished. 'Taddeus!' he cried, rushing into the centre of the chamber.

'Corval?' came a distant reply.

Corval whirled around, trying to locate the source of the voice. It was Taddeus, he could recognise the preacher's strident tones, but he could not see him.

'Corval?' came the voice again. It was coming from beneath him, under the floor.

He dropped to his knees and saw that the surface here was not completely opaque. It was like tinted plex-glass – almost black, but not quite – and there was movement underneath. It was like he was crossing the surface of a frozen lake.

'Audus!' he cried as the shaven-headed pilot rushed past. She was upside down, her feet on the underside of the surface he had his hands pressed against. She was looking around, frantically, but when she shouted a reply, her mouth moved silently. She was yelling but he heard nothing. 'Audus!' he shouted again, but to his dismay she rushed off, not seeming to hear him. He saw the undersides of more boots as the rest of the group ran past, but however loud he shouted, none of them heard.

He scrambled across the floor on his hands and knees, trying to follow, but after a few feet the floor became opaque again and he lost sight of them.

'No!' he cried, smashing the handle of his pistol against the floor.

There was no reply and, after a few minutes of fruitless hammering and crawling, he stood up and dusted himself down again, unwilling to behave like an animal, however dire his situation. He looked at the three doorways that marked the corners of the triangular hall. They were identical. How could he choose?

He paced back and forth, muttering to himself. He should be ecstatic. Draik was dead. The debt was paid. The vendetta was complete. And now he found himself in the ridiculous position of desiring the life that was so obviously out of his reach. He touched the cerebrum cowl, feeling the psychic tremors beneath its surface, crackling and sparking around his third eye, pleading with him to release their power. 'No,' he whispered. 'I cannot.' His gifts were no longer safe. Protecting Draik's party from the madness had been an easy task, but to reach into the warp, as he would once have done, terrified him. He could feel the sickening change taking place beneath his suit. He was a fractured vessel. Unleashing even a fragment of his power would have disastrous results.

A clattering sound rang out through the hall and Corval whirled around, expecting to see another column reforming. But there were no columns left. The rattling sound grew louder, coming from one of the doorways. He backed away, pistol raised.

Tall, spindly shadows flooded through the portal – dozens of them, rushing into the starlight. Corval cursed. They were similar to the pyramid-shaped drones that had attacked when they landed, wrought of lustreless ore and propelled by twitching spasms. Their heads were wide, like triangular anvils, swaying on a jumble of spindly legs. There were cyclopean lights mounted in the centre of their heads, and as they clattered into the room, their cold, blank gaze fell on Corval.

The drones scuttered quickly across the chamber, their legs scraping and screeching, knives sharpening for a meal. Corval fired. His shot was wild but hit one of the drones' legs. The blast ripped it clean off, but the machine did not pause, propelled by the momentum of all its other gangling limbs. Almost instantly, the missing leg was replaced by another. It folded down from the creature's head like an unfurling antenna.

Corval sprinted away from them. The starlight was now refracted by so many facets that the hall shimmered, scintillating and mercurial, dazzling Corval as he veered across the chamber with the spindle drones rattling in his wake. He was making for the nearest of the three portals that led from the chamber, but he could hear from the approaching din that the drones would be on him long before he made it.

'The eyes!' cried a voice from the far side of the hall, back in the direction of the drones.

Corval risked a glance over his shoulder and saw Grekh striding into view, his rifle raised to his shoulder.

The drones paused to look back as the creature fired. One of them flipped back through the dazzling lights, liquid spraying from a hole that had previously been its eye. It clanged onto the floor and the other drones fell on it like hungry predators, their razor-limbs slashing in a frenzy of cuts and lunges, snatching the pieces into unseen orifices until nothing remained, only a faint trail of smoke.

Corval felt the same revulsion he always did upon seeing the kroot, but he was not fool enough to ignore his advice. As the spindle drones whirled back towards him, Corval loosed off a barrage of shots, taking careful aim this time, targeting their arc-light eyes. Every shot dropped a drone. Some toppled in a heap, lifeless sacks of scrap; others thrashed wildly as they hit the floor, shrieking and twitching like crippled insects. Some drones paused to slice up their fallen siblings, but others picked up their pace, juddering through the lights towards Corval.

Grekh was still firing, attempting to walk towards him, but the chamber had other ideas. The kroot had only taken a few steps when the air shimmered and changed around him. Corval's brain struggled to comprehend it. The air split open, fragmenting the kroot along with it, turning the creature into a fan of shards. The more Grekh tried to rush towards Corval, the more he splintered, until he collapsed, shredded into slivers of refracted light.

Corval fired another volley at the drones and ran on, leaping over a chasm and bolting for the nearest doorway. Thanks to the intervention of the kroot, he made it out of the hall, sprinting into a narrow corridor, but he could still hear the drones tapping and clanking after him.

The corridor was a hexagonal tube, more like a ventilation shaft. The ceiling was so low Corval had to stoop as he ran, and the surfaces were made of a different material to the previous chambers – a wire mesh of interlinked strips, like a metal cage. There was light shining from somewhere below, creating a grid of beams that washed over Corval as he ran.

Behind him, he heard the spindle drones crash into the corridor, clattering as they all tried to enter at once. He paused to fire, and saw to his relief that the machines were struggling to follow him down the tunnel. Their razorblade legs slipped through the holes in the wire mesh, causing them to stumble and lurch, toppling forwards rather than running. He added to their problems by shooting out the eyes of the drones at the front, leaving a pile of smouldering metal in the path of the others. Then he ran on with all the speed he could manage, still calling out to Taddeus.

As he ran, an idea started to form in his head. Why not risk the thing he had been hiding from? Without Taddeus to guide him, he was doomed anyway. He would end up just another portrait on Gatto's shard, staring out into the Helmsman at the drunkards and fools. Either the Blackstone would destroy him, or he would simply waste away, starving to death in its labyrinth of halls and passageways. But he had a tool all those other wretches did not. He touched his cerebrum cowl, sensing the third eye beneath, like a finger pressed against a crack in a dam, holding back the tide. For months now, he had not dared gaze into the warp. The degeneration of his flesh was accelerating all the time and he was not fool enough to think it stopped there. As his skin and muscles decayed, the same would be happening to his mind. He would not even dare guide a ship now. What crueller fate could there be for a Navigator? Robbed of the very discipline that lifted him above his peers, as blinkered and dulled as a normal man. 'No,' he muttered, dismissing the idea. 'I dare not risk it.'

He reached an intersection and ducked down another corridor without pausing. They were all identical, so there was no point pretending he knew the best route. He soon regretted his decision, though. The corridor grew narrower and narrower until he was practically crawling. He was just about to turn back when the passageway broadened out and became an angular precipice, like a balcony, looking out over a tall atrium crowded with angular slopes and ravines. It looked almost like a natural, rocky crevasse, apart from the deliberate way the geometric planes and angles intersected. The atrium was topped with the same clear, crystalline ceiling as the previous chamber, and starlight flashed on the expanses of black rock, or metal, or whatever strange substrate the fortress was constructed from. Where the light hit the planes it looked like art – pieces of black and white card, cut and scattered in a monochrome montage.

As Corval studied the shapes, he recalled the surprise on Draik's face as he turned to see a gun pointed at his head. *Why did I hesitate?* wondered Corval. *I spent all these years hunting him down, and then when my chance came I struggled to pull the trigger, despite everything he's done.* He still felt as hollow and blank as he had felt when he watched Draik fall. None of this had played out as he imagined.

The clattering sound of the drones echoed down the corridor and Corval hurried on, looking for a way down into the atrium. He dashed back and forth along the whole length of the precipice, but there was nothing – no steps, or ramp. He was trapped.

The sound of the drones grew louder. He could hear their bladed legs scything against each other as they crushed down the narrow corridor towards him. He looked out over the drop, wondering if he could jump. It was hundreds of feet. He'd be smashed to pieces by the cones and prisms below.

A drone lunged out onto the ledge, its legs scrabbling wildly on the smooth rock as it steadied itself. Corval backed away, firing at its head. The second shot hit home, shattering its eye and sending the drone clattering away. Another emerged, then another, like ants swarming from a nest.

Corval kept firing into the throng of lustreless shells but then his back thudded against a wall. He had nowhere left to go.

The drones charged, their talon-legs flashing as they hurtled towards him. He could not fire fast enough. Dozens toppled before his shots, spinning into the others or dropping from the precipice, but others rushed to take their place.

He clicked an activation rune in his cane and it pulsed with energy.

As the first of them reached him, he smashed the cane into its face, creating an explosion of sparks and splintered metal. The drone fell back into the others and Corval lashed out again, bringing the cane round in a backhanded slash, shattering another eye and engulfing his arm in flames.

Another drone bounded over the two he had downed and slammed into him. It was hard and heavy and the breath exploded from his lungs as he thudded back against the wall. He kicked it from the ledge and halted another one with a las-blast, but then the full weight of the crowd slammed against him.

Pain exploded in his head. His visor filled with blood.

The drones screamed, their legs slicing through him, frenzied, tearing armour, cloth and flesh. *No,* thought Corval. *Not like this.* He would not die so close to the Ascuris Vault. If there was even a tiny chance it might save him, he had to know.

With a whispered oath, Corval opened his third eye and stared into the warp. His cowl blazed, white-hot, channelling the force that ripped through his head. The drones halted, frozen in the act of killing, their heads thrown back and their legs sheathed in webs of blood.

Corval rose from the ledge, incandescent, star-like, radiating warp fire as the drones orbited him, rigid and contorted. He was watching himself from far below, on the slope of a black, sheer-sided pyramid. He was both up on the ledge and down on the pyramid. He watched himself, scrambling to hold his place on the side of the pyramid, and realised he was observing that from a third location – a doorway, down on the ground floor of the atrium. He saw himself in the doorway from a fourth vantage point, then a fifth, sixth and seventh, until his mind grew so fragmented it slipped through his grasp.

He turned in on himself like a paper puzzle, shrinking with each fold until, with a final, molecular snap, he ceased to be.

14

Brittle air snapped through Draik's coat as he tumbled through the darkness. Death could only be moments away, but all he could think of was a name: Numa. A name he thought he'd left behind. How did Corval know it? Did Corval know what he had done?

'This need never emerge.' His father sounded distant and distracted as he led Draik from the duelling cages. For the first time Draik could remember, he looked his age – shoulders rounded by the decades, skin as grey as the Terran sky. 'I spoke to the Novator of House Numa. His grief is… Well, you can imagine. But he knows you were both to blame. There's to be no trial. He has no desire to entertain the palace gossips.'

'Then why must I leave?'

The duke's eyes were dead. He looked through his son rather than at him, waving Draik back into the house.

Draik knew the answer. He was an embarrassment. And he was dangerous. His father was ashamed of him.

Draik shook his head. He was losing himself. He was not on Terra. He was in the Blackstone Fortress, falling to his death. Why was he seeing his father? Without Corval to protect him, the Blackstone was scrambling his thoughts, throwing him into the past.

'Pain is a bond,' said his father, looming over him. The duke was young again, only fifty years old, and Draik was a child of six, clutching a bloody shin, battling tears. 'It locks you to the world, Janus. Trust it. Even if everything else around you is a lie, pain is usually the truth.'

Draik fixed his thoughts on the wound in his shoulder. It was a bright ember of hurt. He had been trying to ignore it but now, remembering his father's advice, he embraced it, savouring the pulse-pounding agony of torn muscle and burnt skin.

It worked. Terra faded, leaving him alone in the darkness, listening to his coat flutter as he fell. He must have been falling for several minutes without hitting anything. How was that possible?

The Blackstone was playing with him.

He strained his neck, looking for a fixed point, or a light source, or anything he could use to orientate himself. There was nothing, so he made his own light. He grabbed a flare from his belt and hurled it. The explosion was bright enough, for a few seconds, to drive back the darkness.

Draik laughed at the absurdity of what it revealed. He was falling past the fractured hull of a vast, Imperial starship, an ancient ironclad, its adamantium plate scorched and warped by centuries of warp travel, its bones picked clean by legions of salvage crews and void creatures. A forgotten monster of the deep, balanced end-on – skewered and hung by the Blackstone Fortress. What kind of chamber could contain such a goliath? Even on the Blackstone this seemed impossible. The ship's hull was mostly burned away, trailing shattered bulkheads and rusting, city-sized plasma drives. The design was archaic, even by Imperial Navy standards. Why was it here? How had it come to die inside the Blackstone? Huge as it was, it looked like a morsel of food, rotting slowly in the gut of an even greater leviathan. No, not rotting, Draik realised – being digested. Whole decks were morphing and reforming, becoming the same gunpowder-grey planes as the rest of the fortress – the Blackstone was subsuming it, turning its companionways into impossible angles and its gunnery decks into baffling, abstract patterns.

The flare died away, sinking Draik back into darkness, but now that he knew it was there he could sense the vast hulk he was falling past – a monumental pool of greater darkness, watching him fall. He reached for the grappling hooks at his belt and attached a cable. Then he looped the cable in a loose knot and attached it to his munitions belt, adjusting the settings before hurling another flare and lighting up the wrecked ship a second time. It blazed from the darkness like a divine vision, haloed by broken spires. Draik pulled a device from beneath his coat. It looked like a small handheld crossbow and he used it to fire a grappling hook across the void, towards the distant hulk.

There was a dull clang as the hook latched on to something. Draik adjusted the cable tension, feeding it through loops in his belt, and his fall turned into a swing – a gentle parabola that sent him gliding towards the ironclad, a tiny point of movement soaring beneath its unimaginable bulk.

However elegant his approach, Draik had no doubts about what would happen if he crashed into the fuselage at this speed. The flare had almost burned out as Draik flew towards the shattered remnants of an observation gallery. As the light failed he singled out a broken joist and fired his second grappling hook at a ninety-degree angle to the first, redirecting his swing and draining its momentum as he glided towards a loading hatch. The door was long gone, creating a gaping, toothless mouth that opened onto a lightless pit.

The flare died as Draik's cable hurled him through the hatch. He crashed into something hard but it collapsed under his weight and he rolled, painfully, across the rubble-strewn floor, his arms wrapped around his head and his knees tucked up to his chest.

Draik came to a halt, surprised to find that he was still alive. There was blood flowing from a cut over his eye and from the gunshot wound in his shoulder but, as he patted down his limbs, he found that the rest of him was intact.

He sat there, in the pitch-dark, taking stock of what had just happened. Corval had meant to kill him. He shook his head, dazed at the betrayal. There was no one in the group he had trusted more. Corval alone had seemed a man of honour. 'Numa,' whispered Draik, his voice echoing through the blackness. What did Corval know?

Draik climbed to his feet and gingerly touched the wound in his shoulder. It was clean, at least. He moved his arm. The shoulder joint still seemed to work. The blast had seared through muscle but left the bones intact. It was agonising to move it, but possible. He took some painkillers from his munitions belt and injected them directly into the muscle. Then he wrapped a bandage around the wound, tying it as tightly as he could.

When he had finished tending the wound, Draik triggered the lumen on his pistol and pointed it ahead of him. It flashed over the bulkheads of a burnt-out companionway. There were a few scraps of machinery lying on the deck plating, but no sign of movement. He edged forwards, treading carefully in case the floor gave way. Because the ironclad was upended, he was actually walking along the wall, and every few feet he had to step over ventilation shafts or around doorways. As he walked, he tried to contact Isola through the vox-bead in his collar. As he expected, the only response was a squall of feedback. Whatever the Blackstone was made of, it played havoc with vox networks. How was he going to get back to the others? Without Taddeus, he had no way of reaching the Ascuris Vault. And without Corval, he had no way of keeping sane. As soon as he had that thought, his mind began to slip. It was as though the Blackstone felt his doubt and pounced on it.

'Without your eyes, you must come alive to the darkness,' said his father, speaking from somewhere up ahead.

Draik was eleven. Already, he had mastered countless training exercises, but none of them had prepared him for this. The dark lantern. His father had never mentioned it until that very morning, giving him no time to prepare.

He stopped to listen. He could hear the old duke up ahead, breathing lightly, preparing to strike. He could hear the dark lantern's shutter rattling against its casing. It was a beautiful antique, like everything else in the Draik villa – an ornate tube of wrought iron, clad in delicate filigree and housing a crystal glow-globe. It was designed in such a way that, when the shutter was closed, no trace of light escaped, plunging the training hall into darkness.

Draik remembered everything his father had taught him, keeping his stance relaxed, knees slightly bent, chin raised, rapier held loosely.

The shutter clanged open and the light blinded him. His father lunged, the rapier heading for Draik's face.

Draik closed the strike, parried and disengaged, stepping back into an en garde position.

The shutter clanged and he was in darkness again.

'You move like a drunk,' growled his father.

The light flashed again and Draik leapt to defend himself, but the training hall was gone. He was back in the ironclad, his pistol's lumen shimmering over piles of rusted cogitators and twisted armour plating.

The memory had been so clear, but Draik had not thought of that day for decades. As he edged on down the cooked companionway he recalled how proud he had been. His father was not one for compliments, but Draik had known, at the age of eleven, he was being challenged in a way that his sister, who was fourteen, had never been. His father did not need to praise Draik. He was rushing through every training regime his father could devise, handling them with an ease that astounded his peers. He had mastered disciplines that the other young lordlings had never even heard of.

The companionway came to an end at a circular bulkhead door. It was dented and scorched, but when Draik punched the controls it whooshed open, and he crawled into the next chamber – a cargo hold. There was a mountain of storage crates heaped against the wall that was now the floor, and several doorways leading off in different directions.

'Which way now?' muttered Draik. 'What's the plan, Janus?' He recalled something the kroot had said. 'The Blackstone always has a plan.' At the time he had dismissed it as exactly the kind of gnomic gibberish spouted by all Blackstone devotees, but now he was starting to doubt things that he had previously been so sure about. He had been as sure of Corval as he was doubtful of Grekh. He had been wrong about Corval; perhaps he was wrong about Grekh too. 'Do you have a plan?' he wondered aloud, his voice bouncing round the cavernous chamber. He crossed to the other side of the room. There was a whole section of the wall that was more Blackstone than void ship. The bulkhead had become a fan of tessellating hexes, a honeycomb of the dull, slate-grey substance that made up the rest of the Blackstone.

'I could wander here for years,' he said, pressing his hand against the cold, angular shapes. 'And I'm already talking to myself. What if you *do* have a plan? How would I see it?'

On a whim, he clicked off the lumen and let the darkness flood over him.

'Honour is everything,' said his father. The old duke's gravelly tones came somewhere from Draik's left, down towards the pile of crates.

Draik should have felt confused, or even disturbed. His father was on the other side of the galaxy. If he was even still alive. And yet, here on the Blackstone, it seemed almost natural to step from one age to another.

'Honour,' he replied, drawing his rapier and stepping towards the voice.

'Without your name, you are nothing – just another face in the mob. And without honour, you are not worthy of your name.'

The dark lantern rattled as the duke flipped the shutter open.

He attacked, low, aiming for Draik's side.

Again, Draik was ready, parrying, disengaging and countering with a graceful overhand slash. This time he kept his position, never slouching or forgetting his stance as the blade came round towards his target. There was a clatter of blades. His father parried but Draik saw surprise in his eyes. He had not anticipated such a fast return.

'Close your mouth, boy. You look like one of the hounds.'

The eleven year-old Draik felt a rush of pride. His mouth was already closed. He had surprised his father so much that the old duke could not think of a genuine criticism.

He pressed on into the darkness, following the sound of his father's breathing. It was heavier now, and less regular.

Draik triggered the lumen. It flashed across a doorframe and revealed another companionway, wider than the last one. 'This way?' he whispered. 'Is that it? Part of him laughed at the absurdity of thinking the Blackstone could lead him. How could a space station *lead* him? How could it have a plan? Draik shrugged. He was lost. And alone. He could sit here and wait to die, or try something.

He clicked off the lumen again.

His eyes were starting to adjust to the dark now. He could see some of the training hall – duelling cages and sparring servitors, hanging ominously around him like partners in a dance. His father was a few feet away; he could not see him clearly, but he saw enough to step towards him. Though he was only eleven, Draik was almost as tall as his father, and the years of training had clad his body in strong, lean muscle.

There was a flash of light as the duke uncovered the lantern, but this time he threw a feint. Draik tried to parry a strike that was not there. He barely had time to sidestep the true thrust.

There was a popping sound as his sparring suit ripped open across the chest. He felt a hot splash of pain. He wanted to cry out: Father, you have cut me! But he held his tongue. An outburst like that would only earn him a deeper wound.

The shutter clattered down.

Draik flicked his lumen back on and saw where his memories had led him. He was in a chamber that bore no resemblance at all to the insides of a void ship – a smooth-sided, triangular prism, a few hundred feet long and leading onto a portal that blazed with cold, blue light.

Draik hesitated, shocked. He looked back the way he had come. Behind him was the ironclad, ahead was the Blackstone. The memory of his training, forgotten until this moment, *had* led him back into the fortress. He shook his head. He was thinking like a devotee. This might just be a part of the ironclad that the Blackstone had transformed more completely than the others. There was no guarantee he had returned to the heart of the vessel.

He strode on down the chamber and stepped through the opening at the far end, shielding his face as the light washed over him.

15

'They're killing everyone,' said Almodath, storming across the embarkation deck towards Audus. He was half dressed in his flying gear, oxygen pipes trailing from his baggy envirosuit as he rushed towards her. His face was white and he was visibly shaken, his hands trembling as he tried to fasten his straps.

The *Benedictus* was the capital ship of Commander Ortegal's fleet, and its primary launch bay was vast. It was crowded with gunships, shuttles and landing craft, but Audus and Almodath were the only pilots present. Everyone else who had taken part in the bombing of Sepus Prime had been called to a debriefing. Audus had been about to make her way there when Almodath arrived.

'What do you mean?' she laughed, unfastening her helmet.

'Ortegal has ballsed everything up,' gasped Almodath, barging past her. He singled out a shuttle behind the gunship she had just emerged from. The shuttle was fuelled and ready for takeoff and Almodath sprinted towards it.

She rushed after him, lowering her voice. There were no pilots on the deck, but plenty of servitors and enginseers, refuelling and repairing the aircraft that had just massacred the regiments on Sepus. 'What are you doing? What do you mean, *killing* everyone?'

Almodath clambered up to the shuttle's access hatch and shoved it open, then paused to look back at her, his eyes wild.

'We killed all those regiments on Sepus Prime for nothing,' he hissed. 'All those poor bastards burned while the contagion was happily heading off-world in a cargo hauler. Some psyker got infected and survived the blasts. No one knows where he went.'

Audus felt sick. None of them had wanted to fly that mission. There had even been a flicker of mutinous talk but she had been one of those who calmed the rabble rousers down. She had reminded her flight crew that the commander was only doing what had to be done; they had to preserve the rest of the subsector from damnation, however great the loss of life.

'They died for nothing,' she muttered, shaking her head.

Almodath forgot his urgency and leant back down to stare at her, his face flushed with rage. 'It's worse than that. I heard that Commander Ortegal was secretly backing the governor who went rogue down there. So he's responsible for the whole mess.'

'Ortegal's no heretic.'

'As good as. He backed the governor so they could get all the insurrectionists under one banner, but the governor was actually spreading some kind of mutant plague. They say he was involved in a *cult*.' He lowered his voice. 'Heresy.'

'But you said Ortegal's killing people *now*. What do you mean? The planet's dead. *We* killed it.'

'He's killing people up here, on the *Benedictus*. Executions! Anyone who flew the mission. Commissarial death squads. He's trying to cover his tracks.'

Audus clutched her head. 'Those people on Sepus! We killed them all. On his orders.'

'On the orders of a liar!' hissed Almodath. 'Come with me, Audus. This shuttle will make it to the Zophirim orbital platform. I can scramble our signal as we fly. They'd never track something this small. The last of the cargo haulers will be leaving Zophirim soon. We can–'

Almodath paused, a surprised expression on his face. He had noticed something on his breast pocket – a small hole.

He reached down to touch it, puzzled. Then groaned as blood rushed through his fingers.

Another hole appeared next to the first. More blood rushed out, lots more, and Almodath fell, hitting the deck plating with a clang, dead.

Audus looked back across the hangar. Guardsmen were rushing towards her, lasguns raised.

The ladder she was holding buckled in her grip as more shots landed.

She bolted up into the shuttle and slammed the hatch, rushing to the control panel and triggering the holo display.

'We're close,' said Almodath.

No, Almodath is dead, she remembered. It was Taddeus she could hear talking.

She shook her head, cursing. Taddeus! She was not on the *Benedictus.* That all happened months ago. She was on the Blackstone.

The name summoned the place. The embarkation deck of the *Benedictus* fell away, replaced by a dark, angular passageway.

'We're close,' said Taddeus, staring at her from the shadows. 'Nothing else matters. To martyr oneself in service to the God-Emperor is an honour.' The preacher had not paused since they lost Draik and Corval, forging on down the passageways with even more fervour than before. The air was still thick and cloying, making every step a struggle, but Taddeus marched on with a grin on his face. Every few minutes he would stop to examine his book or adjust the rosarius on his chest, but beyond that he showed no hesitation, wrenching his bulk through leaning apertures and skewed, intersecting landscapes.

'Martyrs?' said Audus, shaking her head, still trying to escape her thoughts of the *Benedictus.* That ship haunted her. Whenever she thought she might find a way to escape the past, she saw mushroom clouds rising from the marshes of Sepus Prime and heard the screams of the men she killed, crackling over the vox networks, filling her mind with pain.

Isola was watching her, frowning, about to speak, but Audus glared back, making it clear she did not want to talk. Draik's prim little Terran attaché was a symbol of everything she had come to despise – unquestioning loyalty to the Imperium, wrapped up in an immaculate uniform and a haughty pout. She would not explain herself to such a woman. She hurried after Taddeus. She could not quite believe she had ended up in the company of this lunatic again. And now, with Draik gone, there was no one to challenge Taddeus' tedious assertions that the hand of the God-Emperor was in everything.

'We never saw Draik die,' she said. Her voice was strange, so muted and distorted by the Blackstone that she could not recognise it. 'Nor the Navigator. Why talk of martyrs?'

Taddeus shook his head. 'Even if they're alive, they will

be utterly lost. The Navigator might be able to protect their minds but...' Taddeus' words trailed off and he slowed down. He glanced at Pious Vorne, who was keeping pace with him, her flamer lit and ready to fire. 'Are you..? How have you felt since we lost Corval?'

Vorne shook her head. 'I am still with you, your eminence. It is not as bad as last time. I have been reciting the catechisms we practised.'

Taddeus nodded and looked back at Audus and Isola. They both shook their heads.

'Your eminence,' said Isola, her face pale and anguished. 'We must return and look for Captain Draik. We can't abandon him in here. How will he find his way back to the *Vanguard*?'

Taddeus gave her a concerned look and halted, clasping his hands to his chest. 'My child, don't you think I would find him if I could? But where would we look? Which route would we explore?'

Isola looked around at the dozens of openings and passageways that led away into the darkness. She looked so pained that Audus almost felt sorry for her.

'The priest's right,' said Audus. 'Our only hope of survival is...' She looked at Taddeus with distaste. 'Our only hope is to follow the priest to the Ascuris Vault. His visions have shown him the way there and the way back to the Dragon's Teeth. If we wander off without him we'll die in this maze.'

'He is the eldest son of House Draik. I cannot simply lose him.'

'You care about him,' said Audus, 'I understand, but–'

Isola raised an eyebrow. 'You *do not* understand. It is not a matter of caring. Janus Draik was once heir apparent to the Draik family fortune. Have you any idea what that means? House Draik is an ancient dynasty – family estates, fiefdoms, trading rights, entire fleets of void ships, wealth beyond anything you can–'

'I see,' laughed Audus. 'It's *not* that you care about him. I get it. He's a big deal. There's still nothing we can do.'

Isola looked at the two remaining members of the Draik household guard. Their uniforms were scorched and blood-splattered but they still had their lasguns and plenty of charges.

'I could return and look for him,' she said.

'Don't be a fool,' said Audus. 'You saw the same as the rest of us – there's no way back to him. The fortress rebuilt itself. That chamber has gone. *Where* would you look?' Audus was not overly concerned if Isola wanted to blunder off back into the darkness and kill herself, but the two soldiers were a different matter. They were a small group as it was. She did not like the idea of losing any more guns. She needed to keep the group together until they reached the Ascuris Vault. Once she got her hands on the relic Taddeus kept talking about, she could dump the lot of them and get back to the *Vanguard*. According to Taddeus the Eye was not only a priceless artefact, it would also give her god-like omni-science. She should have no problems returning to the ship. She would tell the crew everyone died but her. Once she sold the Eye of Hermius, she would be so wealthy even the Navy would never find her. She would find a world on the furthest fringes of the sector and forget she had ever heard of the Imperium. But none of that would work if Isola split the group before they could reach the vault.

'Think about it,' she said, leaning close to Isola. 'Captain Draik is with Corval. Navigators have all sorts of tricks up their sleeves. Corval's not like us. He's warp-breed. One foot in the real world and one in places I don't want to imagine.

When push comes to shove, he'll find a way to get through. I've seen what those freaks can do. Corval didn't let us see what he's capable of. He'll find a way back to the *Vanguard* and he'll take Draik with him.'

Taddeus had been looking frustrated as he watched the exchange, but at this he nodded eagerly. 'They're probably already back on the shuttle, waiting for us to return with the Eye of Hermius.' He waved his mace down another passageway. 'And we shall not disappoint them. Keep moving, my children, keep moving.'

With that, the priest forced his way on through the darkness, head down, shoulder first, like he was wading through fire.

As the rest of the group followed, Audus thought of something interesting Isola had just said. 'Did you say Captain Draik *used* to be the heir apparent?'

Isola glared at her, but said nothing, striding after Taddeus.

Audus smirked. Perhaps she was not the only one who had made mistakes.

16

'The Terran thinks me a savage,' said Grekh, looking at the small, leather sack in his claw. He was speaking in his own tongue, now that he was alone, and the clumsiness was gone from his speech, replaced by a fluid, rolling torrent of vowels and clicks. 'He doesn't guess that I have my own reasons for seeking the vault.'

But he did not transport you to the vault. The voice was not audible; it was a resonance in his stomach, pulsing through his organs. *So what use was he?*

'He brought me to the Blackstone. I could not have convinced Audus to return without him.' Grekh closed his eyes and pictured the inspirations he had been gifted – so many it was dizzying. His belly was bloated with knowledge. He had consumed a whole army of warrior spirits – not just during this expedition, but on all the previous ones too. He was ablaze with insight. The elders of Akchan-Kur had been right. This place was like nothing he had experienced before. Since reaching Precipice, Grekh had saved hundreds of indwelling souls, cherishing every fragment, every fierce, determined glimpse of the Blackstone's secrets, preserving them all by adding them to his own. Each soul merged with a previous one, meshing and reforming, linking like the walls of the Blackstone, painting a picture that grew more complex with every bite. He had gradually constructed a mental map of the Blackstone's regions and movements. Then he had stumbled across the greatest revelation – even the drones had a kind of sentience. For a long time it had eluded him because their shells were inedible. But then, finally, he had tasted a fraction of the Blackstone's ineffable spirit. It was not the frenzied, hungry mind of an animal, but something deep and glacial, like echoes on a mountainside – fractured and vast, accumulated over millennia. The drones did not possess an individual consciousness, but were pieces of something greater. Were they fragments of the Blackstone? Or fingerprints of the fortress' divine architect? The aeldari he consumed believed the fortress was the weapon of a god – an immortal being called Vaul. But the drones told him something stranger. Their thoughts were alien and obscure, but even a few stolen glimpses of their memories had revealed more to him than those of every explorer he had devoured.

Grekh was seated in a cube-shaped chamber, perched at the top of a clear-sided pyramid. It was an hour since he had heard the others and he could find no trace of their scent. He had tried to help the Navigator get back to them, but the Blackstone clearly had other plans. And there was no way *he* could reach the others now. The Terran had driven him away – angry with him for simply trying to save the wisdom of the fallen. What an absurd idea. Grekh was the oldest of his kindred, and he had travelled the galaxy for decades, but the short-sightedness of humans still astounded him. They would leave corpses to rot, even those of their bravest warriors, without trying to preserve the hidden learning they had accrued – abandoning all that courage and knowledge to the worms. And yet, they would happily consume the spirits of timid creatures, like ruminants and fowl. How could humans hope to evolve when they constantly diluted their essence with the souls of the fearful and the weak, but spurned the wisdom of their heroes?

Even now, after eating all that he could, Grekh would try to learn more from the fallen. He had marked the walls with his scent, leaving clear directions for any of his kindred that might follow, and now it was time to look again at what he had found. He took kindling from his jacket and placed it on the cold, black floor. Then he took out a tinderbox and lit a fire. Once the kindling had caught, he opened the sack and removed the contents, piece by piece, placing them on the fire. First, he added a flake of black enamel, taken from one of the drones – indigestible, but still useful. The flames flickered oddly, turning green as they licked around it. Then he took out a chunk of half-chewed meat and added that to the fire. The flames engulfed it hungrily and began to grow. Then he took out a bleached, crumbling finger bone and added that. Over the next few minutes he added dozens of tiny fragments, clicking and whistling as he did so, using his native language. He had mastered the human tongue decades ago, but for holy rituals he still used the language of his kindred, the Karakh-Kar. Changed as he was by his time with the humans, he had not yet learned to think in their words.

By the time the sack was empty, the fire was crackling merrily, adding an incongruous warmth to the chamber walls.

He let the fire blaze for a few minutes, then took out a piece of stiff, waxed hide and smothered the flames. A thick plume of smoke rose from the charred pieces and he placed the hide over his head, leaning low over the blackened mess, taking long, deep breaths, letting the fumes flood his consciousness.

His head grew light and his stomach growled. He saw the craggy eyries of his home on Akchan-Kur. He saw the farewell ceremony at the Perch of Nine Hawks, standing at the pinnacle, victorious, rain-lashed and surrounded by his warrior kin. The elders summoned him home, insisting that he alone, the oldest of his kind, had the experience to journey to the Western Reaches. The Karakh-Kar had warriors scattered across the galaxy, serving in countless armies. They knew of the Blackstone's presence long before the warlords of Terra.

As the fumes filtered through his nostrils and down into his guts, Grekh sifted through each remnant of spirit, searching for anything he might have missed. The odd, splintered conscience of the drones stood apart from the others. The explorers' thoughts were all similar: eager, greedy, desperate. Such sentiments seemed absurd to Grekh, but he at least understood them. The drones felt something far more profound and interesting. They were part of a vast, galactic puzzle. They radiated violence, but it was not the desperate, bestial tribalism of the explorers – it was a cold, ageless determination. Whatever consciousness drove the drones was manipulating the plans of everyone who entered its darkened halls. Grekh had heard the Terran speak of devotees. He used the word as an insult, deriding the belief that the Blackstone was sentient, but, with every spirit he consumed, Grekh felt that sentience more clearly. No, 'clearly' was the wrong word. As the presence grew larger, it also became more mysterious.

The more it filled his thoughts, the harder it was to grasp. Even now, after scrutinising the thoughts of the drones, Grekh could not be sure what the Blackstone's plan was – only that it had one, and that they were all part of it.

You were not sent here to understand the Blackstone, grumbled his innards. *You were sent to retrieve our heirlooms.*

'There's something larger here. The Terran and the priests did not come together by accident. And it's no coincidence that Draik found me. The Blackstone brought us together for a purpose. Even the pilot is part of it.'

He took another lungful of fumes, tasting the souls of the drones, determining their essence. 'There,' he said. 'There it is.' Embedded at the heart of the drones' thoughts was a single, repeated image: a spherical cage of light. 'The Ascuris Vault.' Grekh had seen it in countless warrior souls before he saw it on the scrap of paper Draik carried. 'That is the heart of everything, and the Blackstone needs us to reach it.'

Then why does it battle against you? Why not give you easy passage if it has a purpose for you?

Grekh shook his head, causing his crest of spines to click and rattle. 'To test us? To ensure we are worthy? Perhaps to be sure that we are what it needs us to be?'

The elders did not send you to solve mysteries – they sent you to find weapons and return as quickly as you can.

'They sent me to explore without fear, because they knew I wouldn't settle for minor victories when there's chance of a greater one. The Ascuris Vault is one of the fortress' stomachs. If there are Karakh-Kar heirlooms in the Blackstone, the vault is where I'll find the most powerful of them. And, at the same time, I can learn why the fortress brought us together.'

He extinguished the fire and scattered the ashes with his claws. Then he checked his rifle and left the cube-shaped room, stepping out onto the polished slope of the pyramid. The fumes were still billowing through his head, merging different acrid aromas into a single, potent note. He sniffed the frigid air, turning until he caught a new scent, carried on the cold breeze from a distant chamber. He closed his eyes and allowed a thought to foment in his guts. It boiled up into his mouth and washed over his taste buds, filling his mind with a clear, powerful image: a weapon and place.

The Blackstone had spoken more clearly than ever before. He nodded, understanding what he must do, then began sliding, slowly, down the slope of the pyramid.

17

Corval's consciousness folded back into his flesh with an audible *snap*. His mind was smashed, trampled and jangling around his skull, but he was alive. He was floating through black liquid. The seals of his antique envirosuit were intact, and as he glided through the blackness he patted himself down, finding that his body was intact too. His mind was a different matter. His third eye was trying to open, flooding his head with dazzling visions of the fortress. It was wonderful and deadly. As his second sight pierced the veils of the Blackstone, the changes in his flesh accelerated. His arms and chest were burning with a terrible itch and he clawed at the thick rubber suit, trying to ease the discomfort. As he thrashed in the void, an image formed in all three of his eyes: a frame, white and shimmering, the lines identical to the ones on Draik's informant's sketch. *The vault.* It was ahead of him, shining through the murk.

He kicked his legs and powered towards it, struggling to

swim through the viscous depths. At first, the light remained steady. Then he recalled Draik's face as he had turned to face Corval and realised he was about to be shot. Angry. Hurt. Betrayed. Corval remembered how he had hesitated to shoot and, as he considered the reasons why, the light fragmented and grew weaker.

There were now dozens of luminous spheres floating ahead of him, so Corval swam towards the nearest.

Finally, he came close enough to see that it was not lit from within, but from above. The sphere was made of something pale and it was catching a shaft of light that had pierced the darkness, lancing down from an unseen source. The sphere looked like a moon, luminous and crumbling, half obscured by clouds. Corval reached out and turned it around.

It was Draik's severed head.

He jolted back in shock.

His breathing became panicked, confusing his enviro-suit and triggering a dizzying rush of oxygen. He kicked his legs furiously, trying to swim away from the head and then bumped into something else.

He turned to face another head bobbing in the abyssal dark. It was Draik's again, identical to the first, except that this one was attached to a butchered torso, trailing ribbons of meat through the void. Again, the pale horror was lit from above by a shaft of wan light.

Corval struggled to breathe, grasping at his throat. His visions of the Blackstone faded as he began drowning in the darkness. He kicked his legs and tried to make for the light.

Another bloodless body thudded into him, sinking from overhead, forcing him down.

He wrestled with the corpse and found himself face-to-face, again, with Captain Draik.

His breathing was now so choked that his suit's controls were struggling to cope. Warnings screeched in his ears. His vision grew dark. His strength failed. The Blackstone was crushing him.

I want to live, he thought, shoving the corpse aside and kicking his legs. *I have a chance.*

None of this was my doing he thought as he swam towards the light, dodging more corpses. *It was all Draik's fault.*

But he was lying to himself. With every accusation he hurled at the dead captain, he became more aware of how he had deceived himself, and why killing Draik had only made him feel worse. When Draik had looked back at him, in that final moment, realising he was betrayed, Corval saw the truth he had suppressed for all this time. They *both* shared the blame. Despair gripped him. No, his own guilt was now deeper than Draik's. Draik's crime had been accidental; his was premeditated.

He looked down at a sea of Draiks. Dozens of identical faces, suspended in a liquid grave, the light extinguished from their eyes.

I'm a lie, he thought. *I have lived a lie.*

As he hung there in the impenetrable gloom, he realised this was the perfect chance to end things. He could stop struggling and sink down into Draik's grave, just another Blackstone mystery. What more did he deserve? He relaxed his limbs and began descending towards the bodies.

He had only sunk a few feet when panic gripped him and he kicked his legs, powering up towards the lights. Even now, full of self-loathing, he wanted to live.

As he swam towards the surface, he saw that the lights above him were moving. At first he thought they were being refracted by the surface of whatever pool he was in, but then he saw that outside the liquid there was a great tumult – vast shapes were rushing back and forth, crashing into each other, revealing and obscuring the light as they collided and fell.

He broke the surface and was hit by an apocalyptic din. He was in an artificial valley – a huge, sheer-sided crevasse split by a river of black tar. At one end, the river flowed beneath an angular archway and disappeared from view, but at the other end, half a mile away, it passed beneath a vast, blazing sphere of light, as big as a palace and identical to the one on Draik's sketch. This time it was real, rather than a vision – towering over Corval as he drifted towards it, still gasping, carried by the black river. A horrible grinding hum was radiating from it, like a radioactive charge, resonating painfully in Corval's head.

The sphere was the source of the light and the valley was attacking it. The walls of the Blackstone were thrashing out like limbs, hundreds of feet long, shedding tonnes of rubble as they crashed against the cage of light. It was as if the buttresses of a cathedral had sprung to life and begun fighting each other. The limbs hit like explosives tearing open a mine, but there was another noise, just as loud, roaring down the valley. It was like the white noise of a detuned vox – the screech of battling frequencies, battering against Corval with even more force than the sound of the avalanche overhead.

As the noise jangled round his head, he realised it was more like the sound of a broken generator – electricity, escaping from coils and charging the atmosphere, burning the air. He knew instinctively what he was hearing: the incomprehensible cry of the Blackstone. It was enraged. Furious about the presence of the sphere, attacking it, trying to crush it with a savagery that was tearing the whole valley apart.

If the vault is the fulcrum of the whole fortress, thought Corval, *why would it attack itself like this?*

He swam towards the edge of the river. As he reached the side, he saw that it was more like a canal, with steep, smooth sides, too high for him to climb. He ducked as a huge shard of wall crashed into the liquid – tonnes of angular masonry that kicked up a wave of tar and sent Corval flailing back the way he had come.

He struggled to right himself as more blocks splashed down around him, filling the air with spray. As he swam, he spied a break in the sheer wall of the canal – a narrow vertical channel, barely wider than he was, leading up to the slopes above.

Corval swam into the channel, pressed his back against one wall and his feet against the opposite side and began to slowly walk up from the liquid. Walls were crashing down all around him as the Blackstone continued battering the distant sphere, but Corval managed to force himself up the channel and finally clambered out into the featureless, black plain at the base of the valley. He could feel the mutation beneath his robes throbbing and growing, but there was no time for the syringe – vast columns were sliding from the walls, exploding as they hit the ground, causing the whole chamber to shudder.

The sphere was like a fallen star, blazing through the tumult, throwing long, confusing shadows, turning the valley into a grid of blacks and whites, making it hard to see what was rock and what was shadow. Corval staggered through the maelstrom, making for an opening in the walls – a pitch-dark triangle, sheltered by a cube-shaped outcrop that had yet to be fractured by the whirling columns.

As Corval ran he felt a mixture of elation and doubt. He had reached the Ascuris Vault, he was sure of it – this spherical cage of light matched Draik's drawing exactly – but the Blackstone was trying to destroy it. So was it really the heart of the fortress? Was Draik wrong?

He had almost reached the doorway when a toppling column threw him from his feet and he landed on his side with a painful gasp. The ground was still shuddering as he stood and bolted through the spinning rubble. The vibrations grew more violent, spraying cracks across the floor. Corval leapt as a chasm opened beneath his feet, then a second. Then, a vast gulf opened directly beneath him and he fell. His head hit something hard. His consciousness folded in on itself again.

Blackness smothered him.

18

Draik walked into a pool of light.

After so long in darkness the glare was painful, knifing into his head. His ocular implant quickly filtered the brightness and allowed him to see that he had entered a long, rectangular hall, similar in shape to a gallery in a Terran palace. Unlike all the preceding chambers, this room was made of a polished white material, gleaming and lustrous, suffused with a faint shimmer of gold. The room was hundreds of feet long, and so tall he could see no ceiling. It also lacked a floor. Draik had emerged onto a broad balcony, but it only extended a few dozen feet before halting at an abyss. Continuing on from the edge of the balcony and extending down the entire length of the hall was a narrow aqueduct, suspended on cables that reached up into the unfathomable space above. Running down the aqueduct's centre was a fast-flowing stream of the black, ink-like liquid Draik had seen in previous chambers. The light that had so dazzled him was coming from the chasm beneath the aqueduct: a cool, silvery blaze that filtered up from hidden depths, shimmering across the gleaming walls and the elegant, dangling gantry that led down the middle of the hall.

As Draik hurried across the balcony, he saw dark, motionless shapes around the approach to the aqueduct. He paused to examine the first one he reached and discovered that it was a corpse. The body was a blackened husk, stark and shocking against the ivory floor. It was so badly burned that Draik could not even discern the species of the deceased – humanoid, certainly, but beyond that he could not tell. He rushed to the next body and found it was the same – more charcoal than flesh, and so brittle it crumbled at his touch.

As Draik neared the aqueduct, he saw dozens more bodies and noticed one troubling similarity – they had all died crawling *away* from the aqueduct.

He reached the edge of the balcony and found that there were steps leading up to aqueduct, but no footbridge at either side of the black stream. The only way to cross the chasm would be to enter the liquid and swim across to the other side. The current was fast and heading in the right direction, powered by some unseen pump, or perhaps just the strange gravity of the fortress. Draik would only have to lay himself in the stream and he would quickly float across to the far side of the gallery, but his thoughts kept returning to the charred bodies.

'You're dead,' said a voice. It spoke quietly, but the sibilant whisper echoed around the gallery, amplified by the strange acoustics.

For a moment, Draik thought he had slipped into the past again, tricked by the Blackstone into believing he was on a distant xenos world. The breathy, strangled tone brought back a flood of memories, none of them pleasant. He whipped out his splinter pistol and whirled around, trying to locate the speaker.

He could see nothing.

I'm losing my mind, he thought. It must be an hour or more since he had parted company with the others. Without Corval's protection, the fortress was eating into his thoughts, confusing him. He tried to repeat the trick he used earlier, focusing on the wound in his shoulder, using the pain as an anchor, but it was no use; the voice came again, filling the cavernous gallery with its venom.

'No way forward. No way back.'

Draik looked back to the portal he had entered through. It was gone. That area of the wall was flat and uninterrupted as the rest of the hall, made of the same pearlescent white material. He rushed back over and ran his hand across the cold surface, looking for depressions or marks. There was nothing. The doorway had simply ceased to be.

'I hope you're going to last longer than the others,' said the voice.

It was nearer now and Draik saw movement, just a few feet away – a pale shape, almost indistinguishable from the white floor.

He aimed his pistol at the shape and edged towards it.

'Who are you?' he asked.

'Kurdrak.' The voice sounded amused.

As Draik stepped closer to the prone figure he saw why he had missed it before. As he had guessed from the tone of the voice, it was a member of the sadistic race known as drukhari. He had encountered such beings before and revulsion flooded through him at the sight of its long, cruel face. The thing was humanoid but could never have been mistaken for human. Its features were unnaturally narrow and fine, with wide-set, pointed eyes and tall, spear-tip ears. Its body was impossibly long and lean, like all of its kind, but as Draik looked closer he saw that it was horribly emaciated. Drukhari were always tall and slender, but some of this one's robes had been torn away and he could see bones pressing through its thin, stretched skin. It looked like a skeleton wrapped in thin parchment and there was a brutal wound in its neck where something had been hammered into its flesh.

The febrile wretch tried to sit up as Draik approached, but its arms trembled and gave way. Draik raised his splinter pistol and pointed it at the alien's head. His pistol had come from a similar creature and Draik was pleased at the irony that the thing would die by one of its own weapons.

'Wait,' said the alien. Empty, black eyes stared from its bone-white skin. 'Aren't you interested to know *why* you're dead?'

Draik was repulsed by the idea of conversing with such a monster, but decided a few seconds more would make no difference. The alien was clearly too wasted to ever walk again. It could do little harm now. He nodded.

The alien smiled, revealing a mouthful of needle teeth. Its face was so dry the smile caused the skin to splinter and crack, reminding Draik of the powdered face of a Terran noble.

'Good little mon-keigh,' chuckled the alien. 'It wants to learn.'

Draik took a deep breath, resisting the urge to pull the trigger. Whatever the alien told him would be lies, but lies could sometimes point to truth.

'Help me up,' said the alien, reaching out with pale, spindly fingers.

Draik remained as he was, the splinter pistol pointed at the creature's head.

The alien sniggered and withdrew its hand. 'Clever little mon-keigh. You win a prize. I will tell you where you are. You have reached the heart of Vaul's Talisman.' The alien looked up into the shimmering haze overhead, perhaps seeing a distant ceiling that Draik could not. 'You will breathe your last in a place few of your kind could even imagine.'

'Why am I dead?' asked Draik.

The alien waved at the burnt corpses. 'Because you will enter the canal and burn.'

Draik looked over at the black liquid that was rushing across the aqueduct.

'And, even though you now know that, you will have to try.' The alien closed its eyes and mouthed something in its own tongue. Then it smiled at Draik again. 'Unless you help me, of course.'

Draik had no intention of doing anything other than firing his pistol, but he kept the alien talking, interested to hear what it might accidentally reveal. 'And if I helped you?'

'If you helped me, I would show you the alternative exit that all of your fellow simpletons have missed.' The alien glanced at something it was clutching in one of its hands. 'And then I would offer you the chance to see the true heart of the Blackstone – a place your species could not even conceive of.'

Draik looked around the hall. Every surface was smooth and featureless, apart from the channel of black liquid soaring out across the drop.

'You won't find it.' The alien was clearly revelling in the power it had over him. 'You will sit here, paralysed by indecision, for days, perhaps weeks, until your food and drink are gone and you start to waste away. Then, when you see the end coming, you will realise that you have only one chance – to swim so fast that you reach the other side before you burn away.'

'Is that possible? To reach the other side before the liquid consumes me?'

'Perhaps.' The alien shrugged and nodded to one of the corpses. 'Some of the simpletons made it halfway before they lost their nerve and swam back. Perhaps, if they had persevered, they might have reached the other side.'

'And what is on the other side?'

'The liquid spills into the core of the fortress. It falls away through a sluice gate and the heroic simpleton walks free, rid of the fluid and happily entering the Blackstone's central keep.' The alien shrugged. 'You'll see soon enough. When you're starving and parched, you'll have no option. It seems that your kind were not built to survive in places like this.'

'And your kind *were* built to survive in here? You don't seem to be doing so well.'

The alien's smile faltered. 'I had some business to deal with – a tiresome brother.' It looked around the chamber, seeming to forget about Draik. 'I think that was a long time ago. But maybe not. Strange how this place plays tricks with one's mind.' Then it remembered Draik and scowled, seeming irritated that it had spoken so openly. 'Do you want to know about the other way out?'

'What would you ask in return?'

'That you help me until I recover my strength.' The alien waved at its body. 'I am close to my goal, but my journey has broken me. Watching your friends cook themselves has been amusing for a while, but if I stay here any longer I will never leave. And I am destined to become the master of Vaul's Talisman. If you carry me to the other exit, I will direct you.' The alien glanced at its hand again. 'I am in possession of secrets. You just need to help me to a transportation chamber.'

'And then?'

The alien laughed. 'And then you will try to kill me, but we will deal with that when the time comes.'

Draik still had his pistol pointed at the alien's head.

'I would rather die than offer you help.'

The alien's smile never faltered. 'Of course. Hence my original statement. You are dead, little mon-keigh. Your race is run.'

Draik walked away from the alien. The thing was an abomination. Drukhari were vampiric, sustaining themselves through the agony of others. The alien was too weak to physically torture him, so it was tormenting him in another way. Teasing him with a promise of escape. Making offers that were bound to be lies. He looked at the liquid rushing through the aqueduct, oily and black as it flowed across the gallery. He could not even be sure that it was as lethal as the drukhari said. Perhaps the alien had burned the victims that were scattered around the hall? Perhaps the liquid was as safe as the oil that had washed over Draik in the maglev chamber? He paced up the steps to the start of the aqueduct and approached the edge of the canal. It was about twelve feet wide and the liquid looked identical to the oily substance he had seen before, gurgling and lapping as it rushed away from him.

The alien started laughing, quietly. 'Some never pluck up the courage. Look to your left.'

There was a corpse right near the edge of the liquid. It was not burned like the others, but it was still a husk. It was a man, a privateer of some kind. His face had collapsed in on itself, ravaged by starvation and dehydration, leaving a cold, waxy mask.

Anger boiled up through Draik and his pulse began to hammer. He looked back at the alien and saw, rather than an emaciated creature, his sister, sitting proud and erect on the back of a piebald charger. His mind had conjured no other memories of the Draik estates – just Thalia Draik and her steed, plucked from his past and deposited in this stark, white hall. The horse was snorting clouds of steam and its flanks were splattered with blood. Thalia was trying to catch her breath after the exertion of a hunt. She was twenty and a true Draik – lean, imperious and predator-strong. Blood dripped from her horse, splashing across the polished floor. Thalia sneered down at him from her saddle.

'I've worked it out.'

As she spoke, the white chamber fell away and the Draik estate shimmered into view, replacing the ivory walls with rain-lashed gardens and a spire-crowded Terran skyline, glittering with the landing lights of bulk haulers and atmospheric shuttles.

'Worked what out?' asked Draik. Their father and the rest of the party were galloping back towards the house, followed by a drifting panoply of airborne banners. The pennants were carried on the backs of hooded, wire-limbed servitors, snapping in the smog, adding a splash of proud, heraldic colour to the polluted air.

'Why you're not the heir father thinks you are.' She leant back in her saddle, flinging her damp, tawny hair from her face. 'You're such a diligent learner, Janus – so studious, so quick to learn, so good at practising all those pretty fencing moves. But you're *soft*. Too soft to rule.' Her face grew almost bestial, twisted and snarling as she tied her hair back in a plait. 'When that menial fell, you changed your course. What kind of Draik does that? What kind of Draik loses a kill, just to spare the blushes of a servant? You're no hunter.'

As always, Thalia had a knack of infuriating Draik. 'You rode him down. You broke a man's legs for no reason. You mistake cruelty for nobility, Thalia. The ability to crush a man does not make you fit to lead him.' Draik's steed bucked and pranced beneath him, sensing his agitation.

Thalia laughed, incredulous. 'I didn't even *see* him, Janus. Don't you understand? He does not breathe the same air I do. We are not the same species.' She tugged her reins, cantering away, still laughing. 'Yes, that's it. That's why I find all this so ridiculous. You're too soft, brother. Father will see it soon. You lack steel. That's why you will always fail. That's why I'm the only one who can rule when he's gone.'

Draik charged towards her, reaching out to grab her arm. She laughed, but the sound had changed. Her soft, rich tones had been replaced by a thin, gasping whisper.

At the last minute, Draik halted, his outstretched hand inches away from the crippled alien. The Terran skies faded and Draik snatched back his hand, just before the alien grabbed it. The creature dropped back, disappointed but intrigued.

'Who were you talking to?'

Draik shook his head and stormed back up onto the aqueduct, wondering if the time had come to kill the creature. His pulse was still pounding at the memory of his sister and he was desperate to unleash his fury against something.

'What are you not fit to lead?' asked the alien with a sardonic smirk.

Draik howled a curse and kicked the nearest thing he could find. It was the corpse that had not burned – the body of the privateer who starved rather than brave the liquid. Draik booted it with such force, and the body was so light, that it slid across the polished floor and splashed into the black liquid.

Draik backed away as droplets landed all around him. He glanced back at the alien and saw that its expression had changed. Rather than scornful, it now looked irritated – concerned, even.

Draik realised that he must have unwittingly done something unexpected.

He looked back at the body. It was floating quickly away from him, rushing towards the next chamber.

'It's not burning,' he muttered. 'It's not burning,' he said louder, looking back at the alien. 'You were lying to me. *You* must have burned these men.' He stepped forwards and placed his boot in the liquid. There was a loud hiss and plumes of smoke enveloped him as heat pulsed through his foot.

'Stop!' cried the alien, as Draik wrenched his foot from the canal and staggered backwards.

'Do not kill yourself, mon-keigh!' The alien sounded furious.

Draik stumbled back, pounding his boot on the floor, scattering drops of oil and glowing embers. His boot was blackened but he had removed it so quickly that the liquid had not burned all the way through. His foot was unharmed.

He looked back at the canal. The corpse was moving so fast it had almost reached the other side, but it was still intact. It had rolled a couple of times, but the oil simply slid off, revealing the same greasy cadaver. There was no sign of any burning.

He looked back at the alien. 'Why didn't it burn?'

'It's irrelevant.' Rather than scornful and snide, the alien now sounded unnerved. 'Your only way out of here is to help me, mon-keigh.'

'Tell me!' snapped Draik, pointing his pistol at the alien again.

The creature shrugged. 'Dead things pass. Living things burn.'

'Inanimate things float across?'

'Dead things, yes. What difference does it make? You are breathing. You will burn, simpleton. You will–'

With Thalia's accusations still echoing around Draik's head, the alien's whining was too much for him to bear.

He fired, ripping the alien's head apart with a needle storm.

Blood sprayed across the floor, exactly where it had previously been falling from Thalia's horse, and the headless alien finally lay still. He strode over to it and opened its dead hand. There was a scrap of skin in there. It looked worryingly like human skin and it was covered in notations he could not understand – vile, xenos runes. He felt like casting it aside, but perhaps it was the key to escaping the chamber? He stashed it in his coat as he walked back and forth at the edge of the canal, his anger growing rather than abating, his sister's words cutting him after all these decades. *You lack steel. That's why you will always fail.*

Then, as he thought of the corpse rushing towards the sluice on the far side, an idea occurred to him.

'Dead things pass,' he muttered. 'Living things burn.'

He reached beneath his coat and grabbed the device he had used to save Audus' life. The leather strap of the axial interrupter was cluttered with gauges and dials, and Draik peered at them until he found what he was looking for: a timer.

Then he shook his head at the insanity of what he was considering. He strode back down the steps and walked around the antechamber again, running his hands over the walls, looking again for a hidden exit. The alien was almost certainly lying but there might be another way out. Draik spent nearly an hour scouring every inch of wall he could reach, his optic implant switched to full magnification as he worked. There was nothing, and with every moment that passed he felt his chance slipping away. Isola would be horrified at losing her captain, but Taddeus would not pause. With Corval to protect him, he would not fail as he did last time. The priest might already be approaching the Ascuris Vault. He had no understanding of its true worth, but he would break into it for the sake of his holy visions and the glory of the discovery would fall to Taddeus and House Corval. Conquering the Blackstone was a chance Draik had never expected. This was his opportunity to prove his worth to his father, return to Terra and reclaim his place at the head of House Draik. And he would not let it be stolen from him.

He strode back across the chamber towards the aqueduct.

As he climbed the steps, he turned a dial on the strap, clicking it back a few notches until it started ticking. Then he fastened it to his wrist. He rushed towards the canal, breaking into a run, not giving himself a chance to rethink what he was doing. As he leapt, he triggered the device. Arcs of electricity lanced from his wrist to his heart.

Pain jolted through him.

He heard a muffled splash.

19

'The lullaby again,' growled Bullosus as he blundered through the shadows.

His brothers were behind him. Aurick was carrying a grenade launcher almost as big as he was and Lothar had a lascarbine in one hand and the cage in the other. The toad-thing was wearing an expression of abject terror as it looked around at the Blackstone. The approach vector followed by Draik had looked far too dangerous, so Bullosus had been forced to land miles away at a different docking point. They had been travelling through the Blackstone for what seemed like weeks, and the journey had been brutal. The hired hands they had recruited at the Helmsman had been killed by a staggering menagerie of aliens. Only the three brothers and the singing alien had survived to get this far. Bullosus had a huge arc light strapped to his back, but even that only managed to drive the darkness back a few feet. The echoes of their footfalls made it sound as though they were crossing some kind of empty plateau, but it was impossible to be sure. After everything they had seen, the creature was too panicked by its surroundings to realise it was being addressed.

'Sing!' bellowed Bullosus, glaring back at it.

The bloated little creature flinched, then launched into song. Its voice was usually strong and resonant but here, in the abyss of the Blackstone, it could only manage a thin warble. The sound carried nonetheless, reverberating off unseen walls and echoing in hidden pits.

Bullosus shook his head. The sound failed to calm him as well as it usually did. They had docked with the Blackstone at the same location they always used, but on this occasion the portal had decided to change its shape and Bullosus' shuttle was now a smouldering wreck.

'How will we get back to Precipice?' whispered Lothar, glancing back the way they had come.

'Audus will fly us,' Bullosus grunted. 'In the Terran's ship.'

'Draik? He won't let us set foot on his ship.'

Bullosus nodded at the blade that had replaced his lower arm.

Lothar raised an eyebrow. 'Ah, of course.'

Bullosus looked at the tracker he was holding in his one remaining hand. The tag he had bolted into Audus' chest was giving out a strong, regular signal and, even more usefully than that, it showed the route she had taken. They would soon catch her up.

As they hurried through the gloom, the surface underfoot began to change. Rather than a smooth, slate-like substance, it became fractured and crumbled, crunching under their boots like piles of soot. Pale lights began stretching across the floor towards them – long, grey fingers that grew stronger as they marched on. Soon, Bullosus could see that the light was leaking from around the edges of what looked like closed doors, but if they were doors they were absurdly tall, as though made for giants.

'Who built the fortress?' said Lothar, raising his voice over the song of the caged alien.

Bullosus said nothing, trudging on through the hall. The carpet of flakes became so deep he had to wade through great drifts. They billowed around him as he walked, glinting in the light from the doorways, churning and spiralling like a blizzard.

'There,' said Lothar.

Bullosus had already seen it. Up ahead of them was another doorway, leading directly to the route Audus had taken – and this one was open. The size of the doorways and the billowing clouds made it hard to gauge the distance, but he guessed half a mile.

The blizzard grew more ferocious with every step and they were only halfway to the door when Bullosus began to struggle. The flakes had reached the top of his prodigious gut. It was like trying to wade through a lake of metal shavings. The flakes buckled and snapped under his weight, but they were landing around him all the time, sticking to his face and clogging his eyes.

'Wait,' gasped Lothar.

Bullosus looked back and saw that his brother was covered up to his chest and had ground to a halt. Aurick was the same. The amphibian had stopped singing, looking around in wide-eyed panic at the whirling banks of metal shards.

'Move!' growled Bullosus.

His brothers strained, their faces red with exertion, but however much they tried to push through they could not take a step. Bullosus was about to yell again, when the hall reverberated with the sound of metal pounding on metal. It sounded like someone had struck an enormous bell.

The brothers and the creature all looked around in silence. The flakes were falling even faster now, but the sound was so ominous Bullosus forgot about everything else. It boomed again, metal pummelling metal, hitting with such force that the whole chamber shuddered.

'Something's trying to get *in*,' whispered Lothar, his face as grey as the drifts that were burying him.

Boom. It struck again, with even more ferocity.

Bullosus nodded. Whatever was hammering against the walls was huge.

Boom.

No, he realised. It wasn't the walls.

'The door,' he said, nodding at one of the towering portals.

Lothar hissed a curse.

The metal, or stone, or whatever the door was made of, was buckling.

Boom. The door bowed towards them, starting to rip away from its hinges. The door was hundreds of feet tall, but whatever was behind it was even bigger.

Lothar and Aurick began to splutter as the drifts rose across their chins and into their mouths. They angled their heads back, struggling to breathe, looking panicked. Bullosus tried to reach towards them, but the weight of the drifts was so great he could not move. The flakes had risen to his chest.

Boom. The door was on the verge of collapsing.

'Draik!' snarled Bullosus. If it wasn't for that Terran dandy, he would already have left Precipice with Audus in his hold and his arm still intact. The thought of his injury reminded him of the radium scythe Orphis had grafted to his muscles.

Boom. The door leant forwards.

Bullosus flexed his muscles and triggered the scythe. Heat and smoke engulfed him as the blade tore through mounds of shavings, creating a clear space around the bounty hunter. He wrenched the scythe free, raised it, sparking, over his head, and punched it down. It ripped through the floor like paper.

Bullosus wrenched the blade sideways. He had only meant to create a small opening, but the scythe was blazing with such ferocity that it whirled around him, creating a ragged, circular hole. Bullosus teetered on the edge, staring down into darkness. There was movement down there. Something liquid. Like an underground river.

Boom. The doors ripped free of their hinges and fell.

Bullosus shoved his brothers into the hole and jumped after them, cursing Draik again as he plummeted into the blackness.

20

They met in the outer precincts of the Imperial Palace. A warren of slums and crumbling ruins, crawling with the kind of human detritus the two young nobles had spent their lives avoiding. Draik had never ventured this far from the family estates unaccompanied. As he strode into the Basilica of Saint Scipios, sabre in hand, cloak flung back, he felt more alive than he had ever done before. The atrium soared above him, magnificent – even now, with its walls blackened and its roof gone. Through broken rafters he saw a mountainous heap of catacombs and huts, layer upon layer of city, the tides of history that had drowned this once noble structure beneath hovels, mines and wreckage-strewn landing pads. The air was barely breathable, so thick with fumes that Draik could almost imagine that the basilica was restored to its former glory, its isles and naves swimming with holy fumes, its statues the silhouettes of magnificent priests, blessing the devout legions who had battled their way to the Imperium's blessed Throneworld.

'Beautiful,' said Numa, striding through the fug, approaching from the far end of the nave. He was dressed as finely as Draik and had the same adrenaline gleam in his eyes. Numa was just a year older than Draik and his pale, angular features bore all the same hallmarks of nobility. He held himself with the poise and dignity of a dancer, trailing robes of silk and crushed velvet, intricately braided with the sigils of his house.

Draik nodded, tearing his gaze from the blasted majesty overhead and approaching his friend. As they met in the centre of the basilica they bowed and shared the usual civilities, before drawing their blades and adopting en garde positions.

'Is it true?' asked Draik. 'That you spoke ill of my sister?'

Numa nodded. 'If I have caused injury to your family name, Janus, I apologise, but I stand by what I said. Thalia shows no respect for anything, least of all you. She has spread revolting rumours and lies. She seems determined to tarnish your good name.'

Draik's pulse was hammering and he could see beads of sweat glinting on Numa's face.

'I cannot let such accusations go unchallenged,' he said. 'She is a daughter of House Draik.'

Numa nodded.

For the first time in his life, Draik felt like a man. His father's words echoed round his head. *Without your name, you are nothing. And without honour, you are not worthy of your name.*

'No one must know,' he said.

Numa's serious facade cracked for a moment. 'My punishment would be as terrible as yours, Janus.'

'Then let us begin,' said Draik.

'First blood?'

'First blood.'

They circled through the ruins, stepping lightly over toppled columns and shattered flagstones.

Numa made the first strike, a desultory overhand slash, more like another form of greeting than a genuine attack. Draik parried easily, disengaged, and struck with more fury, thrusting low and fast. Numa grinned as he parried, returning the strike with an equally furious one. The duellists' blades clattered as they danced past archways and architraves, striking with ever-greater speed and ferocity, stirring up banks of dust as they leapt and rolled.

Draik called on every skill he had learned in the training halls of the palace, tempering his violence with elegance and control. He had sparred with his friend many times – even as children they had enacted mock battles across the ballrooms and terraces of their family homes – but this was different. The reason for duelling was irrelevant. They both knew it. Draik took his family name seriously, as his father had ordered him to, but they would have found some other excuse to fight soon enough. The two youths were on the cusp of manhood. The time had come to test their prowess.

The duel quickly became more serious than either of them had expected. What had started as little more than a game took on a deadly earnest. Their smiles faded and the humour vanished from their eyes.

They had been lunging back and forth for nearly ten minutes when Draik stumbled, surprised, as Numa attacked with a move he had never seen before. He rolled, backwards, over a piece of masonry, landed on his feet and brought up his blade in time to parry the blow. Numa's eyes were blank as he lunged again, incredibly fast.

Draik parried again, but fell over another piece of shattered statue.

Numa brought his blade round in a wide slash that was headed straight for Draik's face.

Draik realised, incredulously, that he was going to lose the duel. He hurled himself forwards, moving with wild desperation, his reserve shattered by the idea of defeat.

Numa's blade flashed across Draik's face and pain exploded in his left eye.

Blood flew from his face. Draik had lost the duel, but his momentum carried him forwards. His attack was too fast and clumsy for Numa to anticipate. Draik thudded into Numa and landed a thrust of his own. The two friends ended up face to face, their noses almost touching.

A horrible sense of foreboding gripped Draik as Numa's face twisted into a grimace.

Draik loosed his sword and stepped back.

The blade was embedded, hilt deep, in Numa's chest.

Numa's seconds rushed forwards, crying out in alarm as Numa dropped to his knees, a dazed look on his face as he gripped the sword handle jutting from his breast, crimson bubbling between the fingers of his white gloves.

'Leave!' hissed Draik's seconds, grabbing him by the shoulders and pulling him away.

Draik was so shocked that he did not think to object as they bundled him from the basilica.

As they carried him off, Draik was barely aware of the pain in his eye. He felt as though Numa's blood was washing him away, a crimson tide, hurling him towards damnation. He closed the eye that had not been blinded, giving in to the sensation of weightlessness.

Then the reality of what he had done hit home. He had

left his friend to die. Whatever the consequences, he could not simply flee.

'No!' he cried, opening his eye.

Rather than slum-crowded Terra, he saw a clear, star-filled sky. The kind of sky that had not been seen on Terra for millennia – dozens of shimmering constellations, turning slowly in a sable void. He was about to cry out for his seconds to halt, when he realised he was alone, lying flat on his back in the darkness, agony pulsing up from his wrist, through his shoulder and into his chest. His heart was hammering erratically, skipping and racing as the pain in his side grew.

He tried to sit. The pain tripled and he vomited over his cuirass, groaning. It felt like someone had put a knife in his jugular. His heart stuttered and stopped, then raced and missed several more beats before finally settling into a steady rhythm.

He reached down and felt the device at his wrist, still sparking the electric charge that had stopped and restarted his heart. As he touched it, he remembered everything. He was not on Terra, he was in the heart of the Blackstone Fortress. Despite the agony thrumming through his veins, he laughed.

'It worked.' His voice was hoarse and strange.

He managed to sit and look around. He was on a gridded platform, made of the same onyx-like material as the walls, and behind him was a smooth ramp leading back up to the aqueduct. Black liquid was crashing down behind him, vanishing through the holes of the grid.

A few splashes were landing close to him, so, remembering the charred corpses, Draik dragged himself away from the weir, wincing as arcs of energy sparked down from his wrist and across his chest.

When he was sure he was clear, he took a look around. The grid appeared to be floating in space. The platform ended a few feet away from him and from there on there were only stars, blinking at him from every direction. He unclasped the strap, took a deep breath and wrenched it free. Blood rushed from his wrist but the wounds were not deep. He took a bandage from a pouch on his belt and bound them. Then he climbed, unsteadily, to his feet. He was a mess. His coat and boots were charred and his cuirass was covered in vomit. His clothes were dark with blood and his heart was still skipping the odd beat. He wiped down his breastplate and took a few deep, slow breaths, trying to steady his pulse.

Something had changed. His mind was not his own. Since landing on the Blackstone, he had felt an alien presence staring into his thoughts, but now it was *in* his thoughts, bound to his conscience. Thanks to the axial interrupter, he had been revived, but he also felt altered.

He looked around again. The air was brittle and cold. Even now he could see frost glittering in the folds of his coat. But it was still air. If he were really out in the void, he would already be dead. This must just be another chamber in the Blackstone. He stepped to the edge of the platform and reached out. He was still holding the interrupter and he waved it back and forth. To his surprise, it collided with the stars, causing them to spark and blink. They were not distant, but tiny – a dazzling microcosm, clouds of miniature suns hovering in the air all around him.

He knelt and reached down. His hand bashed against a hard surface. There was a floor, it was just polished to such a perfect sheen that it reflected the stars above.

Carefully, he stepped from the platform. The mirrored floor took his weight but, as Draik stepped into the stars, they detonated against his clothes in a series of little explosions. They sounded like dead leaves – crunching underfoot, harmless and inconsequential – but each miniature supernova burned on his coat, scorching away the cloth and scattering little flames through the air.

Now that he was standing amongst them, Draik could see that the star field was finite. There was a wall in the distance, a few hundred feet away and, if he squinted hard, he could make out the outline of a door. There was no way back, so his route was clear. He took a few steps, still unsteady from his recent resurrection, but sensing that he was moments away from his goal. He picked up his pace but quickly realised a problem. Every star he passed through died, blazing angrily against his face and clothes, and after a few minutes his coat was blistering and smouldering. The stars had even burned through to his skin in some places, leaving painful lesions.

Draik paused. He was not even halfway across, but his coat was already starting to collapse and the shaven part of his head, either side of his topknot, was blistered and smoking as the embers ate into his skull. By the time he reached the other side he would look like a revenant, burned and bleeding, like one of those ruined devotees in the Helmsman. The constellations were more densely packed in the centre of the chamber and his skin was already raw with dozens of burns.

You lack steel, he heard Thalia say. *You will always fail.*

He gritted his teeth and strode on, ignoring the pain as dozens of little fires erupted over his clothes and face, scorching and smoking as they blistered his skin. The pain grew worse as he reached the centre of the chamber. His uniform was ablaze in several places now, and he could barely see through the cloud of fireballs igniting all around him.

It occurred to him that he might die. The flames were

crackling across his whole body. He felt as though he were in a storm of acid. An image of Pious Vorne entered his thoughts. He was still perturbed by the thought that she was willing to burn for her faith despite her perfectly rational fear of such a fate. *If I burn, I burn,* he thought. *But I'm not turning back.*

He broke into a run, charging headlong through an exploding universe, trailing flames and sparks, a brilliant comet punching through the firmament.

21

A tongue lolled across the floor, sinuous and serpentine, reaching towards Glutt. It was leathery and black and trailing the heavy stink of rotting meat. He watched the tongue for a long time, hypnotised by its movements, before realising that it was his. He coiled it back into his mouth, tasting the cold, alien flavour of the Blackstone. Then he looked down at the rest of himself.

As the daemon had promised, his feeble body was gone, replaced by something far more warlike. His legs were like slabs of cooled magma: dusty grey and covered in hard, overlapping ridges, like the plates of a crustacean's shell, bristling with long, serrated spines. There were also more legs than there used to be – seven, to be exact, planted firmly on the ground and ending in blunt, ragged stumps. He reached down to tap one of them and saw that his arm was also changed. It unfolded with a series of clicks, extending dozens of joints. It was clad in the same ridged armour as his legs and, rather than a hand, it ended in a single, scythe-like talon.

He was crouched in the darkness, at the edge of a pool. The pool was a ragged, puckered sore, marring the Blackstone's smooth floor. Rather than water, it contained a thick, puce-coloured substance that was lapping, gently, against hundreds of white eggs.

Glutt stood, his body creaking and groaning like an old door, and saw that he was surrounded by thousands of the eggs. They were all nestled in similar pools of dark red liquid, heaped in piles as far as he could see. He nodded in satisfaction. The daemon was a good teacher. It had patiently taught him the obscure rituals and complicated chemistry required to nurture the virus. In one of these eggs would be the plague that would ruin Commander Ortegal.

Glutt studied the bizarre landscape in awe. His power was now so great that it had even transmuted the Blackstone Fortress. The walls and floor had split as the eggs multiplied, softening the hard-edged geometry of the space station, turning it into a lumpen, sagging garden. Where the red liquid had spilled from the sore-pools, it had summoned weird protuberances from the Blackstone's floor, sending spirals of growth up into the air and draping the doorways with tendrils of fleshy, purple vines. The growths burned with a vivid luminescence, driving back the Blackstone's darkness with pulsing, emerald spores. It was a glorious sight, made all the more delightful by the impotent fury of the Blackstone. He could hear it from here, pummelling the cage Fluxus called the cancrum, unable to break through as Glutt's work took root.

Glutt heard splashing and grunting as something stirred in the pool next to him. He assumed it was an egg hatching and crouched down to look, his tongue unfurling, forgotten, as it slapped down into the glistening mass. As he expected, one of the eggs was bulging and shifting. He plucked it from the pool with his talon and let it roll onto the floor. Rather than breaking, it started to grow, stretching over the shape that was trying to force its way out.

Glutt had seen countless eggs hatch, but none of them had behaved like this. Perhaps, finally, this was the one.

'Fluxus!' he cried.

The egg continued stretching until it was nearly a foot wide. Its shape distorted and, as the shell stretched it grew thinner, it revealed the thing that was twisting and bulging beneath the surface. Glutt gasped as he saw that it was a face – a human male face, fat and jowly and grinning with excitement.

'Are you ready?' the man cried, his voice muffled by the skin-like shell that was stretched over his mouth. 'Are you ready to be judged?'

Glutt recoiled, feeling a deep sense of unease, just as Fluxus came splashing through the pools towards him. Just like Glutt, the daemon had changed during its time in the cancrum. It was now a mountain of flesh – an olive-green sack of blubber and sores that waddled towards him on legs that were hidden beneath rolls of puckered fat.

Fluxus loomed over the pool, its cavernous mouth hanging open as it watched the face in the egg.

'We're close now!' cried the face.

Glutt knew, intuitively, what the man was talking about. Panic gripped him and he plunged one of his talons into the egg. It burst with a moist squelch, revealing heaps of wriggling grubs, but no sign of a face.

'You said nothing could reach us in here!' said Glutt, turning to face the daemon.

'I said the Blackstone would not break through.' Fluxus shook its head. ***'I did not say men would not break through.'***

Glutt looked past the daemon to the ranks of hooded soldiers that were trudging around the pools, watching for any sign of newcomers.

'Then I have to make sure they never get here. He said they were close, did you hear him?'

Fluxus smiled. ***'We are prepared. Remember?'*** He waved at the silent, shadowy figures dotted around the garden. They were hazed by the banks of flies and spores, but Glutt could still see that they were ready, guns loaded and gripped in their clammy fists. It was only now, as the plants bathed them in diffuse, pallid light, that he saw how numerous they were. There were hundreds of masked Guardsmen waiting beneath the dripping boughs.

Glutt nodded. 'No one must get close,' he muttered.

'No one will,' smiled the daemon.

22

Isola tried her vox-bead again, wincing at the screech that sliced into her ear. 'Captain Draik,' she called, 'can you hear me?'

The Blackstone answered. Its deafening, voiceless howl ripped through the bead, forcing Isola to deactivate the unit and slump back against the wall, gripping her ear. Taddeus had demanded a halt so that he and Pious Vorne could pray. Standing still in the Blackstone was lunacy but Isola had no option. What could she do without Taddeus as a guide?

They were in a hexagonal antechamber, thirty feet across, pitch-dark and bitterly cold. Each of the six walls was built around an archway that opened onto rimy, confusing shadows, but the preacher was confident he knew which one to take. All Isola could do was sit and wait. They had placed a lumen at the centre of the room and it pierced the thick pall enough for her to see her companions. She had ordered the two remaining House Draik guards to watch the archways, lasguns at the ready. Taddeus and Vorne were kneeling at the centre of the chamber, their faces lit menacingly from beneath by the lumen as they read from Taddeus' journal. Audus was pacing back and forth across the chamber, toying with her pistol and casting irritated glances at the priests. Her usual loutish sneer was gone, replaced with an anxious grimace. Isola could guess the reason. For the last hour or so, the whole group had become increasingly distracted. The psychic wards projected by the Navigator's cawl were quickly wearing off. Without his presence, the madness was returning. One moment Isola would see Audus and the rest of the explorers, the next she would see figures from her past – parents, childhood friends, even long-dead enemies. She could see from the panic in Audus' eyes that they had little time left.

'We have to move!' snapped Audus, twitching and glaring at the kneeling priests. 'The madness will only grow worse. Do you understand?'

'Do you understand?' said Draik's father, studying Isola across the polished walnut of his desk. They were separated by a galaxy of armillary spheres and star charts, but she could still see a warning in the old duke's eyes.

'My lord?' She hesitated at the doorway of his study, clutching the contracts he had just handed her.

Even in his advanced years, Coronis Draik was a powerful man. His thick pewter hair had receded, but that only lent him a more imposing, scholarly air, with a heavy brow and an intense gaze. His muscular frame was draped in ducal finery, his uniform starched and hung with rows of medals and orders of merit, and his hand rested on a gilded cane, its grip cast in the shape of a dragon's head, the symbol of House Draik.

'Janus must never know the full details of the agreements we brokered with House Numa.'

Isola nodded, but she could tell from the duke's uncomfortable manner that there was something specific he needed to tell her. She closed the door and walked back into the study, halting before his desk.

'They wanted his head, Isola. He murdered their most beloved son. It was all I could do to keep him alive.'

She nodded. 'Of course, I understand, Lord Draik. You have assured them that Janus' Warrant of Trade will take him far from Terra. He will not attend the usual functions and he will not return to Terra unless–'

'He will not return to Terra,' interrupted the duke, 'at all.' He grimaced, massaging his temples, then looked at Isola with pain in his eyes. In all her years of service, she had never seen him show such naked emotion. 'If Janus Draik sets foot on Terra, our contracts with House Numa will all be cancelled – unless I hand him straight over to the Novator and let him avenge the death of his son. The matter is out of my hands. The Paternoval Envoy himself has made assurances to House Numa to that effect.'

Suddenly, Isola understood the stilted, strained conversations she had observed between Draik and his father. 'Janus does not know.'

The duke shook his head, looking at the maps on his desk. 'Nor must he.'

She nodded. 'It would kill him.'

'Quite, Isola.' The duke was rigid with anger. 'Quite.' He was gripping the dragon's head so hard it looked like he might crush the metal. 'All I have ever taught him is that he will one day sit at this desk, commanding the Draik empire, ruling in my place when I am gone. Terra is in his blood, Isola.

He must not know that he will never see it again.' The old man's voice was tight, strangled by his anger. 'And that I will never see *him* again.'

Isola could think of nothing to say. The sight of the old duke displaying such emotion unnerved her. She was keen to leave. 'He will hear no such thing from me, my lord,' she said finally.

The duke nodded, took a deep breath and regained his usual, magisterial demeanour. 'I will ensure that his contracts take him so far from here that he need never guess the truth. The galaxy is vast, Isola, and the warp is fickle.'

She saluted and turned to leave.

'Isola,' said the duke, and she halted at the door again. He was looking out of the window, his back to her. 'Keep him alive.'

'My lord.'

'Let me go!' howled Audus, jolting Isola back into the present.

The pilot's face was ashen and she had gripped her laspistol in both hands, pointing it at one of the House Draik guards.

Both of the guards raised their lasguns and pointed them at Audus. Their expressions were as harried and panicked as hers.

'Stop!' cried Isola, jumping to her feet. 'Remember where you are! The Blackstone.'

The soldiers glanced at her, confused and wary, but they held their fire.

'Audus!' snapped Isola, rushing towards her. 'What are you doing?'

'It's a mistake!' cried Audus, staring at her, wild-eyed. 'Stop the bombing!' She lowered her gun and grabbed Isola's shoulder. 'He lied! Save Sepus!'

'You're on the Blackstone,' whispered Isola, leaning close to her.

Audus froze and stared at Isola.

'You were in the past,' said Isola, still gripping her shoulder.

The priests had halted their prayers. Everyone was staring at Audus.

'What did I say?' she said, her face still horribly pale.

'You talked about someone called Sepus. Or a place called Sepus.' Isola frowned, recognising the name. 'There's a Sepus Prime, isn't there, in this sector? Is that where you come from?'

Audus looked more horrified with every word Isola said. She shook her head, but she looked so anguished it was clear Isola was on the right track.

Isola held up her hands. 'It doesn't matter now. I'm not interested in whatever crime you're running from, but we need to stay in the present or we'll all gun each other down.'

Audus glowered. 'The crime was not mine.'

There was an awkward silence as the various members of the group considered whatever memory had just gripped them. Isola was still dazed by the vision of her final conversation with the duke. His one request had been that she keep his son alive. And now, if she managed to survive the expedition, she would have to contact Terra and inform them that she had failed.

Taddeus slammed his book shut and the two priests stood.

'Hold true, my children.' He tapped the cover of the book. 'We have reached the holy fire. Soon we shall be bathed in the Emperor's flame.' He waved his mace at one of the archways. 'One last antechamber, then we stand at the gates of deliverance.' He looked at each of them in turn. 'Be ready to bow, naked, before the God-Emperor's gaze. Once humanity is cleansed of taint it can stand, unafraid, against the horrors of Old Night. Are you ready? Are you ready to be judged?'

No one replied, but Taddeus did not seem to notice.

'To enlightenment!' he roared, pounding his mace against his deep, barrel chest and striding off into the darkness.

Vorne rushed after him, gripping her flamer, and the rest followed at a more cautious pace, weapons raised and swinging from side to side as they entered the passageway.

The corridor was narrow to begin with, but gradually grew wider. After half an hour or so, they began to hear a low, oceanic crashing sound, like waves breaking against a cliff.

'This is it!' gasped Taddeus. He was sweating, despite the cold, and he paused to wipe his eyes with his sleeve.

'What's that?' asked Audus, glancing back the way they had come.

Isola listened. There was another sound, approaching from behind them. This one was not a colossal roar, but more like the crunch of grinding metal – like a vehicle being smashed to pieces. And there was something else: a voice raised in song, a gentle, simple melody – a child's lullaby. It sounded utterly absurd in the bleak confines of the Blackstone.

They all paused and peered back down the dark corridor, shocked as much by the music as the sound of rupturing metal. Flashes of light shimmered across the walls, like sparks from an angle grinder, tumbling through the air. Isola nodded to her guards and they pointed their lasguns at the clouds of embers.

Then they all flinched as an explosion ripped through the wall. The air filled with flames and shattered fragments, and the guards were thrown from their feet. Isola helped them up and everyone raised their guns, trying to see through the smoke and flames.

'That was a grenade,' cried Audus. 'We need to go!'

Taddeus nodded and rushed on, with Vorne hurrying after him.

Isola hesitated, peering back into the fumes, intrigued to know who else had managed to get so deep into the Blackstone. Perhaps they had seen Draik.

A trio of hulking silhouettes pounded through the blaze. Even through the smoke she could see that they were huge, built like pit-fighters and draped in bulky weapons. One of them had a cage on his shoulder and that was where the singing was coming from.

'Throne,' muttered Audus behind her, backing away. 'Bullosus.'

One of the men paused and pointed a weapon. It was hard to see clearly, but the gun was so big he had to use both hands to lift it.

'Go,' said Isola, waving the others down the corridor and then sprinting after them.

There was another ear-splitting blast, close enough to lift Isola from her feet and hurl her through the air. Shrapnel clattered off the walls and whistled past her ears.

She landed with a painful jolt and turned to fire, her laspistol kicking in her hand as it spat a blind barrage into a wall of flame. Audus grabbed her by the shoulder and wrenched her to her feet. They sprinted off down the corridor, chasing the rest of the group.

They emerged into a circular hall crowned with a domed ceiling, but Isola did not have time to study the details. The rest of the group had halted in the centre of the hall and raised their weapons as dozens of shapes rushed towards them from the shadows.

'Guardsmen?' gasped Isola.

The newcomers were human, and even half-hidden in the darkness she could make out the shapes of Astra Militarum uniforms and weapons. There was something odd about them though: they were shambling and lurching, as though drugged, and there was an odd, liquid hissing sound coming from them.

Vorne spewed an arch of fire up into the air, lighting up the chamber.

Isola grimaced as the light revealed the men staggering towards them. They were rotten husks, their flesh grey and mottled and sagging from their bones. They looked like old rags that had been soaked in water for so long they were disintegrating. Where their flesh was falling away it revealed nests of pale grubs, fidgeting and burrowing in their innards. Most of the men had hidden their heads in mouldering hoods, looking out through crudely ripped eyeholes, but a few of their faces were visible. Their eyes were blue-grey sacks and their mouths were toothless and drooling.

Isola and Audus opened fire. The blasts sheared away chunks of the Guardsmen's flak armour and ripped through their putrid muscles, but did nothing to stop their advance. They staggered slightly but otherwise showed no sign of noticing they had been shot. As they continued lurching forwards, they raised their guns and took aim.

Taddeus raced at them, bringing his mace down into the face of the first one he reached. The Guardsman's head became holy flame as the priest's weapon burned a fierce, sapphire blue.

The Guardsman fell and Taddeus crushed a second, creating another flash of blue flames. The holy fire caught, lighting up the sodden Guardsmen as if they were kindling. The front row reeled back, convulsing, engulfed in flames.

Vorne rushed to her master's side and fired, drenching the Guardsmen in rippling flames and sending more of them to the floor.

More Guardsmen were flooding out of other doorways, approaching from every direction. Isola and Audus joined the priests and the House Draik guards and formed a circle, standing back to back as Guardsmen rushed at them from all sides.

'We need to reach that exit!' cried Taddeus, pointing his mace at a doorway on the far side of the chamber.

Vorne fired again, drowning the Guardsmen in more flames, but Audus had noticed something dreadful – their charred, blackened remains did not lie still when they fell. The burnt bodies rose and rejoined the fight, trailing smoke and ash as they lifted their lasguns and took aim.

There was another blinding explosion, hurling pieces of Guardsmen through the air.

Grub-infested meat landed all around Isola.

'Don't touch it!' cried Taddeus. 'They are corrupted!'

Another blast ripped through the crowd as the Bullosus brothers waded into the fray, hurling more grenades.

Grusel Bullosus saw Audus and jabbed a finger at her. 'Wait there!' he roared, before lunging at the Guardsmen, swinging a blade that was attached to his elbow. The blade sliced through the undead as though they were not there, splitting them into ever-smaller pieces as Bullosus lunged and hacked. The blade burned with a cool, inner light, slicing through the Guardsmen so savagely that there was nothing left to rise – just mounds of butchered meat.

As Bullosus chopped his way towards Audus, more of the shambling figures were pouring from the shadows, crowding the chamber and firing. Most of their shots were wild and untargeted, but a few hit home. One of the Bullosus brothers fell, hit through the neck, gasping as the mob fell on him and tore him down. Then one of the House Draik guards slammed into a wall, his chest torn open by a blast, blood arcing from the wound.

Vorne filled the chamber with fire again, but the blackened

figures just lurched on, dripping ash and flames, surging towards her.

The last House Draik guard fell, a rusty blade embedded in his chest, and the Bullosus brother carrying the caged singer doubled over as Guardsmen fired repeatedly into his stomach, tearing him down and leaving only Grusel still standing. He howled and spun on his heel, firing as he turned, ripping the Guardsmen to shreds with a hail of gunfire and cutting others down with his scythe.

'Keep moving!' cried Taddeus, pummelling his way towards the doorway.

Bullosus had run out of ammunition and hurled his gun at the Guardsmen, but he was still hacking towards Audus with his scythe.

As Isola fired back over her shoulder, she noticed that Bullosus' blade did not just cut through the Guardsmen, but sliced through the Blackstone too, leaving great gouges in the floor. The lumbering bounty hunter was quickly catching up with them, flinging corpses aside and howling as he closed in on Audus. The pilot was too busy defending herself from the Guardsmen to do anything about Bullosus, though, firing into the lurching cadavers and trying to follow Taddeus.

The priest had almost reached the doorway when a dull clanging sound filled the chamber. One by one, each of the doors were slamming shut.

Taddeus cried out in alarm and powered on through the undead, punching and swinging his mace with even more ferocity, but before he reached the doorway it slammed down, trapping them in the chamber. Taddeus howled and whirled around, his back to the door, smashing corpses aside as they crowded round him.

Audus and the others made it to the door and stood at his

side, firing and punching as the crowd of undead soldiers flooded through the hall towards them. Bullosus was still visible, his pale bulk rearing up over the burnt Guardsmen as he slashed his way towards Audus. He was only a dozen feet away now, but he was trailing a mob of the soldiers – they were hanging from his arms and legs, trying to drag him down, slowing his headlong charge towards the pilot. The bounty hunter was cursing as he fought, glaring at the huge crowds of Guardsmen that now surrounded him.

'Bullosus' scythe!' gasped Isola, leaning towards Taddeus as they fought. 'It cuts through the Blackstone!'

The priest nodded. 'Make him a path!' he cried to Vorne.

Vorne fired her flamer, ripping a channel through the undead and creating an opening for the bounty hunter.

'This way!' cried Taddeus, waving Bullosus over.

The bounty hunter lowered his head and charged, smashing through the flaming ranks and crashing into the door behind Taddeus.

'You're mine!' he roared, pointing the blazing scythe at Audus.

She stepped back and pointed her pistol at his head.

The Guardsmen surged forwards, forcing Audus and Bullosus to turn their weapons back on the mob.

'We're all dead if we don't get through this door!' cried Isola, looking up at Bullosus. 'Can you cut it down?'

Bullosus was too busy fending off the Guardsmen to hear.

'Cut the door down!' she cried again, grabbing his arm.

He rounded on her with a snarl, but then seemed to register what she meant. He looked at his scythe, then at the door, then lashed out, nearly taking Isola's head off in the process. The blade carved straight through the door, cutting a long, narrow channel but not helping them escape the teeming mass of Guardsmen.

Audus cried out in pain and thudded into Isola, clutching the side of her head, haloed by a shower of blood. Isola gunned down the Guardsman that had shot Audus and several more at the same time.

'Get it down!' she howled at Bullosus, hammering her fist against the door.

He lunged again and again, thrusting the scythe back and forth, tearing great chunks from the door. It showed no sign of falling or opening, but Bullosus attacked it with such ferocity that he began to rip through its centre, splintering the thick plate and revealing a worrying glimpse of what lay on the other side.

Audus was slumped against Isola, clutching her head wound, but Isola managed to twist and look through the hole Bullosus was making. 'Throne,' she muttered.

There was an apocalypse taking place in the next chamber. Cathedral-sized slabs of wall were crashing into each other, detonating and shattering as they hit, filling the cavernous space with noise and violence. At the far end there was a blinding corona, a sphere of light that threw brutal, dramatic shadows through the mayhem. It looked like the Blackstone was ripping itself apart. It looked like the death throes of a star.

'The Emperor's flame!' cried Taddeus, slamming his mace into the surging crowds of Guardsmen. His face and robes were drenched in blood and filth, but he looked like an ecstatic saint, his eyes reflecting the light of the sphere.

Bullosus hacked at the door a few more times, then stooped and stepped through the gap.

The priests followed, then Isola, half carrying Audus through the hole.

23

There was no need to focus on the pain any more – Draik could feel little else. As he stumbled through chamber after chamber, every inch of his skin howled in complaint. The hall of stars had left his skin blackened and his uniform in tatters. He was in too much pain to examine the rooms that followed. He was vaguely aware of what might have been control panels, banks of raised platforms containing more pools of black liquid, but he made a straight line through every room. His head was bowed and his pistol was hanging loosely in his grip, but even without Taddeus Draik was sure of his route. He felt like a blood cell, racing back towards a heart. Emanating from somewhere up ahead was the grinding, creaking sound of the Blackstone's core. It was the noise he had been hearing, on and off, since they first landed, but since his revival it had been even louder, making him flinch and twitch as he ran.

Draik felt like a stranger in his own body. The change he

had felt after his resurrection was growing more pronounced. The old certainties no longer seemed so certain. He had come to Precipice to raise himself from the mire – to regain his place at the head of House Draik and rule over lesser men. But now – now there was another will driving him on. He still carried a burning desire to reach the vault, but he was no longer sure it was *his* desire. He felt as though there were an invisible cord, dragging him through trial after trial, testing him with all the unyielding rigour that his father had done. Gauging his worth, but for what?

Draik passed through a doorway and cried out in anguish. Ahead of him was the long gallery with the charred corpses and the aqueduct running down its length.

'You're dead,' said the same drukhari who had tormented him earlier.

'No,' he gasped, his voice ragged from his exertions and his head pounding with the Blackstone's pulse. For a moment, he almost faltered. He was a Draik – accepting defeat was as alien to him as the creature that was sprawled on the floor a few feet away. But this was too much. After everything he had endured, to be back here again, no closer to the vault, the same impassable route ahead of him.

He could feel the Blackstone in his head, waiting to see his response; waiting to see if he would break.

'Never,' he breathed.

He silenced the alien with a headshot, killing it for a second time, then sprinted across the balcony, drawing out the axial interrupter, fastening it to his wrist and setting the timer as he ran.

With a cry of defiance, he leapt out across the current and triggered the device.

Pain.

Darkness.

The face of his father. The duke was stern and unyielding. This was before he had given up on his son. He was lunging harder and faster, quizzing him on Imperial governance, burying him under history books, reciting martial treatises and the intricacies of galactic trade.

The face of his sister, bitter and hurt, willing him to fail.

'No!' he howled, his heart thudding painfully back into life.

Sparks flashed across his eye, blinding him.

He rose, jittery and weak, and staggered away from the sluice into the next chamber.

His heart had been violently stopped and brutally restarted and, incredibly, for a second time it had endured.

'You're dead,' said the drukhari as Draik stumbled into the same chamber for a third time: the charred bodies, the drukhari, the aqueduct – everything exactly as before.

Draik dropped to his knees and clutched his head. His skull felt like it was being crushed, groaning and straining. His heart was stuttering wildly after being so ill-treated, and his whole body was jerking and twitching as lines of electricity flashed across his tattered uniform. The Blackstone's presence bore down on him, peeling back the layers of his soul.

'What do you want?' he demanded, his words little more than a whisper.

The alien sniggered.

Draik stood, leant against the wall to steady himself, and shot the drukhari for a third time. Then he tried to run across the room, making for the edge of the balcony and the aqueduct that stretched out from its centre.

He weaved like a drunk, trembling and blinded by after-images.

He almost missed the entrance to the aqueduct and toppled into the void below, but managed to correct himself at the last minute. He lacked the strength to jump, but before he fell into the rushing oil he triggered the axial interrupter.

Killing himself. Again.

24

Something was picking at Draik's skin, clawing and pecking. His eye was closed but he pictured Grekh leaning over him, placing mutilated insects in his mouth, preparing to eat his flesh.

'Get back!' he cried, sitting up.

Shapes fluttered away from him – carrion birds, filling the air with noise as they launched, thrashing their wings and screaming. A pale light was coming from somewhere and, as Draik's vision cleared, he saw that they were not birds, but angular approximations of birds – flat, triangular plates of metal, joined together by blades of the same lustreless ore. Some of them were still on him, jamming their blades into his legs, and he waved his arm weakly, shooing them away.

He looked down at his body and gasped. He looked worse than any of the wretches he had encountered in the Skeins: bloody, burned and covered in lesions. His heartbeat was less erratic but the grinding pulse in his head was louder, causing his teeth to clatter as though he were freezing.

He probably *was* freezing. There was frost all over his exposed patches of skin and his breath escaped in glittering plumes.

The bird-things had scattered, so he tried to sit up and look around. His arms were weak, but he managed to get upright and even stand, swaying slightly as he looked into the half-light.

The Blackstone was playing tricks on him again. He was back where he very first started. Ahead of him was the broad, diamond-shaped plateau they had left the *Vanguard* on. He could not see the shuttle, but he knew that if he walked the half a mile or so to the exit he would see it, waiting patiently on the landing platform, his deck crew inside.

For a moment, Draik wondered if all of his struggles had led him back to his own ship. Then he laughed in disbelief. On the far side of the chamber, a few hundred feet from where they had first entered the Blackstone, was a tall, narrow aperture. It had not been there when they first landed, he was sure of it. Even in the half-light he would have noticed such a specific design. He shook his head in wonder. The stones arrayed around the doorway were formed into a colourless mosaic, an image of a spherical cage, just like the one on the sketch he was carrying. It was a clear, deliberate signal that this was the route he needed. With more certainty than ever before, he felt the Blackstone speaking to him, guiding him, offering him a way in.

He was about to rush across the chamber when he remembered what happened last time – his blood had triggered an avalanche of drones. He looked down at his ruined body. He was a wreck, but none of his wounds looked like they would spill much blood – just the small punctures where the winged creatures had been pecking him and the blisters where the electricity had burned through his skin. The more serious injuries, like the hole where Corval had shot him, had already been bound.

At the thought of Corval his excitement faltered. He still felt shocked and wounded by the betrayal. Even now he could not understand it. What could have driven Corval to such an act? And what was he doing now? What might he do to Isola and the others?

He shook his head. There was nothing he could do but keep going. The Blackstone had offered him a way to reach the vault and he could not go back. He had to seize this chance. Everything else would have to wait.

He headed off through the shadows, struggling to walk in a straight line, keeping his gaze locked on the distant door. As he went, Draik noticed that the winged drones had returned in greater numbers, whirling overhead, clattering and screeching. Despite his exhaustion, he picked up his pace, trying to run as they swooped down towards him, letting out shrill scraping noises as he lashed out at them with his rapier. One of them latched on to the back of his neck, stabbing through his coat and tearing his skin.

He sliced it in two, then fired off a few shots, kicking more of the drones from the air and dispersing the others. Before they recovered enough to attack again he sprinted on, reached the doorway and left the hall.

The other side of the doorway was a wall of blackness so Draik did not notice the absence of a floor. He plummeted through the air and landed with a splash in another channel of black liquid.

He had reached the source of the noise in his head. He was

in an enormous valley – a smooth-sided chasm with a river of oil running down its centre. Up ahead of him, at the far end of the valley, was what looked like a fallen star, turning slowly in the air, spraying lines of silver through the darkness. It would have been a beautiful scene, if not for the ferocity of the destruction smashing through it. Walls and ceilings were collapsing everywhere he looked. It was an apocalypse to match the visions painted on Taddeus' barge. The noise was no longer in his head, but all around him, tearing the air apart with its violence.

The sphere of light was the Ascuris Vault, Draik had no doubt. He could see the spherical cage within the blaze. But there was no time to feel exultant. Slabs of the fortress were crashing down all around him, hurling him across the river on great surges of oil. It was clearly not sprung from the same source as the liquid in the canal, because it was harmless, but he was still likely to die if he didn't find shelter quickly.

He struck out across the liquid, swimming as fast as he could manage, and reached a column that had toppled into the whirling currents. It looked like a vast arm reaching into the depths. He clambered up onto it using his grappling hooks, then stumbled along its length, struggling not to fall as more tremors jolted through the chamber.

At the top of the crevasse he turned and raced through the chaos, dodging and ducking as architecture thundered down all around him. He was making for the distant vault when he saw an incongruous flash of colour in the storm of black and grey: red cloth, embroidered with gold sigils. It looked familiar.

Draik veered off course to investigate. As he got closer, a violent rage boiled up through him. It was Corval's cloak. It was ripped and scorched but still intact, and it was stretching down into another, smaller chasm that had opened alongside the main one.

The force of the avalanche was still growing, like a measure of Draik's rage, as he rushed towards the fissure. He was a few feet away when the floor gave way, sundering with a sound like the crack of brittle bones. He tried to halt but his momentum was too great and he toppled into the crevice.

Draik bounced painfully off ridges and jagged edges before managing to lash out with his grappling hook and halt his fall.

He was hanging on to the hook by one hand, his feet dangling over a maelstrom and his head battered by a shower of falling debris. The hook began to slide, carving down through the wall as Draik grasped wildly with his other hand, trying to latch on to something.

Before he could find a handhold, the hook gave way and he fell.

Draik kicked hard against the wall, diving for a narrow ledge on the far side of the drop.

He slammed hard against it, breath exploding from his lungs, but managed to hang on. He hauled himself up onto the ledge and cursed.

He had reached Corval. The Navigator was a few feet below him, trapped and bleeding, but still alive. Corval was sitting at an awkward angle, pressed onto a narrow ledge with his legs trapped beneath a shard of fallen wall as more debris crashed down around him. The noise was growing louder all the time and it could not be long before they were both smashed into the abyss.

Corval recoiled at the sight of Draik and reached for his pistol. His hand bashed uselessly against the slab pinning him to the ground. The pistol was strapped to his thigh, beyond his reach. Draik whipped out his own gun and pointed it at Corval, gripping the shuddering ledge with his other hand.

His mouth was full of bile as he considered how Corval had brought him to this terrible situation, but before he fired, he cried out over the din: 'Why?'

Corval began to shake. Draik thought he was dying, but then he realised he was laughing.

'Did you think you could outrun your past forever, Janus?'

'What do you mean?'

Corval stopped laughing and shook his head. He slumped against the ragged wall.

'What do you mean?' cried Draik again. 'What do you know of my past?' The violence in the chamber ebbed slightly, as though the Blackstone were pausing to listen.

'Just kill me.' Even through the mouth grille of Corval's helmet, Draik could hear the dejection in his voice. 'I'm a lie.'

Corval reached up to his star-shaped helmet and flicked back the catches, pulling the faceplate away.

Draik almost fell from his perch in shock. The Navigator's face was gaunt, and unnaturally aged, but he recognised it instantly. 'Numa?'

The Navigator shook his head. 'You killed Numa, Janus. Not in the way you thought, but you killed me all the same.'

Draik lowered his pistol, dazed and horrified.

Corval patted his chest. 'The wound you gave me was deep, Janus, but my father would not let it take me. House Numa has resources. They pumped me full of drugs, then they pumped me full of things that have no right to exist.' He grimaced, his eyes full of shame. 'Unspeakable things.'

'They kept you alive?' Draik's mind was ablaze. His father had ordered him from Terra because he had murdered a noble, risking an ancient allegiance between two proud houses. But there *was* no murder.

Corval's voice was full of vitriol. 'They did not keep me alive, Janus, they just gave me a more shameful death.' He pounded his chest, his face contorted by hate. 'Nature will not be denied. The cells of my body rebelled at their intervention.' He touched the sash across his forehead. Like all Navigators, his third eye was always kept hidden – until he used it to pierce the veils of the warp. 'We are a blessed family,' he said. '*Too* blessed.' His voice was full of agony and doubt. 'House Numa is not all that it should be.'

Draik shook his head, confused.

'I'm grotesque!' cried Corval. 'I am damned! The wound you gave me was clean, it would have given me a clean death, but under their care it festered. It became something else, something hateful.' Corval's voice was ragged with emotion. 'You and my father made me a monster, Janus.' He touched the sash. 'I can no longer look into the warp. If I did, the result would be so violent it would destroy me. Do you understand? Do you understand what that means? A Navigator who can no longer see? You ruined me!' He leant forwards, pointing an accusing finger at Draik. 'So I came looking for you. My father wanted me to rot in his vaults, until I was too dangerous to live even there, but I will not die unavenged. So I abandoned Terra and abandoned my name. I stole and I lied and I became Corval. And I hunted you down, Janus. I refused to die until I saw you die.'

Draik's rage faded as he saw the ruin he had wrought on his friend. Then he thought about what this could mean for him.

'My father banished me because I killed you,' Draik muttered. 'If he knew the truth...'

'Oh, he *knew*,' laughed Corval. 'They have no secrets, your father and mine. They agreed that you would never return to Terra. You were too much of a risk. We were both too much of a risk. You were so desperate to be the perfect son that you became the opposite – all those needless duels and ill-considered deals – you were bringing House Draik into disrepute. And *my* father had to be rid of me because of...' His voice faltered. 'Because of what I became. Because of what I am now. Neither of us could be seen. Our fathers ruined us, Janus. And then they had to hide their wretched mistakes.'

Draik pictured his father's face the last time they met, recalling how he avoided meeting his eye. Corval was telling the truth. His father *knew*. More than anything the Blackstone had thrown at him, the revelation crushed him. His father had known Numa was alive, but let his own son leave Terra carrying the guilt for a non-existent murder. No, he realised, that was not true. He *had* killed his friend – the deed had just stretched across the decades, creating this wretched thing before him.

'How could he lie? I did everything he taught me,' said Draik. 'I was honourable. I was honest. I was noble.'

Corval stopped laughing, his tone bleak. 'Nobility. What does that even mean? Look where it got us, Janus.'

There was a loud cracking sound as the ledge holding Draik started to split. Draik looked around for another handhold, but there were none. If he didn't move soon, he would be as doomed as Corval.

'Go,' muttered the Navigator. 'But kill me first.'

'You hesitated,' said Draik.

'What?'

'You could have killed me but you hesitated to shoot. After hunting me for so long.'

Corval laughed again. 'True. I failed even at that.'

'Maybe we're better than them,' said Draik.

'What do you mean? Who?'

'The liars who raised us. Maybe we're better than our fathers.'

Corval looked up at him, confused. Then he looked into the middle distance, considering what Draik had said. Slowly, the anguish faded from his eyes and something else flickered there. Draik could not place the emotion, but in it he recognised the friend he had lost all those years ago in the Basilica of Saint Scipios.

'Do you remember our credo?' he asked.

'To strive, to seek, to find,' said Corval, without hesitation.

'And not to yield,' finished Draik. It was a fragment of an elegy by some forgotten versifier called Lord Tennson, a line of verse from prehistory – from the days before the High Lords and the Imperium, a relic of thought from Old Earth.

'To strive, to seek, to find, and not to yield.' Corval quoted the line again. 'What can I strive for now, Janus?' he said, his voice barren. He touched the sash over his third eye again. 'To die before I cause harm, nothing more than that.'

Draik looked around at the ruined chamber. 'We did not come here by chance.'

Corval nodded. 'I feel it too.'

'Then what does the Blackstone want with us?' said Draik. 'It led you to me and led us both to its heart. Why? Simply so that we can die? I don't think so.' He reached out across the drop, extending his hand to Corval.

Corval looked up at him, shocked.

'Help me down,' said Draik. 'Let me get that thing off you. Our fathers may be liars, but we don't have to be.'

Corval shook his head but then, a moment later, he reached up.

Draik grabbed his hand. 'Can you take my weight?'

Corval nodded.

Draik hesitated. Corval had already tried to kill him. This could be a ruse. If the Navigator loosed his hand Draik would be smashed on the rocks below.

They stared at each other.

Then Draik stepped from the ledge and Corval held his weight, hauling him to his side.

'And not to yield,' said Draik.

Corval nodded.

They grabbed the block on Corval's lap and heaved it aside, sending it smashing into the darkness below. The chamber had begun attacking the vault again, and walls were falling all around them. Draik lifted Corval to his feet and found to his relief that the Navigator's legs were not broken. As Corval replaced the mask of his cerebrum cowl, Draik slammed his hook into the wall and stepped up onto another ledge. Then he reached back and grabbed Corval's hand and they began to climb, helping each other as they went.

A few minutes later, they clambered up onto the floor of the chamber together and ran towards the blazing light.

25

Bullosus was waiting for them as they climbed through the hole in the door. He grabbed Audus and wrenched her away from Isola.

Audus was barely conscious. One side of her head was slick with blood and there was an ugly wound just below her ear. Blood was rushing down her neck, and her face was a ghastly grey colour. Isola was not about to abandon their pilot so easily, but before she could react, the Guardsmen began hauling themselves through the hole in the door, reaching out for their prey with gargled, incoherent cries.

Vorne answered with a jet of flame, turning the hole into an inferno.

The undead soldiers thrashed and hissed, but continued trying to claw their way in.

Vorne fired again, ripping them apart with more flames. Isola staggered back from the door, shielding her face from the heat, feeling the hairs on her skin shrivelling and burning.

The more the Guardsmen tried to break in, the more flame Vorne poured into the hole, until the door was jammed with blackened, charred flesh. The Guardsmen were still clawing and pounding on the other side, but for the moment they were halted.

Isola and the others all turned to face the devastation that was being wrought around them. They had emerged onto a long, flat platform, suspended above the chamber. It was sheltered by a roof, but beyond that the air was filled with spinning fragments of wall and floor. If Isola hadn't known she was in a star fort, she would have thought she was witnessing an earthquake.

Bullosus still had hold of Audus, but he was too dazed by the ruin that surrounded them to think of his prize. The pilot was dangling, insensate, from his meaty fist. Isola saw a chance to snatch her back, but Audus was one step ahead.

Audus stood, quite calmly, and fired, blasting Bullosus from the outcrop and sending him plunging into the carnage below, blood spraying from a hole in his chest.

'If in doubt, play dead,' she said with a grim laugh, glancing at Isola.

Isola was stunned. She had thought Audus was unconscious, but it was a feint – she had just been biding her time until she could kill her pursuer. She nodded in respect.

Audus shrugged. 'If the dumb bastard hadn't been so obsessed with me he could have left this place rich.'

Taddeus did not even notice. He staggered ahead of them down the walkway, shaking his head and whispering prayers of thanks. 'This is what I saw,' he muttered. 'This is what I saw!' He turned to face them, tears glinting in his eyes. 'Enter the light.'

Isola followed, ducking and flinching as great tides of

architecture toppled and fell. There was another noise, beneath the tearing of columns and walls – a crackling, humming sound, emanating from the sphere of light. It sounded like they were trapped inside a vast generator.

'How?' she asked. 'How would we get across there?'

Everywhere she looked, the floor was splitting and shearing. There was a deep crevasse at the centre of the hall, with a channel of black oil rushing through it, but even that was being shattered and smashed, spraying ink-dark geysers up into the whirling dust clouds. As Isola stared in wonder at the destruction, she saw two distant figures staggering through the rubble, rushing towards the ball of light. They were silhouetted by the glare, but there was no mistaking Corval's star-shaped helmet. She stared harder, trying to identify the other figure. It seemed too ragged and hunched to be the captain, but then she gasped as she saw that he was clutching a rapier.

'Draik!' she cried, pointing to the two figures.

'It can't be,' gasped Audus, rushing to her side and peering through the dust clouds. 'Throne, it is,' she muttered, shaking her head in disbelief. 'They really *did* survive.'

Behind them, the Guardsmen were still pummelling the doorway. Vorne fired again, melting more of the blackened lumps, like she was cauterising a wound. 'Burn!' she howled, the fire blazing in her streaming eyes.

'How do we get down?' cried Taddeus, peering over the side of the walkway.

Isola rushed to the end and looked down over the edge. 'Steps,' she called, waving the others over and starting to climb down into the shifting rocks.

'Are you insane?' cried Audus looking at the forest of black towers that was falling all across the chamber.

Isola waved at the scorched door behind them. 'What choice do we have?' Then she paused to look at the wound on the side of Audus' head. 'You should bind that.'

Audus shrugged. 'If I live long enough to bleed to death we'll have done well.'

The combination of Audus' deadpan tone and the savage destruction taking place below dragged an unexpected laugh from Isola. Audus looked back at her, surprised, then laughed too. Then Taddeus and Vorne clambered over the ledge and the four of them began climbing down.

They reached the floor and Taddeus led the way again, picking out a route through the mayhem. They were half-way across the hall when smaller explosions started kicking up around them. Isola snatched a look back and saw that the Guardsmen had appeared on the walkway and were firing. More were stumbling into view and some were already starting to climb down the steps.

'This way!' cried Taddeus, leaping over a crevice and scrambling up the side of a fallen archway.

It was only as they approached the sphere of light that Isola realised just how vast it was. It loomed over them like the prow of a void ship, hundreds of feet tall and simmering with power. The noise was ear-splitting and currents of energy rippled through her uniform. Then, with a cry of delight, she saw the two figures just up ahead, standing at the foot of the sphere.

Her elation faded as she saw what had become of Draik. He looked like one of the undead Guardsmen. His usually immaculate uniform was in tatters, ripped and burned and revealing the ruin that had been wrought on his body. He was covered in blood and scars, and there were terrible burn marks all over him. His face was corpse-grey and gaunt, as though he had somehow starved in the few hours since she last saw him.

'Captain!' she cried, running towards him.

Draik and Corval turned, hearing her determined cry even over the roar of the sphere. Draik was swaying, unsteady on his feet, and his usual aura of cool self-possession had been replaced with a feral snarl. At the sight of Isola, his face became even more contorted and he raised his pistol, taking aim at her head.

'Father!' he cried, as he pulled the trigger. 'You lied!'

26

Draik fired into the whirling clouds, crying out with every shot. The ground bucked and rolled beneath him and he stumbled, his shots going wild. How was the old man here, on the Blackstone? He had clearly seen his father's pompous, self-satisfied face looming through the explosions, leading Audus and the priests towards him. Had he come to apologise? To beg forgiveness? It was too late for that.

Pain sliced through his skull, causing him to lower his pistol and grab his head. A presence battled its way into his already crowded thoughts.

'Focus on my voice,' yelled Corval, grabbing him by the shoulders. 'Remember where you are. The Blackstone is still confusing you.'

Draik looked back at the figures rushing towards them. Somehow, he had mistaken Isola for his father. Thankfully his shots had gone wide. She was still battling through the chaos.

He glanced at Corval, who nodded.

'I'll try to shield you but it's hard, so near the...' His voice trailed off as he looked up at the sphere of light.

Isola, Audus and the priests stumbled towards them.

'Captain!' cried Isola, grabbing Draik's arm, unable to hide her relief that he was still alive.

He returned the gesture, gripping her arm. He had to shout to be heard. 'Forgive me. I saw something different. The Blackstone was in my mind.'

She shook her head and yelled back. 'I understand!'

Draik looked at Audus and grimaced at her wound.

She laughed. 'You look worse.'

Draik turned to Taddeus. Both of the priests had fallen to their knees and clasped their hands over their heads, mouthing prayers.

'How do we get in?' cried Draik, staggering towards them, struggling to stay upright as the ground jolted beneath him.

Taddeus' prayers faltered. The elation faded from his eyes. He tried to walk towards the light, but it was too fierce; the heat forced him back. Overhead, the walls of the chamber were trying the same thing, whipping against the blaze, failing to break through.

'My visions showed a gate!' cried Taddeus. 'An open gate!'

The colour drained from his face as he studied the sphere, taking in its flawless, unbroken surface. He tried again to approach, but the heat was incredible, driving him back. He took out his journal and stared at his notes, flicking the pages back and forth with increasing dismay, shaking his head.

Taddeus closed the book and looked at Draik with dawning horror. 'An open gate,' he muttered.

27

Grekh leapt between falling blocks and spinning shards, his rifle gripped in both hands as he vaulted a crevice and landed on a crumbling slope. The chamber was collapsing all around him, filling the air with a bewildering array of sounds and smells, but the trail was still clear. The Blackstone was speaking to him, its voice raised above the din, leading him on through the carnage. He jumped again as another gap opened before him, then sprinted across an open space, flinching and weaving as walls landed all around him.

Finally, as he passed between the splintered stumps of two columns, he saw his prey.

Bullosus was dead, slumped awkwardly across a broken arch, blood rushing from his pale, blubbery chest. Grekh salivated as he approached. The bounty hunter was a fearless warrior. His meat would be a rich source of inspiration. But Bullosus was not his prey. Through the drones, the Blackstone had given Grekh a clear purpose, a clear prize, and it was hanging from the bounty hunter's elbow. Grekh dodged another explosion, then edged closer to the scythe. It looked as inert as its owner, but Grekh's stomach told him the truth.

He leant over Bullosus' corpse and reached for the blade.

Bullosus howled and attacked. The scythe blazed into life as it rushed towards Grekh's chest.

Grekh sidestepped the blow and the blade slipped across his oily hide, slicing into a wall. Had Bullosus been fit, he would have decapitated Grekh, but he was sluggish and dazed. As he wrenched the blade free, Grekh had already stepped back and begun firing. The slugs thudded into Bullosus' chest and hurled him back across the floor. Incredibly, he managed to rise again, vomiting blood, launching himself at the kroot. Grekh kept stepping backwards, firing until his rifle was empty.

Bullosus collapsed and finally lay still, ripped apart by dozens of shots.

Grekh calmly reloaded his rifle and fired again, just to be sure. Then he took out a hunting knife, dropped to his knees and hacked at the bounty hunter's arm. Beneath all his layers of fat, Bullosus was clad in thick, toughened muscle. Grekh struggled for several minutes before finally wrenching the scythe free from its augmetic brace. He cleared away the slop of bloody ligaments and uncovered the handle, depressing a button to see if the weapon still worked.

It jolted in his hand, glimmering with power.

The trail had died with Bullosus, but Grekh had no doubts about where to head next. He turned to the blazing sphere – the vision that had haunted his dreams since he first reached the Blackstone. He fastened the scythe to his belt and rushed back through the madness.

He had only been running for a few minutes when he saw

the rest of the explorers, hunkered low in a jumble of fallen walls, locked in a desperate firefight with what looked to be human soldiers.

Grekh paused, confused.

Then he ducked, readied his rifle and stalked through the dust clouds, keeping half an eye on the battle up ahead and half an eye on the tectonic collisions taking place overhead. He clambered up a slope and peered through the spiralling fumes, trying to see who had survived to reach the vault. Draik was there, covered in wounds but alive. There was something else, though – he looked changed. The arrogance was gone. At this distance, Grekh could not be sure, but he sensed that there was more to it than that. It looked like the Blackstone had finally reached Captain Draik.

The rest of the group were there too, but Grekh was only interested in Draik. The more he tasted the Blackstone's sentience, the more he knew that Draik was the key. Draik was not here to achieve whatever selfish goal he had set himself; he was here to do the Blackstone's will.

Draik and the others were looking around the rubble desperately as they fired at the soldiers. *They can't get in*, thought Grekh. *They're trapped.* It was only then that he understood why the Blackstone had led him to Bullosus. He looked at the scythe tucked into his belt and nodded. At every turn of the journey, the Blackstone had been ahead of him.

He leant on the top of the slope, took careful aim and fired, picking off several of the soldiers, then leapt from his perch and raced towards Draik.

28

'They'll die soon enough,' gurgled Fluxus. The daemon had merged with one of the larger pools, a bank of gurgling meat draped around the mounds of eggs, covering the birthing liquid like a shawl, its face elongated and distorted. It was becoming one with the garden, mingling with the spore stacks and the streaming sores.

'You said that before,' muttered Glutt, scuttling back and forth, shaking his head frantically. 'And now here they are – at the gates of the cancrum.'

'But what can they do?' Fluxus sounded utterly unconcerned. ***'There is so much of our warp fire sewn into the cancrum. No human weapon could break through. They'll be trapped there until your Guardsmen finish them off. How many of them are there?'***

Glutt crouched over the pool and unfolded one of his chitinous limbs, slicing open a bloated egg. He could use the eggs at will now, like gelatinous scrying stones. Spores spiralled up before him and he wafted them into the shape he required – the scene outside the cancrum.

'Six.'

'And how are they faring?'

'They're trapped,' admitted Glutt. 'They've got no way in. They're firing at the Guardsmen.' He felt a flush of relief. 'But the Guardsmen will not be stopped.'

'Of course they won't. I've no idea how humans got so deep into Old Unfathomable. Perhaps she's so focused on us she overlooked them. But they won't last long against an enemy they can't kill. And there's no way they can break through this shell.'

'I should go out, to be sure.'

'No!' The daemon looked up from the eggs, abandoning its work to give him a warning glare. *'In here, we're safe, but beyond the cancrum Old Unfathomable would crush us. We must stay here until the virus is complete.'* The daemon smiled. *'Then, it won't matter. She can do whatever she likes to us once the virus has spread and your commander is presiding over a cataclysm.'*

'But when will it be done?' demanded Glutt, staring at the eggs.

'Soon,' murmured the daemon, using its long nails to split egg after egg, carefully examining the twitching contents, before stirring them together. *'Each mutation brings us closer, but I'm seeking a combination so potent it will escape the confines of this alien tomb and survive even in the void, passing from ship to ship, infesting every corner of the sector.'*

Glutt looked back at the spore-cloud he had woven in the air. The explorers were pinned down by las-fire but one of them, a priest, was trying to approach the wall of the cancrum. He tried unsuccessfully to break through until the heat drove him back. Glutt nodded, satisfied, and crouched back down over the pool, joining the daemon in its painstaking work.

29

'Wait!' cried Isola. 'What's that?'

Draik peered through the dust. A familiar shape bounded past the Guardsmen, dodging shots and landslides, racing towards the sphere.

'Grekh!' cried Draik. 'Give him covering fire!'

They rose from their barricade, launching another barrage of shots, filling the air with las-beams and flame.

Grekh moved with incredible speed, hurdled the ledge and crashed down beside Draik, breathing heavily but otherwise looking exactly as he did when they had first met in the Skeins.

Corval stepped between them, his pistol pointed at Grekh. The Navigator had been trembling and convulsing since Draik helped him from the fissure. His hand was shaking so badly it looked like he might shoot the kroot even if he didn't intend to.

'Wait,' said Draik placing his hand over the barrel of Corval's pistol. He stared at the Navigator. 'We have both been wrong about many things. Maybe we were wrong about this too?'

Corval shook his head but lowered the pistol.

'They're charging!' cried Vorne, unleashing another wall of flame.

Isola and Audus rushed to her side, adding their shots to hers, but Draik and Corval continued looking at Grekh.

'How did you find us?' asked Draik, shouting to be heard over the deafening sphere.

'The Blackstone. It led me to you,' said Grekh.

Draik shook his head. He was no longer prepared to dismiss the creature's outlandish claims – they no longer even seemed outlandish – but he could not understand how Grekh had navigated such complex, ever-changing routes and arrived here, just as the rest of them had.

'Did you see visions, like the priests?'

Grekh clicked and whistled, looking around, clearly made uncomfortable by the question. 'No,' he said. 'I am not like you, or the priests. I see a different truth. I gain insights.' He grabbed one of the insect cages strung across his chest, whispering an oath. 'But I cannot...' He seemed pained even saying this much. 'We do not share our secrets.'

Shots landed on the ruins behind them, filling the air with more dust and shards.

When the air cleared, Draik studied Grekh. The creature was wearing that same calm expression he had been intrigued by before. Draik finally recognised what it was: nobility. Not the contrived, conspicuous nobility of his father, and all those powdered aristocrats on Terra, but a quiet, unspoken nobility of spirit.

'I understand,' he replied, ashamed to think how badly he had misjudged the creature. He had already thought about

Grekh's strange behaviour – his seemingly barbaric need to consume and taste – and begun to form an idea of the creature's methods. But he would let Grekh keep his secrets. 'When we met, I swore to let you help me,' he said. 'I would be honoured to continue our partnership.'

The fighting was growing fiercer and Corval had to turn away to join the others, firing into the wall of Guardsmen.

Grekh ignored the las-fire, still staring at Draik. 'I....' He hesitated, shaking his head, causing his crest of quills to rattle around his long, hawk-like head. 'The Blackstone brought us together.'

Draik turned and looked up at the sphere. 'Have your "insights" told you how we can enter?'

Grekh nodded, holding up the scythe he took from Bullosus. 'This comes from the same minds as the Blackstone. It can form and reform anything.' He looked up at the sphere. 'Even this.'

'There's a way in?' bellowed Taddeus, wading towards them, sweat pouring from his face and his cheeks blazing red. He looked from Draik to Grekh, frowning. 'What did the alien say?'

Draik looked at Grekh. 'What do we do?'

Grekh was still looking at the sphere. 'There are gaps. If I reach one I can cut.'

Taddeus stared at the scythe, noticing it for the first time. He flicked frantically through the pages of his journal, then held it open towards them. Among the columns of tightly packed script and scenes of fiery revelation, there was a drawing of a scythe, very similar to the one Grekh was holding.

'I have seen this!' cried Taddeus, as if he were addressing a congregation. 'Twelve years ago! I drew this picture twelve years ago from a dream! The God-Emperor is with us, friends! He was with me then and He is with me now!'

'It wasn't made by your Emperor,' said Grekh. 'It is the–'

'No time,' interrupted Draik. 'We have to move.'

The Guardsmen had crested the wall. The fight had descended into a hand-to-hand frenzy. Audus was alternating between shooting her pistol and using it as a club. Corval was bludgeoning Guardsmen with his cane, trailing sparks of energy from its gemstone head. Vorne had unslung a chainsword from her back and turned the air crimson, cutting soldiers down with a torrent of howled prayers.

Grekh nodded and bounded away from them, reaching out into the ball of light, sampling its ferocity, plunging and withdrawing his hand, trailing tendrils of energy.

Dozens more Guardsmen poured over the breach.

Vorne fell to her knees, slashing her chainsword from side to side as the others staggered back towards the light.

'Grekh!' howled Draik, drawing his rapier and leaping into the fray, triggering the blade's powercell and decapitating a Guardsman.

'Here!' cried the kroot, rushing into the light, the scythe held over his head. 'Now!'

They turned and sprinted after him, plunging into the wall of light.

Draik saw Grekh's silhouette in the blaze, swinging the scythe, then he was gone, replaced by a vivid column of blackness.

Draik had a moment of doubt, but it was too late to stop. The black rectangle rushed forwards, engulfing him.

Then silence.

Pure nothingness.

Draik could neither see nor hear anything.

Then, up ahead, he saw a shimmer of flame. It grew quickly larger and brighter, rushing towards him as the black rectangle had done. As the light enveloped Draik, he heard a loud tearing sound, as though the air itself were being ripped open. He stumbled forwards, feeling ground beneath his feet, then the world flooded back into view.

But it was not the world he expected. For what seemed like days, all he had seen were harsh, geometric angles – grey-black polyhedrons, all wrought of the same cold, featureless ore. But now he found himself in an explosion of colour and growth. Towering clouds of flies crossed a mustard-yellow sky, drifting over hazy, stagnant pools and swarming through drooping, wet fronds. The plants were bulbous, pitted hulks. It was a landslide of polyps and tumour-sacks, all of them spewing spores and veined with lights. It was a carnival of grotesque shapes. An explosion of eye-watering colour, made all the more shocking by the monochromatic bleakness that had come before.

He only had a moment to take all this in.

The head-splitting tearing grew louder and a cold blast washed over the back of his neck.

Dull black columns rushed overhead from behind him, smashing in through the opening Grekh had cut, tearing it wider and allowing the violence outside to finally break into the sphere.

Draik and the others dropped to their knees, cradling their heads as arms of darkness roared past, smashing into the fungal garden. Spore sacs detonated, sponges ripped and tumours popped. The Blackstone was skewering the garden with a rain of black spears. The ripping sound grew louder and Draik clamped his hands over his ears, trying to block it out. The others were just as overcome, falling into the wet, pulpy moss. Red, viscous mud oozed up from the turf as Draik sank into it, howling incoherently.

'Draik!' cried someone nearby, barely audible over the din.

It was Isola, dragging herself through the slop, her face twisted in pain. She was pointing to something up ahead.

He turned to see a shape rushing towards him. It looked like an insect, but grotesquely enlarged to the height of a man. It was clad in a plated carapace and it was scuttling across the ground on six twitching legs. There was a human face sunk deep in its abdomen, pale and grinning, laughing hysterically.

Draik stood, firing through the whirling clouds. The needles thudded into the creature's shell but showed no sign of stopping it. There was a flash of light over to the creature's left and it stumbled, thrown off track, its legs scrambling furiously beneath its armoured bulk.

Grekh lurched into view gripping a smoking rifle.

More columns ripped through the air, each bigger than the last. The canopy of leaves collapsed, dropping branches and pale, ugly cankers, filling the air with spores. The black beams were all targeted at one specific point. It was hard to see clearly through the miasma, but Draik could just make out a pallid heap of flesh, like a vast, labouring heart, trying to rise and reach out, spawning limbs and mouths. The black spars smashed into it. All of the fortress' will was bent on its destruction. *This* was the cause of the violence. *This* was the malignant interloper the Blackstone was trying to repel. Draik felt sick as he tried to look at it. Even from here, half glimpsed through the spore-clouds, he knew what it was. Such an abomination could only have come from one place: the warp.

The insect creature near Draik stopped laughing. It turned away from Draik and tried to rush back towards the struggling heap of flesh. Draik saw his chance. He ran through clouds of flies, drew his rapier and leapt at the malformed creature.

The monster saw him coming and raised a barbed limb, blocking his thrust, but Draik had depressed the rapier's powercell. Fire flashed down the blade and sheared through the limb. The face in its the abdomen tried to speak, but its tongue was so mangled and stretched that it thrashed, incoherently, across the ground. The monster lunged, punching a taloned limb at Draik's chest.

He parried, disengaged and struck again, his movements as fluid and controlled as they had been in the training halls of the Draik villa. Draik severed another limb, but as the monster staggered back, leaking black blood, it screeched a curse. Flame-bright pus spat from its eyes, blasting Draik from his feet and bathing his nerves in agony.

He crashed onto his back, but as the pain threatened to send him into unconsciousness, the blast was interrupted.

Corval strode forwards, his cane held before him, deflecting the monster's blast and surrounding the Navigator in a wreath of hissing acid. The creature screamed and more pus jolted from its head, emerging vomit-like from its gaping mouth. The acid punched into Corval's stomach and hurled him backwards. He ripped through the surface of a tree-sized puffball and vanished in a cloud of spores.

Grekh fired again, spinning the monster around. Isola rose from the acid-green slop, firing into the monster's face, causing it to stagger back. Vorne was trying to haul Taddeus from a seething pool and Audus had managed to stand, swaying like a drunk as she tried to reload her pistol.

As Draik and the others battled with the insect creature, the Blackstone waged war on the leviathan in the distance. The limbs of rock outside had taken the hole Grekh cut and wrenched it into an opening like the gates of a city. It was now big enough to show the chamber outside the sphere. It was heaving and imploding, but the Guardsmen were still shambling over the crooked slopes, rushing into the garden with their guns raised.

Shots whined through the air.

'Hold them back!' cried Draik, waving everyone back towards the Guardsmen as he ran on towards the monster.

They did as he ordered, halting the Guardsmen with a blinding salvo, shredding their rotten flesh.

Draik reached the insect monster and leapt, swinging his rapier and plunging it into the creature's face. The monster barely noticed, batting Draik aside and sending him flipping through the air. It loomed over him, swinging back one of its limbs like an axe, preparing to behead him. Then it staggered, hit by dozens of shots.

Audus strode into view, covered in filth and spitting curses as she fired into the monster's face. It reeled from the impacts, then steadied itself and clubbed her down, smashing her into a seething pool. Then it whirled around and gripped Draik with one of its claws, forcing him down into the scarlet mud.

The monster pressed all of its weight down on him and Draik sank beneath the mire, thick, bloody liquid rushing over his face. He thrashed and spluttered, but the creature was incredibly heavy and its grip was unbreakable. Draik sank deeper, his lungs burning, liquid filling his mouth and nose. His struggles grew weaker and darkness spread from the corners of his eyes, leaving only a blurred image of the monster's face, giggling as it held him under.

Draik's consciousness faded. Rather than a rush of memories or a final, death-throes revelation, his thoughts settled on the last mechanical functions of his body: his heart slowing and failing; his fingers stiffening, coldness radiating from his chest. He was vaguely aware that the hysterical creature was reaching forwards, clutching a pale grub. As it came closer he saw that it was a worm. The monster was holding it out towards his chest. The worm was straining and uncoiling, stretching for him.

Then a flame erupted from the shadows, bathing everything in light. Was this the afterlife? Was this the God-Emperor, calling him to the Golden Throne?

The light grew brighter and the monster's expression changed from glee to fear. Its face began to run and slide, like a painting, washed away by rain. The iron-hard grip around Draik's arms loosened and the monster fell back, dropping the worm into the mud. With a desperate effort, Draik shoved himself up, breaking the surface with a choking gasp.

His oxygen-starved brain struggled to comprehend what he saw.

The monster was staggering away from him, claws raised, its carapace dissolving in a beam of blue-white fire.

Corval stumbled into view. Draik was seeing him from behind, but he could tell that he had removed his helmet and dropped his weapons. His robes were torn and ragged and he had raised his arms, as though in prayer. Livid, dazzling light was blazing from his forehead, ripping into the monster, tearing it apart, molecule by molecule.

No, thought Draik, horrified, realising that Corval must have opened his third eye – the one thing he told Draik he must never do. *It will destroy him.* Draik tried to rise, to go to him, but he was too weak. His lungs were full of liquid. He fell back, spluttering and gasping.

Corval kept walking, more determined with each step.

More lines of fire sprayed from his head, crowning him with a blinding halo. While the first beam tore the monster apart, the others sliced into the undead Guardsmen, transforming them into firebrands, engulfing them in colourless flame.

There were hundreds of the Guardsmen and, as they ignited, they raised their arms, mirroring Corval's agony. It looked like a holy vision – a host of damned souls, sundered and cleansed by heavenly fire. With a jolt, Draik realised that it looked like a *specific* holy scene – the one painted on Taddeus' walls and books.

There was thunderclap as the monster and every one of the Guardsmen detonated. Burnt meat and shattered chitin whistled through the air. The light vanished and Corval crumpled into the mud.

Draik crawled towards him, hauling himself over mounds of blackened fungus. As he hauled himself up a sodden ridge he saw the pale, mountainous shape he had glimpsed earlier. It was pierced by spars of black ore. Skewered by the Blackstone.

The tearing sound grew louder.

Draik howled.

As he cried out, the Blackstone wrenched its limbs free, ripping it apart, creating another volcanic bang, filling the air with spores and blubber. The garden began to collapse, toppling and tearing, revealing the cold, colourless walls of the Blackstone.

Draik stumbled over to Corval as the garden fell apart around him.

The Navigator was clearly dead, lying in a hideously unnatural position, half of his cranium replaced by a blackened mess. Draik took Corval's cold, lifeless hand, whispering something no one else would hear.

'And not to yield.'

30

'The flames will hear no plea 'til the faithless soul burns free, 'til the truth is burned in thee, 'til the blind have learned to see.'

Draik heard the words but ignored them. He could think of nothing but Corval – Numa, his friend – dying so far from home, sacrificing himself to save the man who had ruined his life.

'We have to go,' said someone else, and a hand gripped his shoulder.

He dragged his gaze from the dead Navigator and looked up into the concerned eyes of Isola.

'The vault is collapsing,' she said.

She was not shouting. The tearing sound had finally ceased. He could still hear its echo, roaring in his ears, but the noise was gone. He looked around the garden and saw that it was a garden no longer. In just a few short seconds the Blackstone had reclaimed its heart, burying the marshes beneath tons of leaden, night-black ore. The violence was not over, though. The walls were rotating and twisting, dismantling the vault, carving it into something new. If he stayed by Corval's corpse for much longer, he would be crushed.

He nodded and took Isola's hand, letting her help him to his feet.

The rest of the group had also gathered around the corpse. Taddeus and Vorne were staring at it in awe, hands clasped together, repeating their prayer over and over: 'The flames will hear no plea 'til the faithless soul burns free, 'til the truth is burned in thee, 'til the blind have learned to see.'

Audus was stood a few feet back from them. There was no rapture in her eyes. She was not even looking at the corpse. She just looked dazed and exhausted. Grekh was at her side, staring at the tectonic collisions taking place all around them.

'We have to go,' said Isola, gripping his arm harder.

'I failed,' said Draik. 'We found the vault and…' He shook his head, not exactly sure what he had found. Whatever it was, it was quickly vanishing.

'Failed?' Grekh shook his head.

Draik massaged his temples, frowning. 'Then tell me,' he said, looking at Grekh. 'What have we achieved?'

'The Blackstone brought us here for *this*,' said Grekh, pointing his rifle at the sundering walls. 'We were never here for the reasons we thought. Whatever was happening here, the Blackstone needed to stop it. But it could not. Do you see? It needed *us* to do this – to break through where it could not. To let it back in.'

Draik shook his head, but the kroot was only saying things he already felt in his soul. He had been so wrong. This was all fated. No, not even fated – *engineered* by the fortress. It had summoned them to perform this act of surgery, to rid it of this vile cancer.

They all staggered backwards as the ground shifted into a new angle, hurling them down a slope.

They landed in a jumble of struggling limbs in a narrow gulley and Grekh began running, waving for them to follow. They came to a fork and Grekh turned down a path without hesitation.

'Wait!' cried Draik.

In the other direction, the death throes of the vault were still visible, a titanic struggle of crashing peaks. A chasm had opened and Corval's corpse was still visible as it slid into the hole, flames rippling from its ruined skull. They were about to move on when the furthest wall in the vault opened, swinging out like gates, revealing another soaring edifice in the shadows beyond.

There, in the deepest chamber of the Blackstone, sculpted from the darkness, Draik saw the symbol of House Draik, a proud serpent, glowering down at him.

Draik ignored Grekh and raced towards the statue, but before he had taken even a few steps the Blackstone rethought itself, slamming down another featureless edifice, then more, until the vision vanished and even the path vanished, forcing Draik back towards the others and leaving him facing a sheer, impenetrable wall.

He pounded it with his fists, desperate and confused. What was the Blackstone trying to tell him? What did it know of House Draik?

Then the floor shifted and reformed. Angular shapes jolted beneath their feet, folding and snapping. Crystalline spurs clicked together, forming long, sharpened limbs.

'Drones!' cried Isola, grabbing Draik and hauling him after Grekh.

Grekh rushed through a small antechamber and out onto

the diamond-shaped platform they crossed when they first landed. The *Vanguard* was there, its landing lights still glimmering and movement visible on the bridge.

Drones flooded from every corner of the hall, filling the air with the sound of their scraping, knife-blade limbs.

'Ready the engines!' cried Draik, recovering his composure and rushing towards the ship.

The landing ramp clattered down as the drones scuttled across the platform. Draik waved everyone on board then turned to look back. Beyond the swarms of drones, he could see the way back to the vault, the way back to the vision he had seen – the symbol of his own house, stranded in the heart of this ancient, alien structure.

'Captain!' cried Isola, a few feet above him on the ramp.

The first of the drones had almost reached him. He stalled them with a few shots then ran into the ship. 'Go!' he cried as the ramp slammed shut behind him.

The deck crew stared in shock as he ran onto the bridge, drenched in blood and trailing the remains of his uniform. He dashed to a seat, strapped himself in and nodded to Audus, who had already grabbed the flight controls.

The chamber filled with noise and light as the *Vanguard* leapt from the platform, banking hard as it screamed out into the stars.

AFTER

Corval looked down at the mob, stern and proud, his star-helm gleaming in the shifting light.

'Numa,' said Draik, raising his cup to the pict capture, downing his drink. He grimaced. 'How can Gatto serve this bilge water?'

Isola was beside him at the bar, looking up at the menacing slab of Blackstone, studying the portraits plastered across its base. 'Numa?' She sipped her drink with a grimace identical to Draik's. 'You mean Corval?'

Draik nodded, then shrugged, raising his cup again. 'Let's drink to all of them.'

The Helmsman had become even more riotous since their last visit. The bloodbirds were whirling through the flickering light, fluttering around the sweating crowds and clicking their lenses. The roar of drunken voices reverberated off the ramshackle walls, mingling with snatches of song and furious, drink-fuelled arguments. Draik didn't hear any of it.

It was nearly a week since Corval's death and it still dominated his thoughts. He had lost friends before, close ones, but never twice. He felt like his past had died.

'Why are we back here?' asked Isola, leaning towards him as the drinkers next to her starting shoving each other, sending cups clattering across the bar.

'I'm not going,' said Draik, lighting his lho-stick and taking a drag, his eye reflecting the light.

Isola frowned. 'You're not going where?'

'Back to the Curensis Cluster. To the Tann-Karr. I'm going to stay here and see this thing through.'

She shook her head. 'His lordship was clear. The trade routes are set. If we don't meet with the House Draik agents on Mysia Four, you'll be in breach of your contract.'

'Contract!' laughed Draik, dragging on his lho-stick. 'What kind of family is held together by contracts?'

'Don't play games with him. You know he could cancel your stipend.'

Draik shrugged. 'I have my Warrant of Trade. I have investments in my own name. Besides, whatever else it is, the Blackstone is a treasure trove. I won't starve.'

'He could disinherit you – strike your name from the family rolls.'

Draik nodded, calmly sipping his drink. 'He could.'

Isola shook her head. 'Everything you've worked for, all those battles and sacrifices, all so that you could reclaim your place in the family. If you disobey your father so blatantly, it will have been for nothing.'

Draik leant close, as though sharing a secret. 'It always *was* for nothing though, wasn't it?'

Isola flushed, struggling to maintain her usual, icy demeanour.

Draik laughed and leant back, waving his lho-stick in a dismissive gesture. 'Don't worry, you haven't revealed anything you shouldn't. I learned it from another source. I know my father was never going to let me set foot back on Terra.' He could not entirely suppress the bitterness in his voice. 'I've been racing around like a fool, trying to impress someone who despaired of me long ago.'

'It wasn't like that, captain. Your father was not–'

'It doesn't matter. I don't care anymore. What is there back there for me? Let my sister take the wretched crown. She's far more suitable. Power plays and politics. What good does any of it do?' He waved at the crush of figures barging past them – a bewildering mix of explorers, frontiersmen and dead-eyed killers. '*This* is the crucible, Isola, out here. I see it now. This is where mankind will be forged, or die in the attempt. Not in some gilded stateroom full of pompous, gout-ridden worthies.'

Isola had regained her reserved demeanour. 'What did you see in there? When you looked back into the vault – you saw something. What was it?'

'I saw a vision, Isola. Laugh if you like, but I know what I saw. And I know, now, that the Blackstone brought me here. I didn't believe it before, but now I know it's true. The kroot was right. I thought he was a fool, but he was right. The Blackstone was part of my life long before I even heard of it. I may have no future on Terra but I *do* have one here. I'm going back in.'

She licked her lips, looking uncomfortable, but not quite as shocked as he had expected. Perhaps he was easier to read than he liked to think. He wondered what she was thinking. What would she do?

He picked up his drink and left the bar, waving for her to follow.

They pushed through the crowds and he led her towards a gloomy, lamp-lit alcove.

They were almost there when she grabbed him by the arm. 'But look at the state you're in, captain.' She nodded to his impressive collection of wounds. 'You need to rest – to recover.'

He raised an amused eyebrow. 'Rest?'

'And who would go with you,' she said, sounding exasperated, 'if you went back?'

Draik smiled and nodded at the alcove. A circle of familiar faces was waiting for them, hunched over the table, lit by a rusty, sparking glowglobe: Audus, Grekh, Taddeus and Vorne.

Isola halted, shocked, looking at each of them in turn. 'Why? Why would you go back in?' She sat down and looked at the two priests. They both looked horrified by their surroundings, sitting rigidly in their seats and clutching their weapons as though they would rather torch the place than stay for another minute. 'You never found your relic. Why go back? After everything we saw?'

'We found it, child,' said Taddeus. 'The Eye of Hermius. And it was far grander and more powerful than I imagined. I had not grasped the scale of the Emperor's vision.' The priest waved her closer, breathless with excitement. 'Everything I saw, everything I recorded, it all came to pass.' He opened his journal, pointing to the image of a priest, light blazing from his head, scourging the damned. '*Corval* was the prophet. These images show it clearly – the moment of his ascension – his transition to sainthood. It all makes sense now. In that moment, the moment of his death, I saw everything.'

He pointed at the picture again. Behind the saintly, light-radiating figure, there was an eclipse, another kind of halo, a black circle.

'I thought this purely decorative, but Corval showed me the truth. We have found the Eye of Hermius. It's the Blackstone. Do you see? The *Blackstone*! The kroot is right. The Blackstone brought us here. It tested us, seeing if we could cleanse it of that taint, and we proved ourselves worthy. Now we must return and return and return until we find the key to its secrets…' he paused for breath, almost hyperventilating. '…because they are the secrets of the *Emperor*. The Blackstone was sent to us so that we can defeat the Ruinous Powers, to return His light to the Dark Imperium and to cleanse the Great Rift. Here, finally, is the proof that all those heretics are wrong to talk of Him as a corpse-god. The God-Emperor has *sent* us this weapon. And we must master it!' He collapsed back in his seat, staring at Isola, awed by his own words. Vorne had her head bowed, praying furiously.

Isola stared at him for a moment, incredulous. Then she nodded and looked at Grekh.

Grekh looked almost as uncomfortable in the Helmsman as the priests. 'I have to return. I have gained many insights.' He looked at Draik. 'The Blackstone brought us together. There is something greater than relics here. A greater purpose.'

Isola looked at Audus. The pilot was leaning away from the light, her face hidden beneath a hood, but her large, powerful frame was unmistakable. Before Isola could ask her anything, the pilot held up a hand. 'I'm still owed my ten per cent. I'm going nowhere without it.'

Isola looked at Draik with a disbelieving expression. He smiled. He knew what Isola was thinking because he thought the same: Audus' cynicism was an affectation. There was more to her than she was prepared to reveal.

'And what about you?' said Audus, leaning into the light, staring at Isola.

'Me?'

'I told them you work for my father,' explained Draik. 'I told them I was unsure what you would do if I stayed here – if I break my *contract*.'

Isola sipped her drink and looked at him. Then she nodded at the crowds of mercenaries and adventurers that surrounded them. They all had the same desperate, rapacious look in their eyes.

'You know what you've become, don't you? One of them. A devotee. It's insane. Every attempt we make is worse than the last. You nearly died last time. And the Ascuris Vault has been destroyed. It *wasn't* the key to the transportation chambers. So where would we look? What would we look for? What hope would we have if we return?'

Draik noticed that she had said 'if *we* return'. He extinguished his lho-stick and took something from his pocket, spreading it on the table. It was a ragged piece of human skin, the one he had taken from the xenos by the aqueduct. There was something scribbled on it – spirals of text, all written in a cursive, alien script. He smiled, tapping the numbers and runes.

'This time I have something, Isola, I know it.'

ABOUT THE AUTHOR

Darius Hinks' first novel, *Warrior Priest*, won the David Gemmell Morningstar Award for best newcomer. Since then he has ventured into the Warhammer 40,000 universe with the novels *Mephiston: Blood of Sanguinius*, *Mephiston: Revenant Crusade* and the Space Marine Battles novella *Sanctus*, and has carved a bloody swathe through the Warhammer world with *Island of Blood*, *Sigvald*, *Razumov's Tomb* and the Orion trilogy.

YOUR NEXT READ

RISE OF THE YNNARI: WILD RIDER

by Gav Thorpe

When Wild Lord Nuadhu of Clan Fireheart unwittingly awakens a slumbering necrontyr tomb world, he must seek an alliance with the Ynnari if he is to preserve the honour and future of his family.

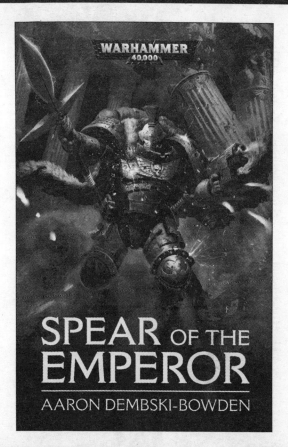